When Love's Knot Enough

Ayesha L. Shoulders

Acknowledgements

I would like to thank my Heavenly Father for blessing me with another opportunity to have my work published. I'm so thankful for this wonderful gift!

To my husband, Alexander Shoulders, thank you for supporting me through the years in my writing career. To my dear son, Alexander Jr. (AJ), it has been a joy being your mom. Never give up on your dreams because they do come true!

To my mom, Sheila Boone, thank you for reading my manuscript. I cherish all the talks we had about this book.

Arianna Allegro, thank you for reviewing my manuscript. Your extra set of eyes really did the trick. Tammy Morris, my San Diego friend, thank you for researching and answering my many questions about the city for this book.

Author Tracy Gilmore, many thanks for your word of encouragement and support during the publication of my book. You were definitely put in my life for a reason. To Rebecca Merritt with Brink Editing, thank you for your editing services.

To all my readers, thank you once again for reading my work. I strive to deliver a book that will linger with you well after the last chapter. Please enjoy and I love you all!

~Ayesha L. Shoulders

And now these three remain: faith, hope and love. But the greatest of these is love.

1 Corinthians 13:13

❧

Prologue

Isaac looked over a deposition for an upcoming case. His brain was growing weary by the hour, as he sorted through the witness' testimony, looking for a technicality to get his client off the money laundering charges. He spun around in his chair, staring at the dark skies outside that reminded him it was well after 9 o'clock. From the big bay window in his office, he could only see a few scattered cars in the parking lot. As usual for the last couple weeks, he was the last one to leave work; brooding over the forthcoming trial he had at the end of the month. The sound of the cleaning crew running a vacuum cleaner in the neighboring office broke the silence in the room.

He turned around and tried to get back to work. He knew deep down why he was having difficulty focusing; it wasn't because of his inability to find a credible witness to vouch for his client's story, or the noise from the vacuum cleaner that was now piercing his skull, but the fact that he was missing his best-friend, Mariah. His job as a defense attorney gave him great pleasures, but, oh boy, she gave him so much more fulfillment.

He and Mariah had been together for three years; however, it still felt like they were in the honeymoon phase. Isaac still gets excited when her number flashes across his phone and, though he would never admit this to anyone, still feels quivers in his stomach at the thought of seeing her again. He knew in the early months of dating Mariah that he had found the woman of his dreams. The woman that he wanted to spend the rest of his life with: for better or for worse.

He felt she completed him and made him whole. Something he had never felt before with another woman in his forty-year life. The closest he ever got to a serious relationship with the women from his past was leaving a toothbrush at their house and maybe one clean pair of boxers; depending on how sane he felt the woman was.

Mariah, however, was different. She was career-oriented, just like him, and self-confident. She was beautiful and had a loving spirit about herself that sucked him into wanting to be around her every minute. She moved about her day without making her day about him, unlike some of the women from his past. She wasn't after his money, nor did she take advantage of the gifts he had given her because she felt she could. Mariah had her own money and confidence in her own abilities to conquer the world. That intrigued Isaac and made him want her more and more. She challenged him. She inspired him to want to be a better man. He was no longer interested in dating around with multiple women anymore. Mariah was the one.

He hadn't seen her for almost two weeks due to this case, and it was starting to take a toll on his well-being. He needed to see his better-half…touch her soft, buttermilk skin, snuggle up close to her where he can smell the scent of her peppermint shampoo that

2

lingered in his nose hairs for hours after they were apart, and just gaze into her adoring brown eyes. He couldn't take it anymore; the time apart was pure torture for him. It felt like he had taken a bullet to the heart and had survived to endure the pain.

Isaac reached for his office phone and called her number. She should still be up; it was Friday night. Isaac felt it was time for him to do what was in his heart. He was ready to call Mariah, Mrs. Isaac Stevens. His only dilemma was getting her to say yes...

Chapter One

Mariah Langston woke up on Saturday morning to the sound of rain beating against her palladium window. "Ugh," she moaned as she set up in bed, running her hands across her face. Another rainy day, that's all she needed. She was really looking forward to getting out of the house and meeting her sister for their usual Saturday morning jog.

"Oh well, there goes that," she thought as she fell back onto her pillow, knocking the cordless phone to the floor that was sitting on the edge of her bed.

She must have fallen asleep last night, still holding it in her hand, after she finished talking to her boyfriend, Isaac. Mariah hadn't seen him in almost two weeks, and she missed him dearly. She was so glad he had asked to meet her for dinner tonight, knowing he was in the middle of a big court case.

Mariah crossed her toned, size four legs under her covers and reached for the porcelain picture frame on her nightstand. It contained a picture that she and Isaac had taken together on her 36th birthday, this past October, at Georges in the Cove Restaurant in La Jolla. She chuckled to herself, remembering how he had surprised her by having Chef Trey Foshee come out singing Happy Birthday, as he presented a sampler of all her favorite dishes in the restaurant. It was one night she would always remember, as the reason she fell in love with this man.

Mariah placed the picture frame back on her nightstand and relaxed back in bed, her eyes catching a glimpse of a pink and black Save the Date card on her desk. It was a Save the Date for her coworker Sandra's upcoming wedding. The thought of going to it made her stomach flip and brought on anxiety that made her want to skip out of the day's events altogether!

She hated weddings. She hated what the whole day of events entailed and what followed afterwards: a marriage that was doomed for failure. She just didn't believe in it anymore. She loathed the fact that she had to attend another wedding, to be a witness in the audience to something she believed was not going to last, or was not going to end in happiness.

Mariah hadn't always felt this way. She recalled growing up as a little girl and being a flower girl in at least five weddings. She used to love getting dressed up, looking like a miniature bride, and walking down the aisle with everyone cooing over how cute she looked.

The big party afterwards was the icing on the cake. She loved being able to sit at the big, adult table and sip apple cider from a wine glass, while the adults had wine, and giggle as her father twirled her around the dance floor in her patent leather shoes. She couldn't wait to grow up to find her own prince charming, sit at the head of her table in a big poofy wedding dress, and ride off at the end of the night in a long, stretch limousine to live happily ever after with her groom.

Boy, did she have it all figured out – what her life was going to be like. She believed it was going to happen in that order too; that is until her second marriage came to an end.

Darren Cox was her first husband. They had dated their entire four years of high school. Mariah remembered Darren getting down on one knee and asking her to marry him at his graduation cookout. He had proposed to her in private, by a creek in the park. At first she thought he was kidding, or maybe had snuck one too many beers while his parents weren't looking. But after she slugged him playfully on the arm and asked him several times to stop joking around, she realized he was dead serious, as he remained down on one knee. Astonished, Mariah said yes – of course at seventeen years old, she was ready to make such a life-changing decision, or so she thought. There was no engagement ring since they were high school kids with no jobs. But, she didn't care! The whole experience was romantic in itself with Darren asking her to marry him under the starry night, at the same creek that he had formally asked her to become his girlfriend.

Once they'd told their parents about the engagement, as expected, they thought they should wait until after college. But Mariah and Darren were pretty convincing with their plans to make it work with school, so their parents agreed to let them get married. They figured Mariah and Darren were going to do it anyway once they both turned eighteen.

Mariah, already obsessed with watching the *Platinum Weddings* television show, planned their wedding in three months. They got married in August and moved into a small, one-bedroom apartment right before starting their freshmen year together at San Diego State University. The first month was pretty smooth as they adjusted to married life, working full-time and going to school full-time. But soon after, the stress-free, pleasurable relationship they had throughout high school turned into nothing but work. It was like they had two full-time jobs.

They recognized early on that they were in way over their heads. With the stress of school, paying bills and not wanting to continue with an unhappy marriage, they decided to call it quits and have the marriage annulled after six months.

Darren decided to stay at home and continue his studies at SDSU, but Mariah transferred to Pennsylvania State University. It was really her first choice college, but she opted not to apply because Darren didn't want to leave the West Coast. After her ill-fated, six-month marriage came to an end, Mariah still had hopes that she would one day meet the man she was destined to marry. Darren would always be her high school sweetheart, but sadly they were not meant to be life partners.

Eight years later, she met her second husband, Arthur Hamilton. She met him at U-T San Diego, a local newspaper company, where he was working as their senior editor. She had to submit an advertisement for her employer, and he was at the front desk when she was putting in her order. He followed her out to the parking lot and asked her out on a date. They immediately hit it off. Two years into their relationship, Arthur popped the question. Mariah was thrilled; she even had an engagement ring to wear this time around.

Mariah believed she had been given a second chance to finally get it right. Well, after celebrating a year-long engagement and beautiful wedding, she found herself living with a husband who allowed the mother of his only child to cause problems in their marriage.

She recalled the final breaking point at their fifth wedding anniversary dinner, where she decided to bring up their marital issues, yet again. It probably wasn't the best time to do it, but Mariah was tired of Bianca using his son Ethan to interfere in their marriage, and she desperately needed Arthur to put her in her place. Arthur listened, but simply sipped on his glass of wine and shrugged at the matter. He didn't see it as a big issue. Once again, Mariah felt helpless, as if her feelings didn't matter. How many times could she have the same conversation and get nowhere? She was fed up.

She decided after trying to give a hundred and ten percent to save their union that it was time to walk away. Arthur just wasn't doing his job as a husband. It was as if everything changed once they got married. That's when Mariah decided marriage wasn't in the cards for her, and she had no intentions of ever doing it again!

Loud thunder exploded outside, causing her to jolt up in bed. *Enough with reflecting on my past*, she thought. She was in a better place now. She was doing things her way these days, rewriting a history that says you have to get married to live happily ever after with someone. Mariah had been given a third chance to get it right with Isaac, and she wasn't going to mess it up this time. Their relationship was solid without marriage. He understood that she never wanted to get married again, and he was fine with it.

Mariah flung her covers from her legs. She didn't want to go out in the rain, but she had a few errands to take care of before meeting Isaac later for dinner.

☓

Hours later, Mariah arrived back at the house with an hour to spare before she was supposed to be at the restaurant. She put away the few grocery items she had picked up, and pressed the button on her voicemail to play back her messages.

Call at 2:30 p.m. ...

"Hi, Sis. Give me a call when you get in...[Pause]...Your brother-in-law is really irking my nerves right now, and I figured I would give you a call before I strangled him. Anyway, give me a call. Love you much," Tina said before the beep sounded.

Mariah shook her head at her sister's message before heading upstairs to her bedroom. This wasn't the first time her older sister called to complain about something her husband had done. Just last week, Tina complained about him leaving dirty clothes all over the floor and his tight budget for household spending. Mariah couldn't imagine what it could be this week. She didn't pay too much attention to it, but recently it seemed like the complaints were occurring more often. Just in case she needed to be on the phone for more than five minutes, she decided to give Tina a call later. She didn't have much time to talk, and she figured Paul would be dead by now if Tina really needed her help to refrain from strangling him.

Mariah went to her walk-in closet to pick out an outfit for the evening. The closet was a close imitation to Carrie's closet from the Sex and the City 2 movie, after she and Big decided to get married. The huge space was filled with Mariah's favorite shoes by various designers in their own built-in compartment shelves and an array of outfits with color coded hangers based on the time of the season. She even had a crystal chandelier installed in the ceiling and a pink suede lounge chair in the middle of the closet. No more shoes in shoe boxes stacked high up to the ceiling for her to make room for someone else's side of the closet. No, those days were definitely over!

After her marriage to Arthur came to an end five years ago, she purchased a two-bedroom two-story house and had her father's construction company knock out the wall to the second bedroom to expand her bedroom and add the large walk-in closet. Clearly, she would never marry again, and she had no interest in having

10

children, so it was a perfect design for her very own dream house.

When her nieces and nephew came over to spend the night, she always set them up in the family room downstairs on her pull out couch or in the sunroom, thus, no need for another spare bedroom. Tina and her parents thought this was a strange design for a house and asked her to reconsider. Her dad kept saying it would be hard to resell the house without a second bedroom. But after her divorce from Arthur, she was not interested in getting input from another man…even if the man was her father.

"Hmmm, this will work," Mariah mumbled as she pulled a pair of black slacks from a hanger and matched them up with a new champagne sparkly bebe top. She added a pair of sparkly champagne three-inch pumps to tie together her outfit.

In another life, Mariah knew she would've been a fashion designer. She loved styling clothes, realizing early on that she took this trait from her mother who retired as a buyer for a local boutique – right after her dad asked her to become a stay-at-home mom.

Everyone in the family always commented on how Mariah was her mother's twin, with her high cheekbones, full lips, and bouncy brownish hair, but Mariah took nothing after her mother's personality. She would never give up her dream of doing what she loved to do, and felt this was partly the reason she chose to study marketing versus fashion design in college. Though her mother would never keep her from following her own dreams, Mariah didn't want to become anything that she knew her mother had resentment about. So she decided to follow her next passion, which gave her the best of both worlds.

Mariah laid her clothes over the bed and turned on some tunes on her iPod. She slipped it into its base so the speakers could blast into the bathroom while she showered. She couldn't wait to get to the restaurant.

Isaac differed from the last two guys she had dated after divorcing Arthur. The fact that she still got excited to go out on dates with him after three years showed just how much he intrigued her.

CB

One hour later, Mariah pulled her Mercedes convertible, another gift she had bought herself after her last divorce, in front of LaManga Restaurant. She stepped out of her car and handed her keys to the valet. She loved LaManga. This was one of her favorite Italian restaurants in San Diego. It was a bit pricey, but they made a Chicken Parmesan plate that was out of this world!

Mariah entered the restaurant, removing her matching champagne, waist-length, light leather jacket as she walked. The evening was a bit chilly outside for mid-April, but it felt toasty inside.

"Welcome to LaManga. Will you be dining alone this evening or are you with a party?" the hostess inquired.

"I'm actually meeting someone. Is Isaac Stevens here?"

"Yes, he is. I'll take you to where he's sitting. Follow me please," the hostess said with a friendly smile as she led Mariah over to a table in the dimly-lit restaurant.

Mariah smiled as she approached the table and thanked the hostess. They were seated right across from the pianist, who was playing classic jazz standards.

"Hi, Baby. You look amazing. As always," Isaac said, wrapping his arms around Mariah and placing a moist kiss on her lips.

"Thank you, Sweetheart. You look handsome yourself," she replied, admiring his button-down, crisply-ironed, mint colored shirt that complemented the complexion of his skin and gray slacks.

Isaac took his seat after Mariah settled in the booth in front of him. He was six feet tall with a firm build from working out faithfully in the gym. He had gorgeous brown eyes, which had attracted her immediately to him, with a close to bald haircut and a well-maintained goatee. He was certainly her cup of tea.

"It's been torture being away from you this past week. I miss seeing that beautiful smile," Isaac said.

"I felt the same way, Honey. How is everything working out with the case?" Mariah inquired, reaching across the table to hold his hand.

Isaac rolled his eyes up in his head and exhaled deeply. "In my

13

fifteen years of being an attorney, I must say this is my toughest case." He lowered his voice with the remaining words and leaned into the table. "With all the extra hours I have put into this case this week, I'm still not confident that I have enough to get my client off. And trust me – no attorney ever wants to admit that out loud."

"Isaac, you're an amazing defense attorney. I'm sure you're going to win hands-down. I'm not used to you sounding like this," Mariah said as she reached to sip her lime martini. Isaac had taken the liberty of ordering her favorite drink before she had arrived. Another thoughtful quality of his that she admired.

Isaac walked over to her side of the booth and slid in next to her placing his arm around her shoulders. "Hey, enough talk about work. I've missed you," he said placing another soft kiss on her lips. He moved her hair behind her ear so he could admire every part of her 'cute button ears' as he likes to call them.

"I've missed you too, Honey. I didn't have my partner to watch *Southland* with me this week. And this week's episode was surreal," she said with a chuckle, commenting on one of their favorite television shows.

"Oh, is that all you missed?" he asked with a smirk, playfully tickling her stomach as the waiter approached their table.

"Welcome to LaManga," the gentleman said with an Italian accent, before going into his speech about the chef's specials for the evening.

"I'll just have the Chicken Parmesan and a Caesar salad with the dressing on the side," Mariah said.

"I'll take the lasagna. Thanks," Isaac added.

"Grazie," the waiter responded before departing from their table.

"I'm so hungry. I didn't get a chance to eat lunch today with all the running around I had to do," Mariah said as she sipped the last drop of her martini. She immediately felt her head begin to spin a bit from the alcohol. She must have been thirsty as well, drinking the martini as fast as she did.

"So, are you still going to be able to accompany me to my coworker's wedding next Saturday?"

"Sure, I'm available. I wouldn't dare let you go alone," Isaac said, as their warm breadbasket arrived at the table.

Mariah reached for the bottle of oil on the table and poured some of the pale green liquid into a small bowl. She sliced herself a piece of bread and dipped it into the oil mixed with Italian herbs and Parmesan cheese, made exclusively by the restaurant.

"Mmm this is so good. OK, I'm glad to hear that since I RSVP'd for two and you're the only one I want to go with."

"I better be," Isaac said with a wink that sent a shiver down Mariah's back.

She was truly happy for once in her life to finally be on the same page with a man that wanted the same things she did. Isaac respected her position in a mature relationship without any unnecessary drama. She could see herself spending a lifetime with him in a committed relationship without any unnecessary strings or rings…

Mariah basked in Isaac's gorgeous looks and intelligent conversation as she ate half the loaf of bread. She was almost stuffed by the time her meal arrived at the table. She vowed never to allow herself to go that long again without eating.

After dinner, Isaac walked Mariah out to the valet stand to pick up her car. He held her closely in his arms and gave her a kiss on the lips.

"Have I told you how much you make me happy?" he asked.

Mariah looked into his eyes and smiled. "Not today, so go ahead and tell me again," she said as the valet walked over with her keys.

"Well, I'll give you the short version since your car is here. You're a special woman, Mariah, and I'm happy to have you in my life. Give me a call when you get home to let me know you made it safe," Isaac said, taking Mariah's hand and leading her over to the driver's side of the car.

"I'll definitely give you a call. Thanks for dinner. I love you," she said.

"I love you too," Isaac responded.

Mariah got inside her car and pulled away from the curb

feeling like the luckiest woman in the world.

Chapter Two

Wednesday afternoon, following a gruesome conference call at work, Mariah left her office for a cup of coffee. She was going to have to head up the initiatives on a lucrative marketing campaign her advertising company was competing for, which meant long hours for the next couple of weeks.

Mariah may have made mistakes in her personal life, but she definitely hadn't in her career. After graduating magna cum laude from Pennsylvania State, she interned for her current company, Armstrong and Associates, Inc., during her summer breaks while in college. She was hired as a Marketing Assistant right after graduation. Mariah worked her way up in the company to the level of Vice President of Marketing.

Mariah dropped a French Vanilla packet into the electric coffee maker and placed her coffee mug on the machine. She leaned against the counter as her coffee was brewing. Sandra Palmer walked into the break room at that moment looking frustrated.

"I guess long hours are due for us in the upcoming weeks," Sandra complained, referring to their recent conference call, as she reached into the refrigerator for a yogurt.

"What are you doing here anyway? Aren't you getting married on Saturday?" Mariah inquired.

"We have hired *the* wedding planner who is tying up all of the last minute loose ends for us. I'm out of here after today though. I have family coming in tomorrow morning. Let me know if you ever need Mildred's Weddings Extraordinaire phone number. My wedding planner has been amazing throughout this entire wedding planning process. I cannot wait to finally meet Mr. Isaac on Saturday. I was so excited to get your RSVP in the mail with 'plus one' included," Sandra said, smiling.

"There will be no wedding planning in my future, Sandra. I've been there and done that and have a book about it in Barnes and Noble on the shelf. I'll leave the whole wedding planning thing to you though," Mariah said as the coffee maker started beeping.

"Hey, I hate it when you say stuff like that. I thought you said you and Isaac were pretty serious. He sounds like a standup guy, just like my Matt," Sandra said.

"Oh no, it's not that. I just don't believe in all of that getting married stuff anymore, that's all. No offense. I can't wait to see you on Saturday though. I know you're going to look fabulous in your Vera Wang gown," Mariah said with a wink before getting her cup.

"Alright, for now…but I wouldn't be so quick to write off marriage, especially when you find the right guy. I see a ring in your future," Sandra said, shaking her ring finger.

"Bye, Sandra. I'll see you Saturday," Mariah said with a snicker as she walked out of the break room. She wasn't really in the mood for defending her anti-marriage beliefs to anyone else at this moment, which was starting to recur more and more now that she and Isaac had been seriously dating for the past three years. She also felt weird having this discussion with someone like Sandra, who was about to get married herself.

Mariah pushed the whole conversation out of her mind and got back into work mode as she re-entered her office. She looked at the scatter on her desk filled with specifications on their potential new client and notes taken from her morning conference call. She picked up her headset and attempted to dial the desk extension to her creative designer so they could get started on their new campaign assignment, when her office phone started to ring.

"Armstrong and Associates, Mariah Langston speaking," Mariah said reaching into her desk drawer for a highlighter without looking at the caller ID.

"Hi, Baby. How's your day coming along?" Isaac asked.

Mariah started to smile and sat down behind her desk. Isaac was the only one at this moment who could bring a smile to her face.

"Hi, Honey. Work is coming along…that's about it for now. I've just been assigned to a major project that will have me busy for the next couple of weeks, but other than that I'm happy to hear your voice. How's your day coming along?"

"I'm just leaving the courthouse. I had to defend a quick traffic case. I'm heading over to the department store real fast on my lunch break to get a shirt to go with my suit for Saturday. What colors are you wearing? I wouldn't want to clash," Isaac asked.

"I haven't given it much thought, to be honest. I'll probably just wear something out of my closet. I have a purple strapless dress that I haven't worn yet with a lace shawl," she said as an email popped up on her computer screen from her boss.

"I hope you remembered to buy a wedding gift at least. You're probably the only woman in the world who's not all that excited about taking a man to a wedding. I have past girlfriends who would have loved to drag me to a wedding," he said with a chuckle.

"Ha-Ha. For your information, I bought the gift weeks ago. And what past girlfriends are you referring to? The only person you need to be thinking about is me," Mariah said matter-of-factly, as she started to respond to her boss' email. She loved how she and Isaac could joke around with each other so freely. It added extra spice to their relationship.

"Awww, is Mariah getting jealous? Well, just so you know, you're the only one on my mind," Isaac said laughing. "I just got to the store, so I'll just pick a neutral color shirt that goes with purple," Isaac said.

"That's fine. I'll talk to you later."

"Sounds good."

Hearing him express his feelings about her so freely made her stomach do back flips. Smiling with happy thoughts, Mariah dialed the extension to her creative designer's desk so they could begin working on the new campaign.

ଔ

Saturday morning came, and Mariah woke up with a bad feeling in her stomach as she rolled over in her king size bed. Yes, king size. She decided a long time ago she was not going to forgo items that were deemed for two people just because she lived alone. She sat up in bed and tried to get the thought of today's events out of her mind. Although she faked to Isaac that she was okay with attending this wedding, it was truly the last place on earth that she wanted to be.

She just didn't get it! People are excused from going to funerals because it makes them sad, so why couldn't she be extended the same pass? Today was going to be a reminder of the two failed marriages for which she had walked down the aisle.

In her opinion, once a couple said the words I do, the wonderful life they had shared together would come to an end. She has experienced it and witnessed it one too many times. Every week it seemed like her sister complained about something her husband did. Even her parents, though they have been married for forty years, seemed to just be going through the motions until death do them part.

Marriage always seemed to change the dynamics of a relationship for her. That's why she was scared to even consider it with Isaac. She loved him too much to put their happiness at risk.

She just had to figure out a way to hold it together today, so she could be there to support Sandra and avoid alarming Isaac. Mariah looked over at her clock on her nightstand. It was 8:00 a.m. She had to get dressed and get over to her sister's house by 9:00 a.m. for their Saturday morning jog.

Mariah decided to ignore the nauseating feeling she was experiencing in the pit of her stomach and went to the bathroom to freshen up. She slipped on a pair of running tights and t-shirt. After dressing, she went to the kitchen to fill up her water bottle, grabbed a towel and her running bag and walked outside to the 65-degree morning weather. Though, the weather was calling for an 80-degree sunny day.

Mariah pulled out of her driveway and prepared for the forty-minute drive to her sister's house. Tina and Paul had decided to build their dream home in an up-and-coming area that was in no man's land away from the city life. The address wasn't even registered on her GPS. Mariah hopped on the interstate and turned to her favorite radio station. She loved to listen to Dr. Gordy in the early morning discussing everyday life topics that affect women. She prayed she didn't run into traffic as she tuned into the discussion about challenges women face when they make more money than their significant other.

Light traffic on the road enabled Mariah to pull into her sister's housing development just 30 minutes later. She turned down the street, noticing two more houses now under construction that hadn't been there during her last visit. She and Tina rotated from month to month working out in the other's city, and this month was Mariah's turn to make the commute. Mariah pulled into her sister's driveway and walked up the gravel pathway. She knocked on the front door eager to see her nieces and nephew before they took off for their run. Tina answered, dressed in her running gear, holding a laundry basket upon her waist filled with clothes. She looked worn out.

Tina looked just like their father, with a round face, pointed nose, which was downright perfect in shape, and thick black hair that went below her shoulders. She even took after their father's tough, firecracker attitude, which benefited Mariah when they were growing up as kids. Tina shot her sister an angry look and stepped to the side so she could come in.

Mariah knew she was about to witness a real life performance of her sister's many complaints. She saw her twin seven-year-old nieces running around the house after each other screaming, and her five-year-old nephew whining on the family room floor because he couldn't get the head back on his super hero's body.

"Is there a reason that it's level ten in your house so early in the morning?" Mariah asked in amazement as she followed her sister to her chef-style kitchen, which was in complete shambles. Breakfast dishes were on the kitchen table, pans from the morning breakfast were still on the stove, and newspapers and mail were all over the counter tops.

"Mariah, don't start with me this morning. I'm really pissed off right now. Paul is still in bed sleeping when he knows I need him up to watch the kids. He left my damn family room a mess after his game night last night. PJ, enough already with the whining! Lexie and Leshia, stop running in the house!" Tina yelled at her children in frustration as she dropped the laundry basket on the floor and started to clear the breakfast dishes from the kitchen table.

"I'll be right back," Mariah said to her sister as she went into Auntie mode and walked into the nearby family room to help remedy the situation. "PJ, let Auntie fix it," she said reaching for his toy as he wiped the tears from his eyes.

"Auntie Mariah, Auntie Mariah," the twins came running at her all at once, knocking her onto the floor with hugs.

"Now, I know you both know you're not supposed to be running in the house, right?" Mariah asked, giving both twins a kiss on the forehead.

"Yes," they said in unison, sitting down beside their brother to brush their Barbie dolls' hair.

"Okay, so I shouldn't see any more running. Here you go, PJ. Next time the head comes off, just insert it back like this, okay," Mariah said, as she handed PJ the toy back and got off the floor.

"Good morning, Sis," Paul said, appearing at the doorway stretching.

"Hi, Brother-in-law," Mariah said as her sister came out of the kitchen yelling for Paul to get up.

"Oh, well, I'm happy you decided to finally wake up. Breakfast is on the stove," she said as Paul tried to give her a hug, and she pushed past him. "Come on, Mariah. Let's go."

Mariah saw Paul roll his eyes at his wife's frustration toward him as he sat down on the couch to entertain the children. She followed her sister outside. They started immediately doing a warm-up walk in the direction of the park down the street from Tina's community. Mariah loved walking out here. They had a section set up for walkers and cyclers with marked trails to tell you how far you'd traveled.

"Tina, I'm not trying to get in your business, but...are you guys okay?"

Tina looked at her sister with a confused glare. "Yes. Paul and I are as much in love as when we first met. What would give you an idea to ask something like that?"

Mariah felt like she had just walked into a twilight zone. What would give her the idea? Was her sister in the same house where they had just left? "Um...it's just you two argue a lot for people who are in love.

"Sis, it's a part of being married. Mom and Dad were no different when we were growing up, and they've lasted forty years. I think you're just being paranoid looking for any reason to avoid

26

marriage again. Do you know what I don't get about you? You believe in love but not marriage, which is so apparent from the fact that you allow Isaac to get close to you. I just don't get why you're afraid to take it to the next level with him. He's nothing like either of your ex-husbands," Tina said matter-of-factly as they crossed the street to the park's entrance.

Mariah was not surprised as the conversation turned to being about her and no longer about her sister. She had to put up with this all of her life and today was not going to be any different.

"It's not that I'm scared. I'm just the only smart one who knows that marriage changes the dynamics of a relationship. Look at you and Paul, for example. Before you guys got married and moved in together, I never heard a complaint from you. It was perfect. And now all I hear is you complain about what he's doing or not doing. This is why I hate the fact that I have to go to this wedding today to bear witness to something that I know is going to come to an end as soon as they say 'I do.' Don't get me wrong, I like my coworker Sandra and I hope the best for her marriage, but I just feel like I know better. Period," Mariah said as she started to speed up the path walking past her sister. She wasn't interested in hearing her sister's response because she knew she was right.

"Mariah, you have it all wrong. Paul and I have special moments together and just because I don't holler from the mountaintop to you about them doesn't mean we're not happy. And you must not like being an auntie because, without marriage,

Lexie, Leshia, and PJ wouldn't be here," Tina said catching up to her.

Mariah shot her sister an aggravated look because she knew that wasn't true. She loved being an aunt and wouldn't give up her nieces and nephew for the world. She just couldn't help feeling the way she felt. She and Arthur, her second husband, would probably still be going strong today if she hadn't accepted his proposal. They had been in love too and had shared wonderful times together just like she and Isaac did now. In fact, she and Arthur didn't start experiencing any problems with the mother of his child until after he married Mariah. The pain she felt from a second failed marriage just wasn't worth the whole ordeal of planning the wedding, getting married, and moving in together to then have to divide up furniture and equity five years later.

She didn't care what Tina said. She knew her sister wasn't happy. But if she wanted to spend the rest of her life living this way and faking it to the world as if she were in marital bliss, then that was on her. Mariah, on the other hand, was happy to do without it and was even happier to have found someone who wanted to share her company as well, without the wedding bands.

Chapter Three

Mariah and Isaac walked into the Hampton's Country Club for the 4:30 p.m. wedding later on that Saturday afternoon. Mariah had to admit the club was decorated beautifully; Sandra definitely hadn't spared any expense on this day. The inside of the club resembled the interior of a mansion, with sitting areas that had expensive antique furniture and a uniquely crafted wooden staircase that led up to a ballroom and terrace overlooking the lake. Yellow and pink orchids were displayed sporadically throughout the downstairs, and soft pink roses in tall floor vases lined the hallway of the club to the outside grounds where the ceremony was going to take place. The grounds outside smelled of freshly cut lawn, and white chairs could be seen through an arch in the shape of a heart decorated with yellow, white, and pink roses.

Just as Mariah was about to step her stiletto down on the steps leading outside to the ceremony area, she got a sick feeling again in her stomach that caused her to pause on the first step.

"Are you okay, Mariah?" Isaac asked, reaching to hold onto her arm.

"I'll be okay. I just haven't eaten anything today," she lied as Isaac helped her down the steps.

"Would you two like something to drink?" one of the servers

asked, approaching them with a tray of champagne flutes.

"Thank you," Mariah said accepting a thin glass. She hoped the bubbles would help ease her stomach.

Isaac accepted a flute, too, and they walked over by the harpist entertaining the guests outside before the ceremony begun.

"Are you feeling better?" Isaac asked after a few sips.

"You know what, I think I need to go to the ladies' room. Will you be okay until I come back?" Mariah asked, giving him a kiss on the cheek.

"I'll be fine. I'm just concerned about you right now," he said, taking her half-empty flute.

"I'll be fine. I just need to go to the restroom. I'll be right back," she said giving him a smile so he wouldn't be so overly concerned. She walked back inside the club. She was almost to the bathroom door when her boss, Keith Gray, came around the corner with his wife, Sarah, laughing with another couple.

"Hello, Mariah!" Keith said, reaching out to shake her hand.

"Hi, Keith and Sarah," she said, mustering up a fake smile. She just wanted to escape and get away from the room full of people laughing.

"Hello, Mariah. It's a pleasure to see you again. I love this venue, don't you? They did a wonderful job with the decorations. I wonder who her decorator is," Sarah said.

Mariah met Sarah on numerous occasions at various company

events. She was a very poised woman and always dressed immaculately. Today was no exception; Mariah felt underdressed compared to her stunning blue ballroom gown with gold rhinestones and a mini train. She decided to go with the simple purple strapless form-fitted dress she had in her closet. Maybe she would have put more of an effort into her attire if she had been excited to attend this event.

"Yes, Sandra selected an amazing decorator for this event. She told me the company, but I can't remember the name. I will see you all outside for the ceremony," Mariah said, politely excusing herself so she could disappear into the bathroom.

She walked inside as two women were leaving and immediately ran over to the sink to wet a paper towel and dab at her face. She was thankful she wasn't wearing any foundation. Isaac liked the fact that she didn't wear a whole lot of make–up, aside for a touch of eye shadow and shade of lip gloss or lipstick. That was one of the things he said attracted him to her in the beginning because he could always see her true beauty and not a made-up canvas.

Mariah discarded the napkin and ran her fingers through her shoulder length curls. She had to figure out a way to get through this day. The wedding hadn't even started yet, and she was starting to feel nauseated. She still had to make it through the cocktail hour, dinner, and dancing without Isaac noticing how uncomfortable she was feeling. He knew she didn't want to get married again, but he didn't know going to weddings made her feel sick to her stomach.

"You have to pull yourself together," Mariah mumbled to herself in the mirror. The yellow light bulb went off in Mariah's head. She could use the stomach ache as an excuse to leave the wedding. Isaac already thinks she's not feeling well because she hadn't eaten anything earlier, so this could be a perfect reason to leave without causing any suspicion. However, Mariah knew deep down that it would be wrong to lie. She liked Sandra and would feel guilty to miss her special day, even if she secretly felt Sandra was making a big mistake by getting married. *Nevertheless, she'll have to learn just like I did*, Mariah thought as the bathroom door opened, and a woman walked in with her little girl. They walked into one of the empty stalls to leave Mariah alone at the sink to pull it together.

"Mariah, you can do this. Today is not the day to rehash your failed marriages to Darren and Arthur. Leave your pain at this sink. You have met a wonderful man who loves you, and you love him. All is better for you in the world now. You're not the one who spent all this money on this day like Sandra did to have to undergo the pain of a divorce later. Rejoice in the fact that you have overcome your own pain and are now in a better place. One who has a great career, her own home, and is making her own decisions in life now without having to consult anyone else," she mumbled under her breath as the bathroom door opened again allowing the laughter and talking from outside to pour in. She took a deep breath, stuck her clutch under her arm and walked boldly out of the bathroom to go meet Isaac.

Worried, Isaac was already en route to meet her as she walked out of the bathroom.

"Honey, are you okay? The ceremony is about to start," he said leading her back outside to find a seat with the remainder of the guests. A horn player started to sound off, signaling the start of the wedding.

"I'm fine now. Nothing a splash of water on the face couldn't cure," she said with a big smile as they took a seat four rows from the front. The seats were picked out by Isaac, close to the ceremony.

The wedding ceremony only lasted twenty minutes, but it was beautiful. Sandra walked down the aisle in a Vera Wang mermaid style wedding gown with her father by her side. They had a small wedding party with three cute flower girls and a ring bearer, all of whom were so adorable they almost stole the show. As Sandra and Matt were saying their vows to one another, Mariah felt Isaac looking at her through her peripheral vision. She turned to face him and saw a warm, loving glare in his eyes that she had never seen before. He mouthed to her the words, *I Love You*, and she repeated the same words back to him with a huge smile as she scooted closer to him. She thought it was going to be hard to get through the day, but the nauseating feeling had disappeared.

The comfort of being in Isaac's presence made Mariah feel so much better, that she was happy that she didn't tell him what was going on when they first arrived. Once the Pastor announced the couple as husband and wife, an explosion of fireworks went off in the air which sent the crowd into a big uproar with applauds and well wishes. *Sandra looks so happy*, Mariah thought, as she walked down the aisle with her husband. The wedding party followed behind them to the pianist playing their exit song.

The wedding coordinator, Mildred, got on a nearby microphone to announce to the guest that the couple would be taking pictures with the family outside. She asked everyone to head to the cocktail bar on the terrace and to the downstairs ballroom afterwards for the reception.

As Mariah was about to get up with the other guest, Isaac pulled her back down in her seat. "Hey, let's hang out here for a quick second. I haven't told you how beautiful you look today. The bride has nothing on you," Isaac said as he kissed the back of Mariah's hand.

"Awww, how cute of you to say that, but this is no Vera Wang dress, my dear," she said with a chuckle, crossing her legs.

"I'm not talking about your dress. I'm talking about you," Isaac said delicately touching her chin. "You are the most amazing woman I have ever met, and I've been around a few in my day."

Normally those last words would have put Mariah on edge, but that's how secure she felt about their relationship. Isaac had always been upfront and honest with her and vice-versa since day one of dating. He never lied about dating a lot of women in the past before he met Mariah or his sincere readiness to finally settle down in a monogamous relationship with her.

When they had first met, Mariah had gotten involved with him as a friend because she wasn't looking for anything too serious. It also took the pressure off of worrying if he would revert to his player days. However, as their relationship progressed, Mariah got to know the real Isaac as a friend and now lover and she knew she didn't have anything to worry about concerning his loyalty to her. This is what made this moment seem so real because she knew he was telling her the truth.

"You're amazing too, Isaac," she said.

"I'm so happy I went to the gym that day when we first met. I still remember to this day how I almost stayed home and would have missed the chance to meet you. What did you think about the wedding?" he asked, changing the subject abruptly. His voice changed from a romantic tone to a more serious one, as he sat up tall in his chair, fixing his suit jacket.

"I thought the ceremony was beautiful. I mean I've had two others myself, so I guess I would be the pro to ask, but I don't know…if they had to do it, I would have just gone to the Justice of the Peace and spent all of this money on a long trip somewhere," Mariah said with emphasis on the words had to do it.

"Yeah, but I bet you were a gorgeous bride. I'm so happy that you're available now and all mine. Come on, let's go grab a bite to eat. Hopefully, this place has some good food," Isaac said, taking her hand and helping her to her feet.

"Yeah, I agree. I'm hungry," Mariah said, walking in the direction of the terrace with his arm around her waist.

Chapter Four

"Aerilis Corporation makes one of the most marketable products in the world. They are a top contender against their competitors, and they need a top contender's level marketing campaign. We need to provide them something edgy. Something exhilarating that will make their customers want to run out and buy this vacuum cleaner as soon as they see it advertised on television or see an ad on the side of a city bus. What they need is something that will attract stay-at-home moms who are busy with the kids and only have a second to spare before the baby wakes up again. It needs to attract busy working professionals who either hate vacuuming, or do not have the time to get it done, but know they have to in order to keep from staring at a dirty carpet," Mariah said, as she adjusted her gold-rimmed reading glasses and walked around the boardroom speaking to her marketing team.

"I can't tell you how important it is for us to win this contract. There are going to be other marketing firms just like us bidding for this potential client. We only get one shot to make a lasting impression. Let's focus more on the fact that this is a new generation of vacuum cleaning. Shoot, I've seen the darn thing. It's amazing! It's almost as if you push a button and the vacuum cleaner goes by itself!" Mariah said with enthusiasm, as she sat back down at the boardroom table at the front of the room.

"So you don't want us to focus so much on the general features, but more on the new features the vacuum cleaner has to offer in this market today?" Arbela, a Marketing Analyst, asked.

"You've got it, Arbela! I want the customers to know they are not losing any of the features you'll see in your every-day standard vacuum cleaner, but highlight the new age features the most," Mariah responded.

"I definitely think we have enough to get started," Peter Graham, Marketing Director, said as the others at the table nodded in agreement.

"Good. Well, let's have a meeting on Thursday around 9 a.m. to check to see what you have come up with. The meeting with the Aerilis President is in three weeks, so we have to make this top priority. I'll have Susan send out a meeting request to the team for Thursday morning. Have a good afternoon," Mariah said as she rose from the table collecting her folders and paperwork.

"Mariah, Keith wants to see you real fast in the other boardroom," Susan, the office administrator, said, poking her head in the room as everyone else was walking out.

"Sure, on my way," Mariah said, following Susan to the boardroom around the corner. She had meeting after meeting all day today. She hoped this meeting would be a quick one so she could grab a bite to eat.

Mariah walked into the boardroom, already filled with other senior executives in the company, and took the only available seat in the front next to Keith.

"Alright, can everyone hear me on the phone? We're now ready to get this meeting started," Keith said, turning up the volume on the telecom phone as the participants on the phone acknowledged the fact that they could hear him fine.

Great, Mariah thought. This was going to be another long meeting if they were having a teleconference call with the other senior executives located in their Michigan, Texas, and Los Angeles offices.

"I would like to start off by thanking you all for making time in your busy schedule to attend this short notice meeting. I love meetings like this because it allows us to take a break from budgets, trend reports and things of that nature. We can now take the time to recognize one of our very own in this dominating, competitive marketing industry," Keith said as the other members in the boardroom cheered at his comment.

"As I was saying, we're here today to recognize one of our own peers. This person doesn't know it yet, but she has been nominated by her peers to be our Spotlight Senior Executive of the Year," Keith said as Susan walked over to present him with a plaque. "This person has been ever vigilant throughout the years in ensuring Armstrong & Associates' strong position in the Marketing industry, as well as helping us to get to be the top 10 company out of 500 businesses. This is a pretty big accomplishment. She started out with us fresh out of college and has worked her way up to being someone who is a valuable asset to this company. Mariah Langston, congratulations and we appreciate all of the hard work that you do for us," Keith said, turning to present her with the plaque and an envelope.

Mariah was in complete shock as the other members in the boardroom stood up to clap for her. She couldn't believe it. Her hands were slightly shaking with a rush of adrenaline running through her body as she accepted the envelope and plaque. She had seen so many senior executives win this award over the years and never thought she would be in the elite rankings to be in line with them. The majority of the recipients were men who had been with the company for a minimum of twenty years. This award was definitely a big deal in her career.

"Speech, Speech, Speech!" she heard cheers from the back of the room.

Mariah stood up to thank her colleagues. "Thank you all for this award. I have enjoyed working with each of you during my fourteen years here. You have all played a major part in my success, and I look forward to the great accomplishments we're going to achieve together for Armstrong and Associates this year! Including securing the Aerilis contract," Mariah added, as the room exploded with applauds and cheers in agreement.

She took her seat feeling elated and well-respected amongst

40

her peers; all the hard work and sacrifices she had put in over the years was now paying off. Not to mention this award will definitely look good on her resume.

"You will be formally honored at this year's banquet in August, which will be held in Las Vegas. As a recipient of this award, all of your travel accommodations will be paid for, including a limo ride to the banquet. Congratulations," Keith said, shaking her hand.

At the conclusion of the meeting, it seemed as if everyone in the room wanted to personally congratulate her, which Mariah didn't mind at all. However, she couldn't wait to call Isaac and tell him this great news. As soon as she was able to make it back to her office, she closed her door so she wouldn't be disturbed and immediately started jumping up and down as she dialed Isaac's number.

"Isaac, you will not believe what just happened!" she screamed as soon as he came on the line.

"Hi, Mariah. What's going on?" he inquired.

"I just received the Spotlight Senior Executive of the Year award! This is such a major accomplishment. Most people don't get this type of recognition until they've been with the company for twenty years. I'm so excited right now that I can't contain myself, not to mention stoked about the nice bonus that comes along with this," she said, fingering the envelope she received in her hand.

"Wow! That's amazing, Mariah. I'm so proud of you. You definitely deserve it. I'm happy to see your colleagues recognize the amount of work you've been putting in around there. We have to celebrate," Isaac said.

"Yes, we do! How about LaManga tonight?" she asked, excitedly.

"Oh no, this is a special occasion. I don't want to take you to a place that we go all the time. How about tomorrow night, 7:30 p.m. at the Sheridan Room?" he asked.

"Wow, the Sheridan Room. Sounds perfect. I can't wait. Before you go, I just want you to know you're the first person I called to share this news. I know I don't say this a lot, but I really appreciate having you in my life. You're definitely one special man and I'm lucky to have found you," Mariah said.

She noticed a small delay with Isaac responding and hoped she didn't pour out too much of her feelings. They have told each other on numerous occasions how much they mean to one another, but this time seemed different. Mariah hoped he took it for what it was and didn't read anything more into what she had just said. She was excited about her award and it was definitely causing her to speak more freely than she normally would.

"Mariah, you already know I feel the same way about you. It means a lot to hear you say that though," Isaac said finally.

Mariah felt like she could breathe again after hearing his

response. He felt the same way about her. She could even tell he was smiling through the phone as he made his comment.

"Well, I'll let you get back to work. I look forward to seeing you tomorrow night. I'll give you a call later on tonight," Mariah said.

She hung up the phone feeling like she was on top of the world. She had a successful career, a successful relationship – for once in her life - and she was making all the rules without anyone's input in her decisions. Yes, she was definitely in a good place. She controlled her own destiny.

Chapter Five

Friday evening, Mariah walked into the Sheridan Room looking like a million bucks. She had on a beautiful black fitted Michael Kors asymmetrical dress with her hair pinned up in a neat bun. The Sheridan Room was a five-star restaurant and Mariah felt very special to be celebrating here.

"Hello, I'm here to meet Isaac Stevens," Mariah told the hostess at the podium.

To her amazement, she was directed to the Quantum Private Room. She couldn't believe Isaac had actually reserved a private room for her celebration. She was just happy to be eating a five-star meal with the other attendants at the restaurant enjoying the view of the harbor.

Mariah thanked the hostess and did a double take when she saw the ambiance that had been set up for her. In the center of the room was a dinner table for two with a tall glass vase filled with her favorite flowers, two dozen white tall stemmed calla lilies. The presentation on the table was immaculate. Gold rimmed china plates, gold tableware, and tall crystal flutes were displayed perfectly on beautifully printed linens.

"OMG," was all Mariah could mouth as the lights in the dimly lit room turned up, displaying the lighted trees in each corner of the room and the wide glass floor—length window overlooking the harbor. A soft saxophone started playing a simple melody through the speakers as Isaac entered from the back of the room in a crisp three-piece black suit.

"Isaac, wow, I didn't know you were here already. This room is exquisite. Thank you so much," Mariah said, rushing over to give him a big hug. He smelled good and his fresh haircut and clean appearance made her proud to have him as her man.

"The best for the best, Baby. I'm so happy you like it," he said holding her close in his arms.

Mariah bent in to give him a kiss on the lips. She felt so safe in his arms; his strong grip encompassing her as they kissed. "Mmmm, you definitely know how to treat a woman. I can't believe you pulled this off in such short notice," she said as their lips parted.

"I try," Isaac said with a smile.

"So what's on the menu?" Mariah asked, excitedly walking over to the table. She hadn't eaten since breakfast, due to all the meetings she had all day at work and she was starving – as usual.

"Oh tonight's just the beginning, Honey; we have a lot to celebrate. Your award, and us. I'll be right back," Isaac said, pulling out her chair for her to sit down.

"Okay," Mariah said, placing the napkin on her lap. Isaac walked out the back of the room again. He reentered five minutes later with two waiters. One held a bottle of Dom Perignon and the other carried a platter of baked shrimp.

Mariah watched her glass being filled.

"Would you like cheese?" the other waiter offered her after adding the appetizer to her plate.

"Please," Mariah accepted.

"Enjoy," the waiters said, exiting the room.

"This looks delicious," Mariah said, tasting the baked crispy crust over the shrimp.

"Oh, I hope you didn't mind me taking the liberty of ordering the appetizer in advance. I thought you would enjoy it," Isaac said fingering his fork over his food.

"Definitely, thank you. It's delicious," Mariah said smiling. A few minutes passed and she noticed how quiet Isaac had become, barely touching his food.

"What's wrong, Honey?" she inquired.

"Oh nothing is wrong. Everything is so right," he said, smiling as his phone rang. He took the call and excused himself from the table.

Mariah nodded and sat finishing up her appetizer, enjoying the saxophone playing over the speaker. The music changed to a slower jazz guitar as the waiters reappeared to collect their appetizer dishes.

"You can leave his plate. I think he is still working on his appetizer. Are we going to get a menu for dinner?" Mariah inquired.

"Yes ma'am. Mr. Stevens asked for us to hold on the dinner menu for right now, but I can bring you one out if you would like?" the gentleman asked with a Norwegian accent.

"That's fine. I can wait," Mariah said, wondering what was taking Isaac so long to return to the table. She walked over to the floor-length window that extended the whole left side of the room. The harbor looked gorgeous tonight, lit up, showing off the ships and boardwalk with night walkers. Tonight was ever so perfect.

The door opened and Isaac came back in the room. He walked up behind her and turned her around. She was surprised to see her parents, sister and brother-in-law, and Isaac's parents enter the room followed by a few of their close friends.

"What's going on?" Mariah asked, confused.

"Mariah, I told you I wanted to celebrate your award tonight and us," he said, speaking loud so the others could hear him.

"You're an amazing woman. My family and friends can all see how you have made me a better man. I didn't know what we share was even possible until I met you, and this is why I brought our family and friends here tonight. To congratulate the woman in my life for receiving such an honorary award at work for her hard efforts and......," Isaac said, reaching into his pocket for a red box.

He bent down on one knee and took her hand. Mariah felt the

room begin to spin and at that moment she couldn't breathe.

"Mariah Langston, I don't want to go another second without knowing for certain that you're going to be by my side in life forever. You're the one I want to grow old with. Would you please do me the honor of becoming my wife?" he asked, looking at Mariah with the most sincere eyes she had ever seen.

Mariah wanted to pass out when she heard the happy squeals from the others in the room. Isaac opened the box to reveal a beautiful solitaire center stone surrounded with a karat of diamonds on a platinum band. She looked around the room at all the happy faces. Her sister was standing beside her husband with her hand over her mouth in awe, tears in her eyes. Her parents stood looking proud. Even Isaac's mom was in tears.

Mariah wanted so badly to rewind the time back to earlier today. She wished she had an easy board to erase this very moment. She thought she and Isaac had an understanding that they weren't interested in all this jazz. They were supposed to be doing things the way they wanted to, without anyone's opinion of where their relationship should go next.

"Mariah, are you going to leave me down here or are you going to give me an answer?" Isaac asked nervously, still smiling.

"I'm sorry…I'm just so surprised. I wasn't expecting this," she said.

"So, are you ready to become Mrs. Stevens?" he asked, still

down on one knee holding firmly to her hand.

"Y-Yes," was all she could mouth as everyone in the room started to clap and squeal with excitement. Isaac rose to his feet to put the ring on her left hand.

"Everyone, we're getting married!" Isaac yelled.

At that moment, everyone rushed to hug them and to examine the engagement ring.

"Baby Sis, you're getting married," Tina said. Mariah wanted to hit her in the stomach for making such a comment. She acted as if she hadn't been a bridesmaid in her past two weddings.

Mariah felt embarrassed. She was obviously a failure at marriage and found it hard to stand proud in a room full of people who were already rushing her down the aisle by asking when the wedding date was going to be. She felt worse when her father, the comedian of their family, made a light joke that he was glad she had a good paying job this time around so he didn't have to pay for another wedding. Her mother nudged him softly, but Mariah was glad that she and Tina were the only ones who heard it over all of the other conversations going on in the room. The waiters re-entered the room with bottles of champagne and more flutes.

Mariah was fuming inside. She had gone against everything she said she would ever do again in her life to help Isaac save face. Finding it hard to hold up the phony expression any longer, she excused herself to the restroom. Isaac was happily talking to his best friend, Christopher, who was now the best man in the wedding. Isaac didn't even notice how tense she had become.

Mariah walked out of the room and ran into the bathroom across the hall. "UGH!" she screamed as soon as she got inside. Luckily no one else was in there. She walked over to the granite sink and leaned against it, tears starting to fall down her face. "I can't believe this is happening again," she mumbled as the door swung open and Tina walked in.

"You...you knew about this didn't you?!" she questioned her sister immediately, turning around with daggers in her eyes.

"What's wrong? I knew about what...the proposal?" Tina asked confused, rushing to her sister's side.

"Yes, about this damn proposal. You of all people know I never want to get married again. How is it that you hear men are so afraid of marriage, yet I continuously keep finding the ones who are so willing to propose to me? For Pete's sake, Isaac knew I never wanted to get married again, so why would he do something like this?"

"You're so ungrateful, Mariah Elizabeth Langston. Did you hear what you just said? Obviously these men see something special in you that they want to make you their wife. Now I understand your past marriages didn't last, but that has nothing to do with you and Isaac. I know women who would kill to be in your shoes right now. You've got to let go of this fear you have allowed to manifest in your mind about marriage or I'm sorry, Mariah, you will lose

Isaac," Tina said sternly to her sister.

"Me?! Me?! It's always my fault!" Mariah yelled, tears falling down her face as she reached for a Kleenex on the sink.

Tina threw her arms up in frustration. "Whatever Miss Drama Queen. You're hopeless."

"Let me tell you something. You can say what you want about me because you're my older sister, but I know what I want and what I feel is right for me and that's all that matters. And this is not it!" Mariah yelled, pointing to the ring on her finger.

The reflection from the shiny diamonds illuminated in the room as the light hit it. She looked at the gorgeous ring and for a split second she became honored and excited all at once to wear such an exquisite ring. But then the images of walking down the aisle to say I do, to later experiencing a relationship change from better to worse brought Mariah back to reality quickly. She couldn't go through this again.

"Mariah, I didn't know Isaac had called us here tonight for a proposal. He said you had won an award at work and he wanted us all here to celebrate. Why don't you just enjoy yourself tonight and relax. You don't have to get married tomorrow," Tina said, giving her sister a hug.

"Okay," Mariah said as she held onto her sister dearly for support.

"Now, let's get your face cleaned up. I don't want Isaac or

anyone else seeing you looking all frazzled...especially Mom!" Tina pointed out while raising her eyebrows. Their mom seemed to have ESP when they were growing up; she knew something was wrong with them before they showed any signs of it.

Mariah nodded her head in agreement. She knew her sister was right.

"You have a wonderful man who loves you, Mariah. And this is one hell of a ring. If your ring is the size of how much this man really adores you, then he loves you a whole lot," Tina said trying to shed light on the situation as she wiped her sister's face delicately from the tear stains.

"Thank you. It is a gorgeous ring. Okay, I guess it's time to go back out there," Mariah said, blowing air out of her mouth to relieve stress as she looked at herself in the mirror. Her stomach was still churning inside, but she was going to do her best to make it through the rest of the night. That was all she could promise at this point.

Chapter Six

Mariah rolled over in bed and looked at Isaac sleeping. It was 7 a.m., Saturday morning, the day after his proposal, and she felt like a mess. Against her wishes last night, Isaac had insisted that she spend the night with him. After the party, Isaac wanted to take a walk on the harbor boardwalk together. Mariah was finding it harder and harder as the night progressed to continue to hold up her fake happiness routine, but she agreed to go to make Isaac happy.

She felt agitated inside the whole time, longing for the night to hurry up and be over with. She almost cracked toward the end of their walk when Isaac kept asking questions about their engagement. If she had any idea that he was going to propose to her and what date did she have in mind to get married? Luckily, they had reached the end of the boardwalk near the parking lot at that point, and she was able to avoid answering those questions. Mariah was more relieved that she could finally make it to her car alone and sort out the details of what had just transpired. But the so overjoyed Isaac wanted to spend even more time together and asked that she spend the night with him at his place.

Mariah thought she would scream at this point and used every excuse from being tired to having to work out with her sister in the morning to try to get out of it. All she could remember seeing was the disappointed look on Isaac's face and decided to give in yet again. She dreaded the drive over to his condo. For the first time since they had started dating, she wished she could make a U-Turn and go back to her house. She didn't know how much longer she could keep up this charade of being happy about the engagement. It was one thing to pretend you're happy in a room full of people or walking on a boardwalk with so many distractions going on around you, but to be alone with Isaac was going to be tough.

Isaac liked to look in her eyes when she talked to him, as if he was always searching her soul to verify whether or not what she was saying was the truth. She didn't know if that came from his profession of being a defense attorney, but she knew she didn't feel up to facing him and his interrogating eyes when they arrived at his condo last night. The fact of the matter is that she was deceiving him. She had accepted a proposal in front of their friends and family that she knew she was not going to go through with.

Tina used to say when they were growing up that she was a very good actress. She used to always get Mariah to be their spokesperson for getting out of doing chores or pretending to be sick so they could stay home from school. Mariah was able to fool her parents back then and as she stepped into Isaac's condo last night, she felt she had fooled him too. Mariah felt like she deserved an Academy Award for her performance. No one at the engagement party had even picked up on her disgruntled mood. She decided to take it up a notch and pretend she was extremely tired so she could go straight to bed, which Isaac, surprisingly, didn't mind. All he wanted to do was get into bed beside her and hold her in his arms.

Mariah placed the events of the prior evening in the back of her mind as she rolled over away from Isaac and looked at her ring finger. The sparkly diamond was still shining on her left hand.

"Good Morning, you still can't believe it, huh?" Isaac asked rolling over and kissing her on the shoulder.

Mariah was startled. He had caught her looking at the ring. "Yeah, Honey. This ring is gorgeous," she muttered, sitting up in bed and stretching. "I hate to leave, but I've got to get up now in order to make it back to my place to get my workout clothes. It's my turn to drive to Tina's this month," she said climbing out of bed.

"Okay, I love your dedication. I guess I could stand to hit the gym myself if I want to look good standing next to you on our wedding day," Isaac said, flexing his arms in the bed.

Mariah tried to ignore his comment as she pulled off his T-shirt she had slept in and slipped back into her dress from last night.

"I was starting to think when you were sleeping that I don't really think we should have a long drawn-out engagement. I'm already forty, you've been married before, and we've already been together for three years," he said.

Mariah turned to face Isaac as she was putting on her earrings.

"Yes, I've been married before, which is why…never mind. I'll call you later, okay?" she said walking toward the door.

"Mariah, what were you about to say?" Isaac inquired.

She turned around and tried to hold back her tears. The last thing she wanted to do was hurt Isaac or lose him for that matter. "Isaac, when I first met you I said I never wanted to get married again and you were fine with it, so I'm just confused right now. What's with the change of heart?"

"I was fine with it until we left your co-worker's wedding. I saw how you were looking like you wanted it to be you. I didn't want to deny you a chance at marriage again, especially when I've been ready to ask you this question for some time now. I want to marry you. I want you to become my wife. I just assumed that the idea was never possible until I saw your reaction to your co-worker's wedding," Isaac said, rising out of the bed and walking over to her.

Darn! The Academy Award act again! Shucks, if she had just told him how she felt or didn't put on that front like she was happy at the wedding, then she wouldn't be in this situation right now.

As Mariah was about to object to this whole engagement and finally come clean and tell Isaac how she really felt, he went into his lawyer mode and started to talk over her.

"You're scared and I don't blame you. I never thought I would be getting married at all before I met you. But you're a very special woman, Mariah, designed specifically for me and I can promise you that I will always be here for you until death do us part. You don't have to worry anymore," Isaac said, putting his arms around her.

Mariah wasn't convinced, but she wasn't in the mood to fight him on it. She would break this whole engagement off soon enough. She just had to find the perfect way to tell him so they could at least still be together afterwards. She would find a way to make him see that marriage was overrated and they were fine just the way they are. As Mariah unlocked arms with Isaac, she headed to the front door where she had placed her heels from last night.

"Let me slip some pants on so I can walk you out!" Isaac yelled from the bedroom.

"Honey, it's okay. I'm already running late. I'll call you later," Mariah said, opening up the door and rushing out before Isaac could get ready and follow her to her car.

She rode the elevator down to the parking garage and walked over to Isaac's visitor parking spot. It was now after 8 a.m. The sun was just starting to come out as she drove onto the main street toward the interstate. Mariah didn't have enough time to get home, change, and make it to her sister's house before 9 a.m., even though Isaac only lived twenty minutes from her house. She wasn't really in the mood to work out today anymore. She had to figure out what to do about this engagement. She looked down at her ring as she stopped at a red light. The diamonds sparkled in the sunshine.

Mariah remembered this was the very same time of year when she got engaged to Arthur. His ring wasn't as over the top as the ring Isaac had given her. But now that she thought about it, the proposal wasn't either...

It was a rainy Saturday morning. Mariah was cooking eggs and turkey bacon. She separated yolk from whites as Arthur came into her apartment, back from the grocery store. He had run out to get orange juice for breakfast about thirty minutes ago.

"Hey, sorry it took me so long," Arthur said, walking into the kitchen and placing the carton of juice on the island in the center of the room.

"I was wondering what happened. The store is only around the corner," Mariah said, emptying the bowl of egg whites into the frying pan. She turned her back to Arthur as she continued to prepare breakfast.

"I'll put the plates out on the table. Would you mind heating up some of those fried potatoes and onions you made last night for dinner to go with breakfast? They were really good," Arthur said, heading to the nearby dining room.

Mariah started to smile at her man as he complimented her on her cooking. She enjoyed having him around this week, cooking for him and spending close time together as he was having renovations done to his house. They had been dating for two years and she was secretly hoping he would hurry up and pop the question. However, if there was one thing she learned from her mother, it was you never force a man to marry you. So until he was ready to ask the question, she would just enjoy moments like this

58

playing house with her boyfriend. Mariah heated up the potatoes and put all the food contents into separate bowls, on a silver serving tray that her mother had brought for her as a house warming gift some months back. Mariah took it to her dining room table. She went the extra steps with presentation of her food so that Arthur could see what it would be like if he lived with her permanently.

"Everything looks great, Mariah. Thanks," Arthur said as he started to dig in.

"I forgot the orange juice, one sec," Mariah said rushing back to the kitchen to get the carton of juice.

As she picked it up, she noticed a slip of paper taped to it. Displayed across the front were typed words in a large red font, WILL YOU MARRY ME? Mariah dropped the carton of juice to the floor. She turned to where Arthur was sitting at the kitchen table.

"Mariah is everything okay?" he asked, turning around in his chair with a huge grin on his face.

Mariah looked at him with the biggest smile on her face. Arthur got up from the table and looked down at the carton of juice on the floor. He picked it up, placed it on the counter and took Mariah's hand.

"So, will you marry me?" he asked.

"Will I marry you?! Yes!" Mariah yelled as she jumped up and down and leaped into his arms.

Arthur held her close then reached into his pocket and took out a ring box.

"This ring was given to my grandmother by my grandfather. I had the center stone reset. He placed the ring on Mariah's ring finger.

She was so in love that he could have put a piece of lint on her finger and she would have been happy. She looked down at the antique-style ring reset with a princess cut center stone. It was different and not what she had envisioned her engagement ring would look like growing up as a little girl, especially since she and her first husband could only afford plain wedding bands the first go around. But she was happy because she was wearing the ring from the man she loved, and whom she was going to spend the rest of her life with. She would wear the ring proudly.

"Do you want to sit down and finish breakfast together?" Arthur asked.

"Are you kidding me?! I can't eat right now! I'm too excited! I have to call my sister and my mom!" Mariah yelled as she ran to pick up her wall phone. She was so excited that she couldn't contain herself and couldn't wait to share the good news.

Mariah pressed on the gas as the light changed to green and she veered right onto the interstate. Looking back she realized there was no getting down on one knee like Isaac had done, and the ring that Isaac had given her was the one that she had envisioned she would always have growing up as a little girl.

The only problem was that Isaac's ring came years too late. She couldn't go back in time and erase her past. The fact of the matter was that she had been married twice before and things changed in both situations after she had said the words "I do."

It was as if the love that bonded her in both relationships wasn't enough to hold them together forever. She loved Isaac too much to risk their relationship deteriorating to the point that they ended up in divorce too. Mariah just couldn't imagine that, much less deal with it, knowing how much she cared about him.

She and Arthur were supposed to be together forever too, but now they were living in the same city no longer married. Mariah refused to take the risk of adding Isaac's name to that list. Luckily for her, Darren, her first husband, got a really good job at a software company in New York right after graduation and never moved back home.

When she pulled up in her driveway, Mariah realized she had been thinking about her marriage to Arthur more than how she was going to get out of the engagement to Isaac and still salvage their relationship. Although she no longer had feelings for Arthur, she couldn't get past the fact that they were supposed to fight with all they had to make their marriage work.

As much as she loved Isaac, and couldn't see her life now without him, she was still scared. If her marriage with Arthur had just worked out, this could have definitely prevented the humiliation of having to get married for a third time to someone else. How was she supposed to trust that she and Isaac could fight to make things work when the going got tough, when she wasn't successful in doing so in her two previous marriages? Where had she and Arthur gone wrong?

Mariah stepped out of her convertible and walked up to her front door. She was going to dial a number that she never thought she would have to dial again. It was fine time she got the answer to this question. Maybe this would change everything. Maybe.

Chapter Seven

Mariah pressed the doorbell and waited for Arthur to answer the front door. She noticed how nervous she had become standing on his front stoop. She started to tap her pink and white Nikes on the steps. After Mariah had called and canceled her workout plans with her sister, she decided to pay a visit to her ex-husband Arthur. Mariah tried not to dress too appealing to give Arthur any ideas. He used to compliment her on her long, smooth, toned legs so she opted to wear jeans on this 80-degree day. She wore a pink velour short-sleeved top. Although she was dressed very casually today, her hair was in a perfect form with bouncy roller set curls. The last thing she wanted was for Arthur to think she had completely fallen apart after they split up. Mariah heard footsteps heading to the front door.

Arthur stood before her in a white tank top, a pair of Nike shorts and Nike flip flops. He hadn't taken the time to get dressed up for her either. She hadn't seen him in years, but he was still strikingly handsome. He had let his facial hair grow out in a goatee and still had a toned physique. He smiled showing off his dimples and pearly white teeth. Mariah found herself staring back at his gray eyes.

"So what did I do to deserve your company today? You didn't want alimony so…what's up?" Arthur asked sarcastically, leaning against the doorframe.

"Are you going to let me in or am I supposed to talk to you from the stoop? You said you weren't busy when I called," Mariah inquired, becoming testy by his tone of sarcasm.

"Well, I can see you're still pushy," Arthur said as he stepped to the side to allow her to walk inside. All of a sudden, Mariah became really sensitive over his comment as she walked past him and headed for the living room. She could hear the NBA play-offs coming from the television. Was he trying to imply that her pushiness was one of the reasons their marriage didn't work?

She didn't need to be shown where the rooms were in this house; she had lived here with him for the entire time they were married and had decorated every room. As she entered the living room, she noticed it was no longer the same. The brown and red décor she had chosen for the living room now consisted of a two-piece black leather sofa set, giant tan throw rug, big screen television, a fake floor plant, and two wall murals.

Mariah sat on the far side of the couch. Arthur sat at the other end of the couch and reached for his can of beer on the coffee table.

"Would you like something to drink?" he offered.

"No, thank you. I don't plan on staying long. So, how are things going for you?" Mariah asked, finding it rude to just get to the nature of business without creating some type of small talk.

"Things are going well actually. I can't complain. I just signed a three-book deal with my publishing company. I'm working on the sequel to my last book," Arthur said, leaning back on the couch.

"That's awesome! I can't wait to read it. The first book was really good. My email address is still the same so feel free to add it to your listserv to notify me when your book comes out. I'm still working at Armstrong and Associates, but I'm now heading up their marketing department," Mariah said, smiling as she stuck her hands between her legs sitting on the edge of the couch.

Arthur was a writer who wrote articles for magazine companies when they were married. He had always talked about venturing over to the fiction genre, so she was happy to hear it was happening for him.

"I will do that. I'm happy to hear that all is going well with you at Armstrong, too. You were always a good executive there and it's good to hear that they appreciate you," Arthur added.

The air in the room started to become tight and it was apparent that the small talk was turning into overkill. It was obvious that Mariah hadn't shown up after five years to discuss what the other was doing in their careers.

"Okay, well I'm sure you're probably wondering why I called you out of the blue. I would like to talk to you about something," Mariah said as she ran her left hand through her hair.

Arthur's eyes came in contact with her ring and at that

moment she realized she was still wearing it. "Well, well, well, congratulations are definitely in order. When's the big day?" Arthur asked with a snicker on his face.

Mariah knew that look too well. She knew even though they weren't together anymore and hadn't seen each other for some time now; it still did something to his ego to see another man's ring on her finger. She had been his wife just five years ago.

"Oh," she said looking down at the bulky diamond shining on her ring finger as if she had just received it straight from the jewelry store. "Yes, I'm engaged and this is why I need to speak to you."

Arthur's eyebrow rose at her comment. He turned off the game and gave her his undivided attention.

"I just accepted my boyfriend's proposal and I'm having a tough time with it. This would be marriage number three for me, and I'm scared that what happened to us will happen to our relationship once we get married," she said, taking a breath.

She saw Arthur looking at her inquisitively, probably wondering why she was here talking to him about this.

"The reason I'm here is because I'm trying to figure out where we went wrong and why we couldn't stop it before we ended up in divorce. We really didn't have any problems until we got married," she added, resting back against the couch.

Arthur shifted in his seat with a confused expression on his face. At this moment, she felt stupid for even coming over to his house. How could she have expected him to want to help her figure out what went wrong in their marriage, so she could prevent it from happening again in her life? He was of no help to save their marriage five years ago.

"I don't know, Mariah. We got married and starting arguing about things that didn't even make sense. I tried to the best I could to make you happy, but I guess it wasn't enough," Arthur said, brushing it off as if he had amnesia about what really happened.

"Stop it, Arthur! You're not going to put this all on me. You know darn well there was more that could have been done on your end. We started to argue a lot about you and the mother of your child because she was jealous of our marriage and you didn't stand up for us," Mariah said, folding her arms.

"All right, Mariah. I made a lot of mistakes in our marriage. I should have been stricter and put my foot down in a lot of instances concerning the mother of my child," he said.

"I just figured things would eventually iron themselves out, which obviously never happened. Maybe we should have sought counseling for our issues and maybe I should have been more aggressive to get Bianca to respect our marriage. However, back then I felt I was making the right decisions in order to keep the peace and make you happy. I guess I was wrong and by the time I figured it out, it was too late."

"So why didn't we go to counseling?" Mariah asked, eager to hear his response. Is this something that men are even willing to do? Albeit Arthur and Isaac are like night and day with certain characteristics, they are both men and she wanted to hear the answer.

Arthur scooted closer to her. She didn't know if it was a good idea to be sitting that close to her ex but they were divorced now so she figured she would allow it.

"Mariah, I do not regret the years that I spent with you. I learned a lot through it all, and I will say looking back, that I could have done more before agreeing to go separate ways, like going to counseling. But I've always been the type of person who doesn't live with regrets. You know that about me. After we signed the paperwork to end our marriage, I haven't thought much more about what we could have done to fix us. I have accepted that it is over between us and learned what to do next time, if faced with the same challenges. Clearly, you have moved on as well, else you wouldn't be sitting here with another man's ring on your finger," he said, lifting up her left hand to show off her ring. "I recommend that you stand your ground like you did in our marriage and never settle. You were a good catch and I was too blind to see that it was worth fighting for back then. I just wanted peace from all of the bickering that was going on and I took the easy way out. If given the opportunity to remarry again, I would definitely fight to the end for my marriage."

"Well, lucky for you for finally figuring out what you should have done back then," she said matter-of-factly, remembering how

Bianca used to do pop-up drop-off visits with Ethan when they were heading out for planned vacations. She even remembered on multiple occasions how they either had to change their plans, or bring Ethan along to accommodate Bianca to keep the peace, as Arthur so kindly put it back in the day.

"I'm sorry I didn't step up as the husband you needed me to be back then. Maybe in another life we could get it right, but for now I would say move forward with marrying this guy if he truly makes you happy," Arthur said with a sigh.

Mariah looked up at his sincere eyes. This was the first time he had ever apologized for his part in the things that went wrong between them. She also felt this was easy advice for him to give since he had only been married once in his lifetime…unlike her.

"I accept your apology and you're right he does make me happy. I'm just so scared that what happened to us will happen to my marriage with Isaac if I decide to go through with it. No, he doesn't have any kids with a cuckoo mother, but my first husband didn't have any kids either. I don't know, maybe I'm just embarrassed to be getting married again for the third time and I'm only 36 years old," she added, starting to feel so vulnerable that she just came clean with all of her deepest feelings.

At this particular moment, it didn't matter that Arthur was her ex-husband. He had once been her confidant, and she decided to lean on him again for moral support. She felt so alone and had no one else to talk to about what was bothering her. Arthur was the perfect outlet because he was a neutral person in this situation.

Arthur blinked a few times as if he were trying to find the right words to say. Mariah remembered that look very well. It's amazing how you can learn so much about a person that you know what their facial expressions or body movements mean in every situation. "Mariah, you're a smart woman. I doubt very seriously that you would have accepted that ring if you doubted this was something that you really wanted to do. I think you need to let go of the past and just live for today. Who cares if this is your third marriage, if you're with someone who's right for you."

Mariah shifted in her seat, giving some thought to what he was saying. He's definitely right about one thing. She was smart and knew herself well enough to know that if she really didn't want to give the idea of getting married again a second thought, then she would have returned the ring by now. She obviously loved Isaac so much that she would visit her ex-husband to seek advice.

"That's probably the most profound thing that anyone from my family has said to me. My dad is making wise cracks about being happy that he doesn't have to foot the bill for another wedding, and my sister is proclaiming that I'm pure crazy to feel the way I do," Mariah said as she dabbed at a tear forming in her eye. This whole ordeal was really starting to take an effect on her spirits. "Thank you, Arthur. I really appreciate this talk."

"Hey, anytime. I might have sucked as your spouse, but I do remember there was a time when we were friends. I will always care for you, Mariah. I honestly want the best for you. And don't worry about your family. Do what makes you happy," he said, gently turning her chin to face him.

"Thanks again. Well, I feel like I have taken up enough of your time. I'll let you get back to the playoffs," she said, rising from the couch. "I remember how much you loved the game."

"Yeah, this is a good one too. The Lakers are up by twenty points!"

The two started walking toward the front door. Mariah opened it and turned around to face her ex-husband. "Do let me know when your next book comes out and when you do a book signing for it. Take good care of yourself, okay?"

Arthur hugged her and waved good-bye as she walked over to her car. Much to her surprise, the weight of the proposal and anxiety of getting married again had disappeared. She felt good. She felt like giving the idea of getting married again a try. Mariah looked at her engagement ring. She definitely would enjoy wearing this ring while planning a wedding.

Mariah started to back out of Arthur's driveway as her phone started to ring in her purse. She pulled to the side of the street to answer it before getting on the interstate. It was Isaac's parents' number. Perfect timing! She definitely would not have answered while at Arthur's house. She decided that was one visit she would just keep to herself.

"Hello, Mrs. Stevens," Mariah answered.

"Hi, Mariah. How are you doing today?"

"I'm doing okay and yourself?"

"I'm fine, dear heart. I'm calling to see if you're available the Friday after next for an engagement party? Mr. Stevens and I would love to throw one at our house with close family and friends to celebrate your engagement," Mrs. Stevens said with excitement in her voice.

"That actually sounds great. I do not have anything planned off the top of my head for that night."

"Great! I will let you and Isaac know when to arrive as soon as we put everything together. Thank you for letting me and his father do this for you. I do not want to step on your parents' toes considering the parents of the bride handle most of the planning for the wedding. I'm just so excited that my only child is finally getting married," Mrs. Stevens said.

"Oh, it's no problem, trust me. Thank you for the gesture," Mariah added. She knew her parents hadn't planned on throwing anything. This was going to be all her doing if anything was done.

"Okay, well I'll speak to you soon. Have a good evening."

"You do the same. Thank you," Mariah added, before disconnecting the call.

A party – well, this is another step in her engagement process and she was going to take it on in full stride. She started to smile at the idea and realized this gave her an opportunity to do something that she loves to do – go shopping! Since she and Isaac were going to be the highlight of the party, she couldn't go dressed in something she already had in her closet. Before heading back to her side of the city, she decided to go to a nearby shopping center that she had loved to visit when she and Arthur had lived together.

Chapter Eight

Tina hurried downstairs to finish preparing dinner. She sent the kids to her parents' house for the evening so she and Paul could have some much-needed time alone. After the proposal last night, it made her take a look at her own marriage. There was a time that she and Paul were smitten just like that, to the point that they couldn't keep their hands off each other.

Tina used to dress up in various fantasy outfits to give Paul strip teases all over the house – her favorite room being the laundry room where she could really get dramatic. And Paul was no slouch with his deep body massages that would leave her body feeling tingly all over. Yes, those days were worth remembering, although they seemed to be a distant memory now.

Three years ago things started to change. And it didn't help when she quit her job last year as lead chef at a seafood restaurant to start-up her own catering business. Since quitting, she had done some private parties through referrals from previous customers, but it wasn't landing her the big gigs that she had anticipated when she first left her job of fifteen years.

Paul was supportive, but lately Tina could tell he was starting to become overwhelmed with carrying all of the bills for the family. He was a construction foreman and the economy wasn't in the greatest state for the construction business. He was actually meeting with his boss this afternoon to see if they had won a bid on a new contract.

Tina knew if their finances didn't change soon that she would have to put her dreams on hold and go back to work in someone else's restaurant. She desperately hated this thought at this point in her life, at age forty.

She tried to pretend to everyone else that she and Paul were still in marital bliss, but deep down she knew they needed help. She felt like they were drifting apart after sixteen years of marriage.

Paul's car pulled up in the driveway. Tina rushed to light the candles. She took her seat at the dining room table and waited patiently. Her heart began to race as Paul walked through the front door. She couldn't believe how fast it was beating. This was her husband for Pete's sake. Not some stranger she was meeting for a first date. *Has it been that long since they had a romantic evening together?* she thought as Paul appeared at the kitchen doorway.

Tina rose to her feet and smiled. Paul was startled at the dimmed lights coming from the adjacent dining room and the romantic place setting for two. Tina walked over to greet him. She threw her arms around his neck and placed a kiss on his cheek.

"Tina, what's this?" he asked with a confused look on his face.

"Well, I thought we needed to be alone tonight. Come and sit down. I made your favorite dish," she said.

"O-kay. Where are the kids?" Paul asked as he washed his

hands at the kitchen sink before joining Tina in the dining room.

"They're at my parents. So, how did your meeting go? Did you win the bid?" Tina asked eagerly. She placed the salmon grilled with fresh peaches and red onions on their plates with a side of wild rice.

Paul was still taken aback with the attention he was receiving but decided to let it go as he cut his salmon. "Yeah, we won the bid. We're going to be the builders for a new housing development. We start next week on the model homes."

"See, I told you everything would work out! You just have to have a little faith," Tina said, giving him a wink.

"This is good, Tina. Thanks for making dinner. But really tell me what's going on. You're all dressed up, and you have our wedding china out with the candles lit…did you get a new job or something?"

Tina dropped her fork causing it to make a clinging sound against the plate. How dare he ask if she got a job as if she wasn't trying to launch her catering business? She was sick of him not taking her efforts serious.

"Paul, why can't I just do something nice for us? It's not like we get that much time alone with the kids. Why can't you just relax and enjoy the moment?"

Paul calmly placed his fork down and leaned back in his chair. "So now you want to spend time together. When did this start?"

"What do you mean?"

"What do I mean? Are you seriously trying to play me like I don't know what's going on here?"

"No Paul, I don't know what you mean. So why don't you enlighten me, since I'm the one who slaved over this meal to do something nice for you."

Paul started to chuckle, which almost made Tina's blood pressure spike. "Your sister gets engaged last night and all of a sudden you want to care about your marriage. When for months you haven't thought two squats about me."

"That has nothing to do with it! Are you serious?" Tina lied, chuckling this time at his insinuation.

"Nice touch exposing your breast for me tonight in that dress, seeing as I can't remember the last time I got any."

"Well, maybe if you would've sat through this meal with a better attitude you would've gotten some tonight," Tina snarled back at him. She was pissed that he brought her sister's engagement into this, as if she was afraid of her sister upstaging her by getting married again.

"Thank you for the dinner, Tina. But I'm going to head over to your parents' house to pick up the kids. At least they appreciate me," Paul said.

"Why are you going to get the kids? And what do you mean by that. I do appreciate you."

Paul shook his head and headed towards the front door. Tina jumped up from the table and ran after him. The last thing she wanted him to do was pick the kids up early and send warning bells to her mother that something was wrong.

"Paul, wait! Let's sit and talk about this. I'm sorry. I'm just trying to get things back the way they used to be, that's all."

Paul turned around to face his wife. "Tina, you have been complaining for years about how you're unhappy about this and how you're unhappy about that. You wanted a bigger house, so I got you this one. You wanted to start your catering business, so I supported you in your decision to leave your job…when you know we needed the money. And not once do you ask about the things that concern me…or much less just say thank you! Damn! The world doesn't revolve around you, Tina."

Tina stood at a loss for words. She was shocked to hear Paul speak to her like this. She thought she showed him gratitude for being a supportive husband. But then again, if she hadn't, she just figured it was his job to listen.

"Paul, I do appreciate you. I'm sorry for being so stuck in my own mess that I've been neglecting you. Can you please leave the kids at my parents' tonight and come back to the table to enjoy our dinner. I made a cobbler for desert," she said leaning against the door with alluring eyes.

"I need to clear my head. I'll be right back," he said.

"Will you at least leave the kids at my parents!?" Tina called after him.

Paul nodded his head yes as he got in the car. Tina smiled as she closed the door. This was not going to be as easy as she thought. It was time for her to go to the basement and pull out one of her old cat suits. She definitely had her work cut out for her tonight.

Chapter Nine

A week later, Mariah walked into the 94th Aero Squadron restaurant to meet her mother and sister for lunch. Tina had volunteered herself to be the Matron of Honor, as if Mariah would have picked anyone else, and wanted to meet her and their mother to discuss wedding plans. By the time Mariah had arrived, her sister had already settled outside under an umbrella table facing the Montgomery Field airport. She walked over to their table on the grassy embankment, which was stationed amongst World War I replica airplanes. Mariah enjoyed coming here. The restaurant was designed as a WWI French farmhouse, and she hoped the cute duck pond around the exterior grounds would serve as a good distraction as she prepared to talk about the wedding with her sister.

"Hey Tina, you look refreshed and happy today. What's going on? Did you and Paul have a date night last night or something?" Mariah asked as she placed her purse on an adjacent chair.

Tina gave her sister a friendly scrunched-up look. "No date night. I just got to sleep in today that's all. Paul decided he wanted to take the kids out today since he was off. They are going to the aquarium and then over to his parents' house for a visit. I have the whole day to myself."

"That's good. I'm not a mother, but I think it's very important to have time for yourself. Where's Mom? I'm ten minutes late, so I assumed she would have already been here. I offered to pick her up, but she said she would just meet us here," Mariah said.

"Same here. I called the house just before you arrived and Dad said she had already left about thirty minutes ago. At least we know she is on her way. I'm sure she just made a stop somewhere. How are you feeling since I last saw you at the proposal party?" Tina inquired, changing the subject abruptly.

"I'm feeling better. I've decided to at least give the whole marriage idea a try. I'm not one hundred percent comfortable just yet, but I do love Isaac and I'm trying not to let my insecurities get in the way. Oh and before I forget, his parents are throwing us an engagement party next Friday at their house. You and Paul are invited, of course."

Mariah reached into her purse to retrieve the shiny envelope to give to her sister. "Mrs. Stevens asked for your address, but I told her I would just give it to you since we were meeting today."

Tina reached for the invitation and immediately dropped her mouth open. "Wow, snazzy. I can't wait for the party, by the look of this fancy invitation it is sure going to be an event that I do not want to miss. You know Paul and I will be there to support you guys," she said, opening the shiny vanilla envelope engraved with gold writing to display the beautiful cream and gold invitations.

"I thought the same thing when I first saw the invitations. His mother does have great taste."

"His mother and your soon-to-be mother-in-law. I never really asked how your relationship is with his parents. The Stevens seemed like a very nice couple at the proposal party.

"Oh, I love his mom. She is so sweet. His dad is cool and very down to earth. They both have always shown me nothing but love ever since we first started dating," Mariah said, looking down at her watch. She wondered what was taking their mother so long. Their parents lived only twenty minutes away from the restaurant, which was the reason they picked this location.

"We can go ahead and order if you're hungry. I'm sure Mom will be here shortly," Tina said opening up her menu.

At that moment, Mariah wondered what was going on. Normally Tina, with her Type A personality, was always the person in their family who was obsessed with being on time. She would start fussing whenever someone was not as punctual as she was for an appointment. However, today she was cool and collected. Mariah thought it was strange, but decided her sister was probably a bit more relaxed because she was able to sleep in this morning.

Mariah opened up her menu to scan the seafood section. She decided to order the broiled fish and vegetables. Ten minutes later, the waiter took their orders and was leaving just as their mother approached the table.

"Sorry, I'm late girls. I had to make a quick stop," Mrs. Langston said, bending over to give both Tina and Mariah each a kiss on the cheek before taking her seat.

82

"Hi Mom, no worries," Tina said, closing her menu. "I ordered your favorite dish anyway."

"Thank you, Tina. I got caught in a bit of traffic on my way over here," Mrs. Langston responded.

"Well, now that we're all here. Let's get down to the wedding business. As Matron of Honor, I need to know all of your plans, Mariah, so I can be of great assistance to you. First things first, have you picked a date so I can plan your bridal shower around it?" Tina inquired.

"No, we haven't decided on a date yet, but there will be no bridal showers, or tea parties, or anything of that nature. I've already had two in the past and there is no need to have another one this time around. I would really love for you to go looking for dresses with me and just stand by my side on our wedding day," Mariah responded.

Tina made a disappointed face and looked over at her mother for support. "Okay, Mariah. Whatever you say. I was really looking forward to throwing you a nice bridal shower, but I understand. If you can at least send me an email with your bridesmaid's names and contact information, that'll be great. I can make contact with them concerning the wedding details as you make them."

"No, I'm not planning on having bridesmaids either this time. I know Isaac's best friend from his childhood is going to be his best man, but I'm really hoping I can talk him out of having anyone else stand up with us. I really want it to be simple this time around, okay?" Mariah asked, feeling uncomfortable with the strange looks she was receiving from her mother and sister.

"Honey, this is your wedding and you should plan it however you want. But you have to take into consideration that it is Isaac's wedding too. Just relax a little bit, okay?" Mrs. Langston suggested, reaching for her hand on the table.

"I'm relaxed, trust me," Mariah lied.

"Mariah, just get back to me on the date. It seems like you and Isaac still have a lot to sort through. I would still like to throw you a bridal luncheon. I think it will be a nice touch before the wedding with you, Mom, me, and Mrs. Stevens. Does that sound alright?" Tina inquired.

Mariah nodded in agreement. She could handle one small social event.

"Mariah, I cannot tell you how proud I am of you. I still remember like it was yesterday when you were four years old and you used to dress up in my shoes and jewelry and parade around the house," Mrs. Langston said with a chuckle. "I just want you to know that your father and I really like Isaac and we think he's a good catch for you. And if you and Isaac need anything along the way, you know your father and I will always be there for the both of you. With that being said, I wanted to present you with this gift to wish you the best of luck on your upcoming wedding day."

Sweat started to bead on the back of Mariah's back as she

accepted the jewelry box from her mother. Her body started to heat up inside. She had on a sundress, but you would think she had on a cashmere sweater in May from the way she was feeling. She also realized that this was the reason her mother was late. She was off picking up this gift. Tina had a huge grin on her face, which let Mariah know she knew about this the whole time. That's why she was so calm and collected while they were waiting.

Mariah opened the box and immediately wanted to scream. It was a pearl bracelet with her birthstone linked in the middle. Mariah tried to hide her anger. This was their mother's famous touch. Mrs. Langston liked for her daughters to wear her gift on their wedding day – Something New.

When Mariah first got engaged, their mother gave her their grandmother's necklace. She had been saving it for her since she was a little girl. For her second engagement, she received her great-aunt's diamond earrings. Tina received a bracelet that was another family heirloom as her gift for her wedding. However, the pearl bracelet that Mariah received today was store bought. It had no connection to their family and it proved one thing. Mariah had used up all of the special gifts from her previous failed marriages; thus the reason she felt so angry inside at this moment. Her mother had to go out and buy something this time to show her congratulation.

"I hope you like it," Mrs. Langston said.

Mariah tried to muster up a happy smile so that she didn't hurt her mother's feelings. "Mom, it's beautiful, but you really didn't have to go out and spend money on a gift. I would have been happy to wear grandma's necklace again."

The look that Tina shot her let her know that the attempt she tried to make to not hurt their mother's feelings did not go over so well.

"Mariah, you know I like to give you girls something special to wear on your big day, but if you do not like it I can just take it back," Mrs. Langston said softly.

"No, Mom, it's not that at all. Okay – here it is. I'm still not feeling comfortable with getting married again. I've been married twice before and I just feel like everyone is going to look at me as crazy for getting married again. Like I'm some type of failure or something," Mariah said, closing the bracelet box and looking down at her water glass.

"Sis, I've never heard you say that before. I thought you were worried about getting married again for your own purposes. I had no idea you were worried about what other people might say. Who cares about that anyway? You're marrying a perfect man designed for you, so please don't worry about what other people may say about it," Tina said, getting up from the table and going over to comfort her.

"Mariah, baby, I'm sorry that the bracelet put you in an uncomfortable position. Don't let situations from your past hold you back from blessings you have received to go forward in the future. I didn't raise you or Tina to be concerned with what other people have to say about you, and I do not want you to start thinking like that now. You're a beautiful, successful woman and Isaac knows it. This is why he wants *you* to be his wife. It really doesn't matter what anyone else thinks," Mrs. Langston said reaching for her hand again.

Mariah held onto her mother's hand. "Thank you. I'm not just concerned about how it looks. I'm really worried that once I say I do, the beautiful relationship that Isaac and I have built together will come to an end. I'm really trying to fight these feelings so we can get married, but it keeps popping up, no offense Mom, at moments like this. It's just a reminder of all the other gifts I received and how they were wasted on marriages that ended. But I can assure you; I love the bracelet and will wear it happily."

Mariah was happy when the waiter arrived at their table with their food. She felt like she had put a damper on the whole mood at the table. This was so not her intent when she had arrived at the restaurant today. Mrs. Langston sat with a worried look on her face in silence and Tina looked uneasy as if she didn't know what to say next. Mariah tried to make herself enjoy the flame broiled fish on her plate, but right now all she really wanted to do was get up and leave. Silence went on for about ten more minutes before Tina tried to spark up another conversation.

"You'll never believe what PJ came home and told me he told his teacher the other day," Tina said with a slight snicker in her voice so Mariah knew it was going to be funny.

Unfortunately, she didn't get to hear it because she immediately tuned her sister out. All she heard was the faint sound of her mother laughing in the background as her mind drifted back to her issues. Mariah loved Isaac with all her heart. This was the one relationship in all of her adult years that was built on a solid foundation without any problems, and she didn't want to lose it. Even their first moments together showed how they were onto something special...

Mariah walked into the gym and signed the attendance book. She had five minutes to catch the Zumba class she liked to take once a week. Mariah walked into the nearby studio. The class was normally full with a minimum of twenty people, but today only ten people were stretching in the room, waiting for the instructor to arrive. Mariah was happy that the class wasn't full so she could get a good spot in the front. She dropped her bag on the floor and started to stretch as the door opened and one of the trainers walked in.

"Hi everyone, the Zumba class is canceled for today. I apologize for the inconvenience, but the instructor has called in sick," the trainer said.

Mariah had been looking forward to this class, but she got up off the floor and grabbed her bag. She would just have to run on the treadmill for forty-five minutes. She left the studio and scanned the open gym for an empty treadmill. There was one in the back of the room. Mariah headed over to the machine quickly to snag it before someone else did. She took her towel out of her bag and laid it on the arm of the machine. All of the treadmills had mini flat screens attached to them so she turned to one of her favorite channels, set her machine for a high incline workout and started moving.

"You're fired up and ready to go. I wish I had that much enthusiasm about my work out today," someone said next to her.

Mariah glanced over and almost did a double take. She looked over at one of the most handsome men she had ever seen. His smooth skin and beautiful smile sent a shock through her body as she tried not to run her eyes down his muscular arms and legs speed-walking on the treadmill.

"Hi. I'm not doing anything special. I'm just over here because my class was canceled," Mariah said, shyly looking back at her TV screen.

"I'm sorry to hear that. I almost didn't make it in today myself. I just wasn't feeling up to hitting the gym, but I haven't been all week so I figured I would come do at least an hour," the fine man said.

"Yeah, I hear you," Mariah added, trying to catch her breath as her treadmill picked up speed with an incline walk up the hill. She really wanted to hop off the machine and continue the conversation with the mystery man next to her - in the cafe. After her divorce, she wanted to take time for herself. She bought a new house and was putting more time into her career. However, two years later, she was now ready to test the waters again.

"I'll let you get back to your workout. It was nice talking to you," the fine man said as his machine came to a stop. He was finished and was about to walk away, but Mariah didn't really want him to leave. She wanted to find out who this fine gentleman was.

"Okay. It was...so...whew...nice to meet you too," Mariah tried to

get out in one breath, pounding her feet against the treadmill.

The fine man walked away. She couldn't help looking back to see what direction he was going. But the man headed into the weight room and that was the last that she saw of him. Mariah attempted to get the man out of her head as she focused on the two miles she had in front of her.

About forty minutes later, Mariah tried to gain her composure after her high-intensity walk on the treadmill. She grabbed her bag and headed to the front entrance. Her legs felt like noodles. She was exhausted and sweat was pouring from everywhere on her body. She signed out at the front desk and ran her towel across her face. Right before she could open the front door, the fine man appeared again.

"We must be on the same schedule. I'm heading out now, too," he said, showing off his beautiful white teeth.

Mariah was so tired that she couldn't even muster a smile. "How was your workout?"

"I got a good one in."

"That's good."

"So what's your name?"

"Mariah. And yours?" she inquired. Mariah knew she looked like a hot mess. Her hair was now a sweaty ponytail with strings matted to her face. But if he still wanted to know her name, she was definitely going to give it to him. They walked out to the parking lot.

"My name is Isaac. Do you come to this gym a lot?"

"Yeah, I try to come at least five times a week. Providing that I do

not have to work late," she added.

"Wow, that's dedication for you. Well, I'm not trying to be fresh with you, but you do look great. You definitely look fit," Isaac said.

Mariah smiled shyly as she crossed one leg over the other leg to prevent from passing out. She really needed to sit down, but she didn't want to miss out on this conversation.

"Mariah, I don't want to hold you. I'm sure you're exhausted. If it's okay with you, I would like to take down your number and give you a call. We could continue this conversation over dinner or something," Isaac said.

"Sure. I would like that," Mariah said, as Isaac reached into his gym bag for his cellular phone.

And the rest was history. Three years later the man she was so eager to meet that day at the gym wanted to make her his wife. Mariah came back to the present with one thing in mind. She knew she wanted to always have nothing but special memories where Isaac was concerned. Looking down at her engagement ring, she realized this could be the one thing that caused her to eventually lose out on these special moments, if she went through with this wedding.

"It is a beautiful ring, Sweetheart. I know you're going to make a beautiful bride. And don't worry about marrying Isaac. This time around you are going to have a fairytale ending. I feel it in my bones that Isaac will be for keeps," Mrs. Langston told her, squeezing her hand and slightly nudging her with her shoulder.

Mariah looked up and smiled at her mother. She sure hoped she was right. She made herself a promise after leaving Arthur's house that she would give the wedding her best effort and take one day at a time. So regardless of how uncomfortable she felt after receiving the bracelet from her mom, she decided she needed to honor that commitment. She just hoped she wasn't making a big mistake.

Chapter Ten

The following Friday evening was a beautiful, perfect night. It was the last weekend in May, and the weather was warm outside with a slight breeze. Mariah was applying her make-up in the bathroom when she heard a knock on the front door. She figured it was Isaac there to pick her up for their engagement party. She answered the door dressed in a turquoise strapless cocktail A-line dress with her hair pinned up with curls surrounding her face. The look on Isaac's face let her know he approved her attire.

"WOW! I don't know if I want to take you out tonight. I may just want to stay home with you in my arms. You look amazing," he said, planting a kiss on her cheek as he entered the house.

"Thank you, Honey," she said, walking bare feet back to the bathroom to put her lipstick on. "So who's going to be at the party tonight? I know my parents and Tina and Paul are coming."

Isaac took off his lightweight blazer and sat down on the couch. "Um, my aunt and uncle are coming in from my mom's side of the family and a ton of my parents' friends will be there I'm sure. Christopher is going to be there as well as a few of my other friends," he added.

"Oh, okay, that sounds nice. Yes, your parents have a ton of friends," Mariah said, walking out to the kitchen.

"So, have you given any thought to when you would like to

set the date? I know we both have been busy the past two weeks with work, but I think we sort of need to decide on a date before we go to this engagement party," Isaac inquired.

Mariah walked over to the couch and sat down beside him. After the dramatic lunch date with Tina and her Mom last week, she had been trying to maintain a positive attitude about the wedding plans. She was actually in a good mood tonight about the engagement party. "I've always wanted to go to Fiji and it's not too humid around mid-September, early October. How about we set the date around that time?"

"I didn't know you always wanted to go to Fiji. That sounds like a nice honeymoon idea. Okay well, Fiji it is and let's get married the first weekend in October. That's five months from now so I guess you need to get started with the planning. This is great! We killed two birds with one stone tonight," Isaac said excitedly, pulling her close to him in a bear hug.

"Oh, I thought maybe October next year. Honey, we're both busy at work right now. Do you think we would be able to plan a wedding so soon?" Mariah inquired, putting on her most sincere face. She was just getting used to the idea of getting married – baby steps. She was definitely not in the mood to leap head first into the wedding planning stage. She needed to move slowly at this thing.

"Are you kidding me, Mariah?" Isaac asked, sarcastically. "There is no way I want to wait over a year and five months to get married to you. Can't we hire one of those wedding planning people to do it for us? Matter of fact, I'm sure my parents' have a friend who may even be at this party tonight who probably owns their own wedding planning bridal thing business. We'll just have to ask my mom when we get to the party."

Mariah's face dropped as Isaac got up from the couch to prepare to leave for the night. Isaac was not her typical man. He knew that they could hire someone to plan the whole shindig for them, so she had to think fast to try to buy herself some more time.

"How about we get married in January then? I don't know…beachy islands are so overrated and everyone seems to do that for their honeymoon. Besides, it would be better for me to take a vacation around that time. Most of our clients at work are still on leave for the holidays," she added, getting up from the couch to put on her heels.

"Okay – January would work for me. I guess I can wait a couple more months before making you my wife. An eight-month engagement is not too long," Isaac said pulling his cellular phone out of his pocket to look at the calendar for January. How about January 12th? This will give us a week to get over the New Year's celebration."

Mariah sat on her bar stool to slip on her heels. "That works for me. We can figure out what's nice in January another time for a honeymoon. At least we have a date," she added with a shrug.

"Yes, we have a date," Isaac added with a wink.

CB

The drive to the Stevens' residence took about twenty minutes since they lived in La Jolla. The wind started to pick up the closer they got to the beach, but Mariah loved the smell of the salt water as she stepped out of the car for the valet. The Stevens' had gone all out for this party.

"I don't know if this is the wedding, Honey, or an engagement party?" Mariah asked Isaac as he escorted her up the steps.

"You know how over the top my mom can be sometimes. Let's just roll with it," Isaac whispered in her ear with a chuckle as they approached the front door.

Isaac had followed in both his parents' steps to practice law. His father was a retired lawyer in private practice and his mother was a paralegal there. They have a lot of acquaintances from business associates to close family friends who have watched Isaac grow up to the man he is today. They all seemed to be at the party tonight too.

As soon as Mariah and Isaac entered the house with over fifty people dressed in their best cocktail attire, they were greeted and congratulated with hugs and questions of when the big day was going to be. Mariah was glad that they had ironed that detail out before leaving her house else it would have been an awkward pause. The caterers erected a buffet table at the back of the house near the entrance to their sunroom. The table displayed heavy hors d' oeuvres and a beautiful dessert table filled with different fruit filled tarts and pastries, bride and groom decorated chocolate dipped strawberries, miniature cakes decorated with gold wedding bands, and red velvet, carrot, and chocolate cupcakes.

Mariah and Isaac got caught in a conversation with Isaac's godfather, who was his father's best man in his parents' wedding. While the two men were discussing Isaac's opinion on a popular court case that was going on in their area, Mariah caught a glimpse of her sister in the corner of the room. It looked like she was having a heated conversation with her husband, Paul. She couldn't hear what they were saying over the music, but neither looked happy with the other at that moment. Paul walked off and Tina waved her hand in the air as to say "whatever," before sipping on her champagne.

"Mr. Wilson, it was a pleasure to see you again. I see my sister in the corner and I'm going to go say hello," Mariah said, squeezing Isaac's arm as he nodded and went back to the discussion he was having.

Mariah tried to make it across the room without getting stopped again by someone congratulating her on the engagement. After successfully accomplishing this task, she noticed her sister's demeanor suddenly change as she approached her. She felt like she was looking in the mirror when she was proposed to at the Sheridan Room. Her sister was obviously upset about something but seemed to put on a pretend face that everything was all right.

"Hi, Mariah. This is one amazing party. You and Isaac can just say "I Do" right here tonight," Tina said, raising her glass to her sister.

Mariah tapped her sister's glass with her glass. "Is everything okay? Where did Paul walk off to?" she asked, casing the room for her brother-in-law.

"Yes, everything is fine. He went outside for some fresh air. You know how antsy he gets in a suit and tie. I can barely get him in one for church," Tina said, laughing.

Mariah was not falling for it. Her sister was hiding something.

"I'm enjoying this food. I should have brought my business cards to pass around. Isaac's parents' friends must do this type of thing all the time. You know I'm trying to get my catering business off the ground. Hook your sister up with some clientele," Tina whispered in her sister's ear.

"You're not passing out business cards at my engagement party," Mariah hissed at her sister, noticing Tina's attempt to change the subject.

Mariah scanned the room for her parents. The last she saw was her dad sitting on the couch eating and her mother sitting beside him waving at everyone. Her mother and father were nothing alike. Her father was comfortable sitting at home on his couch watching television and her mother was more of a free spirit who liked to get out and try different things. It was probably killing her to be glued to the couch next to her dad all night because he was not social. Mariah definitely took after her mother.

"Let's go find Mom unless you want to wait for Paul to come back?" Mariah asked, eyeing her sister's reaction for any loyalty to wait for her husband's return.

"Oh, he'll be fine. Paul is a big boy. Let's go," Tina said, leading the way over to where their parents were sitting near the food table.

"There you go. I have someone I want you to meet," Isaac said, grabbing her arm before she could make it across the room.

"Tina, go ahead. I'll meet you over there," Mariah said calling out to her sister over Kenny G playing over the speakers. Tina looked back, nodded and headed over to where their parents were sitting. Mariah followed Isaac over by the dining room area to four women who were decked out in pearls and diamonds over their Sunday best dresses. They were all very attractive women, one resembling Isaac's mother.

"Aunt Patty, this is my fiancée, Mariah. Mariah, this is my aunt Patty and my mom's sorority sisters Angela and Laiya," Isaac said introducing her proudly to everyone.

"Hello, Mariah. It's a pleasure to finally meet you. I have heard all about you from my sister and she speaks of great things. I can tell you make my Isaac very happy too," Aunt Patty said, giving her a hug.

"Hi, Aunt Patty. Thank you so much for coming tonight to

share in this special occasion with us. Isaac is definitely a great man. I'm the lucky one," Mariah said looking up at her fiancé.

Wow, he is her fiancé and she was actually fine with saying that word tonight. This step-by-step process was really starting to work for her. She was having a good time tonight and didn't mind any wedding questions. Maybe she would go out and look for a dress tomorrow, too.

"I don't know where my husband is in here, but you'll have to meet his uncle later," Aunt Patty said.

"Excuse me, I'll be right back," Isaac whispered in her ear before walking off.

"Where's the ring?" Aunt Patty inquired eagerly.

Mariah showed off her ring finger as the women began to shower her with compliments.

"So, when's the big day?" Angela, Mrs. Stevens' sorority sister, inquired.

"We have decided on January 12th," Mariah said smiling as the women started to marvel on her decision to have a winter wedding.

"I got married in the winter myself, although it seems like centuries ago now. It makes for great pictures," Aunt Patty said.

Mrs. Stevens walked up smiling. She looked beautiful in her champagne knee length dress and her hair was cut in a neat bob around her face. "I see you have met my sister, Patty, and my best girlfriends."

"Yes, we're finding out about the wedding day plans. So, are you guys going to have a big wedding? I'm pretty sure you've been dreaming about this day since you were a little girl," Angela inquired. All of the women started to nod in agreement remembering how they were excited to plan their own weddings.

Immediately, Mariah felt the most uncomfortable feeling she had felt all night. Was she supposed to say that this was not her first rodeo? She honestly didn't even know if Isaac had told his mother how many times she had already been married. Not wanting to lie in front of his mother, she opted to tell the truth. Just in case Mrs. Stevens already knew she had been married before.

"Well, I've been married before, so this isn't my first wedding," Mariah said, trying to keep the smile pasted on her face. She felt so embarrassed and hoped the conversation would stop there.

"Oh – okay. It can happen to the best of us. You can still plan a big wedding if that's what you want. I'm sure the second time around will be wonderful. You have a great man," Angela said, rubbing Mariah's shoulders.

"Well, this will be my third marriage. But you're right, I have the man I'm supposed to be with next to my side now," Mariah said. At that moment she felt like she should have just kept her big mouth closed. Angela's eyes widened and then dropped down to the cocktail glass she was holding.

Aunt Patty shot her sister a glare out of the corner of her eye as to say, "Where did Isaac get this girl from?" Laiya blinked a couple times and cleared her throat. Mariah was standing side by side to Mrs. Stevens and didn't have the heart to look over at her reaction.

"Well, this is a great party, Patricia," Aunt Patty said after what seemed like an eternity of the women standing there in silence.

"It was a pleasure meeting you all. Hopefully, we'll see each other again before the wedding. Excuse me," Mariah said deciding to seek Isaac.

She couldn't help but hear Aunt Patty whisper, "If there will even be a wedding, with her luck."

Mariah wanted to run out of the house. She was pretty sure they were over there gossiping about what she had just said. Mrs. Stevens never seemed to be the gossiping type, but her sister sure seemed to be. Mariah spotted her fiancé talking to Christopher and a couple of their other friends from college by the stairwell. She grabbed his arm and whispered in his ear to meet her outside. Mariah didn't even wait for an answer. She walked outside to the backyard and plopped down on one of the lawn chairs. She could have used a light jacket at this point, but she was too busy fuming inside at herself to even notice how chilly it had gotten, as she folded her arms.

Isaac showed up five minutes later smiling from cheek to cheek. "Sorry, I got stopped on my way out here by some woman who said she used to babysit me when I was growing up. My mom seemed to have invited everyone we know. I'm sure my first-grade teacher is in here somewhere," he joked as he sat down across from her. As soon as he looked at her, his smile immediately disappeared from his face.

"I feel like such a fool," Mariah said, tears welling up in her eyes.

"Sweetheart, what's wrong?"

"Your aunt asked about our wedding plans and alluded to this being my first wedding, and I spilled the beans that this is not only my first wedding, but my second either. You should have seen the look on your aunt's face. I didn't have the heart to witness your mother's reaction because she was standing right beside me when the whole fiasco took place. I didn't know if you had told your mom about me being married before and I didn't want to lie," Mariah said.

Isaac got up and kneeled down on his knee in front of her. He rubbed her leg as an attempt to comfort her. "No, I have not told my parents because none of that matters to me. I'm marrying you not them. And you don't have to feel like you have to tell everyone about your past."

"Gosh, I wish I would have known. Do you think your mom likes me anymore? I wish you could have seen the look on your aunt's face and what she said about me under her breath as I walked away," Mariah hissed, wiping the tears from her eyes.

"Oh, yes she still likes you. Don't even think like that. And my aunt can't talk. My uncle stayed at the bars more times than he did at home when I was growing up, so don't you worry about her either. Nobody is perfect or has the perfect life they pretend to have, Mariah. Don't get sucked up into all the foo-foo you see going on in the house right now either. Everyone inside might all look like they have it together, but you don't have friends as long as my parents have without getting to witness tough times in everyone's life. I know a man in the house right now who has been married at least five times and the fifth one was a woman twenty years younger than him," Isaac said, smiling.

Mariah immediately grabbed his face and placed the longest kiss on his lips. She was so in love with this man. He would do anything to make her smile. "I love you so much, Isaac. Thank you. I hate to say it, but I feel better after hearing all of that. Is that mean?" she asked, placing her hand over her mouth to shield the smile on her face.

"No, it's not mean. And I would do anything to make you happy. I'm in it for the long haul, Baby. Til death do us part," he said pulling her up from the lawn chair.

Mariah felt like the luckiest woman in the world as she fell into Isaac's arm for a kiss under the clear night skies.

"And If my aunt wants to mumble things under her breath

about you, then she doesn't have to come to the wedding either. You're my family now and don't you forget it," Isaac added.

"That's good to hear. I feel the same way about you."

They walked back to the house to finish enjoying their engagement party together. Isaac made it his business to stick by her side for the rest of the night, which made Mariah very happy. She wasn't going to let anyone else's comments intimidate her again tonight – even from his Aunt Patty.

Chapter Eleven

Tina sat at her kitchen table sipping on a cup of tea as her kids were running around the house playing and screaming at the top of their lungs. Normally she would have yelled at them for playing in the house, but today she didn't care what they did just as long as they didn't burn it down. She tuned them out as she looked out at her backyard and tried to envision her life somewhere else without children...and without her husband.

She was in Paris, somewhere in her own restaurant, on one of her busiest nights. Tina was serving a shrimp and crabmeat pasta special and the orders were just pouring into the kitchen for it. She was instructing a staff of twenty cooks as they were flourishing over pots and pans. She could hear the banging sound of pots and pans, the chatter of French voices, and the chopping of knives as they were hitting the chopping boards. Tina could smell the savory aroma of her famous tomato soup that she was serving as the soup du jour.

One of her waiters came into the kitchen to tell her that one of the customers wanted to speak to her. She walked out to see Wolfgang Puck sitting in the crowd. He wanted to personally congratulate her on her opening and to ask the recipe for her pasta special of the day. Tina chuckled to herself as she came back to reality. She sipped on her cup of tea. She was definitely not in Paris with Wolfgang Puck requesting her presence at his table, and she didn't own her own restaurant.

Tina wanted to be her own boss and business was slowly picking up, but she desperately needed to put her best foot forward this year. She was already five months into the year and things weren't really going as she had hoped in her career or her marriage. As much as she hated to admit it, she and Paul were turning into her parents – just going through the motions of being married. But she wanted more for her life. She secretly wanted the same excitement that Mariah and Isaac shared.

Tina loved how Isaac had closed out the engagement party last night by thanking everyone for coming and publicly confessing his love to Mariah in front of everyone. This is why she wanted her sister to get over the issues she was having with getting married again and just go for it. Tina could tell how much Isaac loved Mariah. When she told her sister at the Sheridan Room in the bathroom on the night of her engagement that she knew women who would kill for what she had, she was secretly talking about herself.

The front door opened and closed and Tina looked at her watch. It was 5:00 p.m. and she knew that was Paul coming in from work. He had to work this Saturday to meet a deadline to get one of the model homes up and built. Tina exhaled loudly out of her mouth as she waited for him to enter the kitchen. The kids had quieted down and were now watching an episode of Tom and Jerry from what she could hear from the family room.

Paul entered the kitchen wearing a dirty orange t-shirt and jeans. He put his keys on the key hanger by the refrigerator and opened it to get a bottle of water.

"Hi," he said as she waved her hand in the air and tried to smile. They still weren't really speaking after the disagreement at the engagement party last night.

"How was work?" Tina asked. She was definitely her mother's child. Her mother raised her and Mariah to always make the first move to try to mend any confrontation in the house with their man because her motto was, "Keep your man happy or some other woman will."

"Work was busy. It looks like we're going to meet the deadline though. How was your day?" Paul asked leaning against the island. It didn't seem like he really cared about her day, but just felt obligated to ask about it.

"I took the kids out earlier to the park and came back here to try a few recipes. I have some samples in the fridge if you would like to try them," she said.

"Yeah, maybe later. I'm going to go take a shower," Paul said turning to leave the room.

"Paul!" Tina called out to him.

Her husband slowly turned around with a reluctant look on his face as if he was bracing himself for another argument. He used to look at her with love in his eyes and now it was a look she never thought they would ever have for one another. It was a blank look with no emotion or love behind it.

"Would you like to talk after you finish taking a shower?" Tina inquired. She didn't know what she was expecting him to say, but she definitely didn't like the way they were treating one another.

"Yeah, I think we need to talk, but not right now. I'm really tired and all I want to do right now is take a hot shower and lie down for a bit," he said before leaving the kitchen. He didn't even wait for her to give a response.

Tina exhaled and looked back out at her backyard through the big bay window. She tried and that's all she could do. Maybe she could pick back up to where she left off fantasizing about being in France and Wolfgang Puck congratulating her on the opening of her new restaurant. She needed something to cheer her up right now, even if it was a dream…

Chapter Twelve

Two weeks later on a Wednesday morning, Mariah walked into her office with just enough time to prepare for her meeting with Sandra. She sat behind her desk and turned on her computer. Things had been going smooth lately at work since she had sealed the deal on the Aerilis project. The Aerilis President had contacted her boss last week to inform the company that he was interested in the proposal they had submitted. Mariah was meeting with Sandra this morning to tie up some loose ends before they entered into a contract.

Mariah pulled up all of the files. She sat back in her chair waiting for Sandra to arrive when her eyes looked down at her lap and the glare of her engagement ring caught her attention. She immediately gasped, took her ring off and placed it in her desk drawer.

"Whoa," she breathed a sigh of relief as she almost let the cat out of the bag.

Although she had been making every attempt to settle into the fact that she was now engaged, she still wasn't ready to come out at work just yet. She was taking it one step at a time.

She had met Tina on her lunch break this past Monday to go dress shopping and tried on a few dresses. At first, trying on dresses for the third go round felt like overkill since she had already purchased two dresses in the past for her previous weddings. She reminded herself that this was Isaac's first wedding so she set her mindset as if it was her first wedding too – it sort of was, with him.

"I'm here, I'm here," Sandra said interrupting Mariah's thoughts as she walked into her office. She entered with her usual smile and upbeat spirit balancing a clipboard and a couple stapled booklets.

"Oh, you're fine. I just got here myself, maybe thirty minutes ago. How is your husband doing, and married life?" Mariah asked, making room for Sandra's documentation on her desk.

Sandra sat down and pasted the biggest smile on her face that spoke of a person living in marital bliss. "He's doing fine. We're closing on our house this weekend, so we're pretty excited."

"Sandra, Congratulations! Wow – I guess people will start bothering you guys about kids next. I still remember your father's speech at your wedding and how he can't wait to receive the call that he's going to become a grandfather – hint-hint," Mariah said with a chuckle.

Sandra waved her hand in the air still smiling as she reflected on her father's speech. "Yes, our parents are so ready to become grandparents, but I think we're going to wait a year before embarking on that adventure. We're just enjoying each other as newlyweds right now."

"This all sounds so great. I can't tell you how happy I am for you. Well, let's get started so we can hopefully have this to Keith before noon," Mariah moaned, rolling her eyes in the back of her head.

"I agree," Sandra included with a moan.

About an hour into work, Mariah heard a tap on her door, which was open, and saw Isaac walking through it with flowers.

Mariah was so engrossed in analyzing figures on a spreadsheet that she didn't even notice he had walked in until Sandra acknowledged his presence.

"Hi. I thought I would surprise my fiancée for an early lunch. Your secretary said your calendar was clear for this afternoon when I called this morning. I wanted it to be a surprise, so I asked her not to say anything to you about it," Isaac said, presenting Mariah with a bouquet of flowers.

"Engaged?! When did this happen?! You didn't tell me and we've been sitting here for two hours," Sandra squealed, turning to face Mariah with huge eyes.

Mariah was in complete shock as she accepted the beautiful flower arrangement. All she could do was smile and try to come up with an explanation quickly, but it was too late because Isaac had zoomed in on Sandra's comment.

"Yep, it's been almost two months now – right after your wedding," Isaac said, standing proudly in the background. He still didn't pick up on anything being out of the ordinary.

Sandra looked back at Mariah with a confused look on her face. They had been in contact with each other on numerous occasions and not once did Mariah have on a ring or allude to becoming engaged. Yes, Mariah was cold busted. Not only did she not have her ring on now, but it was in her desk drawer. How was she going to get it out of the drawer without Isaac noticing? If she opened the drawer, Isaac would see her slip the ring back on. And if he didn't, Sandra would pick up on the fact that she hadn't noticed a ring earlier. Mariah had no idea of what she should do, but she knew she had to try to get that ring back on and get Sandra out of her office without drawing any attention to herself.

"Well, congratulations to the both of you! Let me see the ring!" Sandra asked, her expression quickly changing from confused to excitement.

"Ummm…I kept hitting my hand this morning, so I took it off to keep from damaging the stone," Mariah said, trying to play it off as she reached into her drawer for her ring and then slipped it back on her ring finger.

"Wow! That's a whopper ring there. I can't believe I could have missed that in the past month," Sandra said, eyeballing her ring.

Isaac's facial expression became a blank stare – one that Mariah had seen very few times when he was about to get upset at something.

"Thank you, Sandra. Hey, do you think you can finish up the

113

last page of the report on your own while I go grab a bite to eat with Isaac?" Mariah asked.

"Sure – take all the time you need, Mariah. I'll have this finished in ten minutes. I'll send you an electronic copy when you get back, then you can send it over to Keith," Sandra said rising from her seat to collect her documents. "You'll have to give me the details on your proposal when you get back. So modest," Sandra said.

"Congratulations again. Enjoy your lunch," Sandra directed to Isaac before heading out the door.

Mariah wished she had a magic wand at this second to zap herself out the room. She had to come up with an excuse -- and one that made sense – fast!

"So, you kept hitting your ring this morning so that's the reason you took it off?" Isaac asked sarcastically, taking the seat in front of Mariah's desk.

"Yes, Isaac. Thank you for these gorgeous flowers. You're too good to me," Mariah said, smelling the roses.

"So who does know about your engagement, Mariah? I mean I don't expect you to shout it from the rooftop at work to every Tom, Dick and Harry, but it seems mighty strange the one person you work so closely with doesn't even know or has seen your ring, since we got engaged," Isaac inquired sternly.

Mariah got up from her desk and closed her door. "Isaac, I

have no idea what you're implying, but I have told people."

"Oh really – does Cheryl know? If anyone would know, I would think your secretary would definitely know since she has to see your hand when she comes into your office. Surprisingly, she didn't say anything to me this morning about it or when I walked past her desk on my way to your office."

"Yes, of course she knows!" Mariah lied. She didn't intentionally mean to lie, but accidently lied to try to deter an argument and move on quickly to leaving for lunch.

After she and Isaac had returned from lunch, she was going to make it top priority to walk around and announce her engagement to everyone. She just needed to get past this dreadful moment.

"Okay – Well, let's go see, shall we?" Isaac said jumping up from the chair.

"NO! You can't," Mariah said, stopping him.

"That's what I thought. And just so you know that move was called a bluff. I had no intention of asking Cheryl. I guess I bluffed you like you have been bluffing me the past couple of months," Isaac said standing in front of Mariah with a hurt look on his face.

"Isaac, I love you so much. Please let's go to lunch so I can explain it all. It's just my stupid issues of feeling embarrassed about getting married for the third time. Trust me it's no big deal. I have it all under control now," Mariah said, tears forming in her eyes.

"Mariah, remember when I told you in my parents backyard

that I was in it for the long haul? Well, I meant it. I told you I didn't care and that I wanted you to be my wife – that's all you should have been concerned with and not what everyone else thinks about you or your past."

"Isaac, I have been trying to do just that. You have to believe me. I just haven't told anyone at work yet. I was a little insecure because they knew about my past marriages. But I'm going to do it now. I promise," Mariah said, wiping her eyes.

"It really hurt to see you take that ring out of your drawer the way you did…like it was nothing and here I was trying to buy you the best ring I could afford. With time, I guess I could get that image out of my head, but what I can't and will not stand for is a liar. Mariah, you have had ample time to tell me you were still having issues. I could have worked through those issues with you, because that's how much I love you. We have set up countless nights talking about our plans together and not once did you ever say anything," he added, trying to contain his voice so it was not heard outside the office.

"I was scared to come out and tell you because I thought it was all or nothing with you and I didn't want to lose you. I have honestly been trying to work on my fear of getting married again, so that's why I didn't say anything."

"Well, like I said before I can deal with a lot, but not lying. You flat out lied in my face when you didn't have to when I asked you about Cheryl – who knows what else you have lied to me about. I'm done. I no longer want to get married, or be in a relationship with you anymore. May I have my ring back, please?" Isaac asked, holding out his hand.

Mariah couldn't believe her ears. Was she dreaming? She wasn't about to let Isaac walk out of her life just like that – was he crazy?!

"I'm sorry Isaac, but I'm not giving you this ring back. We're going to get married and we can work through this," Mariah said, sternly.

Isaac got close to her ears to make his retort. The severity of his tone could have cracked frozen ice. "Mariah, I don't think you really want to go there. I'm asking nicely for my ring back. But, if you do not want to hand it over willingly, I'll be happy to file some paperwork when I get back to my office to get it back."

Mariah was in complete shock. Who was this man standing before her right now? She thought he loved her and would do anything to keep from hurting her. Well, she must have been wrong to ever assume that. "No need...take the damn ring. I can't believe you're acting like this over a misunderstanding," she said sliding the ring off her finger and handing it to him.

Isaac placed the ring in his jacket pocket. "Just think I'm doing you a favor. This way you don't have to worry about sliding it on and off every time you have to go to work in the morning. Take care," he said walking out of her office without a second glance back.

Mariah closed the door and slid down to her knees. She started crying so uncontrollably that she started to shake. She couldn't believe what had just happened because of her own insecurities. What was she going to do now?

The ironic part of this dramatic episode was that she was spending so much time in trying to avoid a marriage to the one man she loved the most. However, right now she would give anything to be his wife or much less girlfriend again for that matter.

She had to try and get him back. She climbed to her feet and walked over to her desk to pick up her office phone. She immediately dialed Isaac's cellular phone number hoping he would answer the call. The call went to voice mail after several rings. Mariah dialed the number again to get the same results. She slammed the phone down and turned off her computer. She reached for a Kleenex to dry her face, so she could walk through the office suite to get to the parking garage without drawing any attention to herself.

Mariah opened her office door and headed straight for the elevators trying to avoid eye contact with anyone. She took the first available elevator down to the building garage and made it just in time to her car before she started balling again. She couldn't believe what had just happened. She couldn't lose Isaac in this way. She reached into her purse and dialed his number again to get sent directly to the voice mail this time. He must have turned off his phone to keep her from calling him.

"Ugh!" Mariah screamed, hitting her steering wheel. The horn made a loud buzz in the quiet garage. She laid her head against the steering wheel as the tears started to fall on her leg like a rain shower.

The heat in her car was starting to suffocate her, so she rolled down her window and rested her head against the headrest. Mariah didn't know what to do, but she had to come up with a game plan to get her man back. Her mind was spinning out of control. She felt so embarrassed to have Isaac catch her in a lie like that. She didn't know what she would even say to Sandra about this whole matter when she saw her again, but right now that was the least of her worries. Isaac was the best boyfriend she had ever had in all of her years of dating. He wasn't a selfish person and had always been honest with her from day one.

Mariah had lost his trust and now she had to figure out how to gain it back. She started the car to drive to her parents' house. Normally she would never get her mother involved with anything in her personal life, but right now she needed to confide in someone who wasn't judgmental. She needed someone who would give her an honest opinion and she couldn't trust her sister because all she would hear was a bunch of I told you so.

Mariah drove quickly to her parents' house. She ran into the house not even caring about her tear stained face and muffled appearance. She saw her dad sitting in his favorite chair in the house watching television in the family room.

She yelled out, "Hello," to him as she darted past the family room towards the kitchen where she could hear her mother's voice.

"Mom, I need to talk to…" she said before even getting to the entrance of the kitchen doorway. She stopped in midsentence when she saw her mom and sister sitting at the kitchen table talking. Tina looked worried and her mother seemed to be comforting her about something. They both looked up at her and tried to change the looks on their faces.

"Hello, Mariah. What are you doing here in the early part of a work day?" Mrs. Langston asked.

"Mom, I came over to talk to you. What's going on here? Did something happen?" Mariah asked, concerned about the image she had just seen on her family members' faces.

"Hi Sis, oh everything is fine," Tina answered with a phony smile.

"This reminds me too much of the times when I was growing up and Dad and Mom would pull you into the kitchen first to talk to you about something that they thought I couldn't handle. If you all haven't noticed, I'm a grown woman now and if something is going on I would like to know about it," Mariah said. She felt offended that they would lie to her face about everything being all right when something was clearly going on. She wasn't in the mood to deal with any nonsense right now.

Mrs. Langston looked over at Tina, who in return looked back and raised her eyebrow at her. "There is nothing going on that's serious. I'm just a little down because one of my catering jobs fell through and money is starting to get tight at the house. I may have to go back to work," Tina said matter-of-factly, turning back to her sister with another forced smile.

Mariah immediately sat down at the table and tried to comfort her sister. "Sis, I'm so sorry to hear that. If it's money you guys need, you know I'm here for you. I can give you some money to at least give you a couple more months to try and make your business work. I will do anything for my nieces and nephew if you guys are in a financial bind right now."

Tina waved her hand in the air and got up to get a glass of their mother's famous homemade raspberry lemonade from the refrigerator. "Mariah, I really appreciate that, but you know Paul would never agree to accepting money from you. I can go back to work at a restaurant part time and see how my business ventures go by the end of the year. We'll be fine, so please don't worry about us. So what's up with you? Aren't you supposed to be at work?" Tina asked, joining them back at the table.

Mariah looked down at her bare left hand. Tears started to form in her eyes and she immediately fell apart at the kitchen table.

"Mariah, what's wrong with you?!" Mrs. Langston screeched.

"I'll be fine. It's just….that…I'm not engaged anymore," Mariah said, showing them her bare left hand.

"What happened?" Tina inquired with no compassion in her voice. She had a look on her face as if she knew it was her sister's fault.

"Excuse me," Mariah said giving her sister a glare. She didn't appreciate her tone at this moment after she had just showed her the upmost kindness regarding her situation.

"I'm just saying I can't wait to hear what happened that's all. It seems mighty strange that Isaac was just confessing his love to you in a room full of people not too long ago. All of a sudden, now he doesn't want to marry you. It just seems odd that it would have been something that he did that would cause the engagement to be called off," Tina said, matter-of-factly.

"Tina, stop it right now. Have some compassion for your sister," Mrs. Langston said sternly to her daughter.

Mariah on the other hand was speechless. She was sick of her sister's judgmental attitude when it came to her life. She was not a little girl anymore and refused to continue to put up with her big sister's opinions or attacks on her decisions. Enough was enough.

"Let me tell you something. I don't know who you think you are or who you think I am, but you have no right to speak to me in that way. I would appreciate you giving me the same consideration that I just gave you. You don't hear me saying that you put your family in a bind by quitting your job to start a business. And how you're putting unnecessary pressure on your husband to afford a house that you had to have built when there was nothing wrong

122

with the house you guys owned before. Oh, I'm sorry. It didn't have the large chef style kitchen that you needed for your business that's non-existent," Mariah said, rising from the table with her arms folded.

"Mariah, now you need to stop it too! Apologize to your sister!" Mrs. Langston requested.

"Oh, that's okay, Mom. I don't need an apology. In fact, I can't wait to hear what Mariah has to say about the wedding being called off. I can't wait to hear how it's all the guy's fault once again that she can't keep a successful relationship. You would think the third time would be a charm, but I guess not in her case. Poor Mariah. What are you going to do now?" Tina asked sarcastically, leaning against the table on her elbows with a pretend sad look on her face.

Mariah's eyes became so enlarged that they seemed like they were going to pop out of her head, as her mother started to yell at her sister for making such a comment. She would have never guessed that she would wake up this morning to encounter such a day. First, Isaac breaking up with her, and now she was getting into the worst argument she had ever had with her sister.

She had never hauled such words at her sister before and neither had Tina, telling her how much a failure she thought she was in the relationship department. Mariah always felt she was a failure, but to now know that her sister felt the same about her made her feel like the worst person in this world. Maybe it was best

123

that Isaac got out before it was too late. She loved him too much to mess up his life too.

A tear started to form in Mariah's eyes and she immediately wiped it away before her sister got the gratification of seeing her cry. "You know what, good luck with your business venture and your household affairs. I'm not even going to stoop to your level. Mom, I'll call you later," Mariah said turning on her heels to head to the front door.

"Mariah, come back here!" Mrs. Langston called after her.

"Let her go, Mom," Tina said.

Mariah walked past the family room to see her dad sitting asleep in his favorite chair. There was a big argument going on in the kitchen and he didn't even hear it.

She hopped in her car and sped down the street. Maybe marriage just wasn't for Mariah. She knew this would happen. Maybe it wasn't meant for her to marry Isaac, after all.

Chapter Thirteen

Isaac got in his car and turned on his ignition. He reached into his pocket and pulled out his cellular phone to see Mariah's office number flashing across the screen. He hit the End button and turned off his phone. He didn't want to hear her voice. He pulled out of the parking garage to her office building and started driving down the street. He had no idea of where he was driving to. He just knew he had to get out of there and fast.

Isaac started to speed down the street with frustration as *Real Love* by Eric Bonet came on the radio. This song used to remind him of Mariah all the time. He immediately turned it off. As he approached a busy intersection, he saw a sign blinking for a tavern and decided to make a U-Turn to go back there. He knew today was not going to be a good day to sit in traffic. He needed to clear his head and get out of the car before he got a reckless driving ticket. Isaac waited for the light to turn green and immediately made a U-Turn into the tavern parking lot. He grabbed his wallet out of his cup holder and headed inside. He walked directly to the bar and sat down.

"How are you doing today, sir? What can I get you to drink?" the bartender asked in a deep southern accent.

"Rum and coke, please and two shots of tequila."

"Sure thing. That'll be $20.00."

Isaac reached into his wallet and took out twenty-five dollars. "Keep the change," he said to the bartender.

"Thank you very much. Drinks on the way," the bartender said.

Isaac ran his hands over his face. He felt like he was in a bad dream from which he desperately wanted to wake up. He tried to be honest with every woman in his life even when it would be uncomfortable for him. He believed in Karma and didn't want to be hurt when he was finally ready to settle down.

Some of his friends tried to downplay it and said that you didn't always have to tell a woman everything, but he tried to stick to the values that his mother had instilled in him – honesty is everything. He just didn't understand why it didn't work in his and Mariah's relationship. All he wanted to do was show Mariah how much he really loved her and that she didn't have to feel insecure anymore. Why wasn't it enough? Isaac thought as the bartender returned with his drinks.

He immediately chugged both shots. The alcohol burned as it went down. He needed something to numb the pain he was going through right away. As a man, he hated to admit that he was heartbroken and devastated that the woman he thought he knew and wanted to share the rest of his life with had been deceiving him. Isaac took a long swing of his rum and coke. He wasn't a big drinker and normally would have to sip his drinks, but today he

126

wanted to get it down as fast as possible and his body was rolling with it.

Isaac reached into his pocket and pulled out the engagement ring he had given to Mariah. He looked at every inch of it before dropping it onto the bar. It made a clinking sound as it hit the countertop. The alcohol was starting to take a toll on him.

He felt something wet on his face and he realized it was a tear. He immediately wiped it away. He wasn't about to sit here in public and start crying. He had to pull himself together. Isaac coughed to try to play off the tears and took another quick swig of his drink. He took it straight to the head and immediately emptied the glass. His chest started to hurt as the alcohol flowed through his body.

"Excuse me. Is anyone sitting here?" someone asked, coming up behind him.

Isaac looked next to him to see a short young woman with a low-cut, fitted tank top exposing her breast standing there. He wondered what she wanted, but he knew deep down what time it was. There were only four people sitting at the bar including himself and there were six bar stools separating them from him.

"Nope," he said, taking his empty glass to his head to see if he could get the corners left in his glass. He wasn't going to give this woman any extra attention.

The bartender reappeared and offered to bring him another drink. Isaac accepted and reached into his wallet for a $10.00 bill to pay for it.

"Okay – Thanks. So what are we drinking?" the woman asked, taking the empty seat next to him.

"I don't know about We, but I'm drinking a rum and coke," he said, nonchalantly.

"Hey you don't have to be nasty. I'm just trying to be friendly. I've been in a car, driving for six hours straight without any human interaction. Excuse me for trying to engage you in a conversation," the woman said, scooting down another seat and reaching for a menu.

Isaac looked over at her. He exhaled loudly and tried to come across as a gentleman. "I apologize for the rude tone. I'm just in a bad place right now," he said.

"I can tell. But trust me you're not having nearly as bad a day as me," she said, looking at the menu.

The bartender walked over to the woman. "Hello ma'am. What can I get you today?"

"I would like a well-done cheeseburger with ketchup and pickles only and a glass of water with lemon please," she said closing the menu.

"Okay – Sounds good. Could I get you an order of waffle fries to go with that?" the bartender asked.

"No, that'll be all," the woman said.

Isaac looked back over at the woman wondering why she was

ordering such a small meal if she had been driving all day. She opened up her wallet and he could see her thumbing over two twenty dollar bills she had inside. He saw her open the change compartment, pull out a few dollars and lay it on the counter. She then proceeded to count quarters to add to it for her bill. She obviously just had enough to pay for her burger.

"Could I buy you something to drink and an order of fries to go with your meal?" Isaac offered.

The woman looked up from counting her money. "I'm fine. Thank you," she said and then looked back down at the money she was counting.

"Okay," Isaac said, sipping on his new glass of rum and coke.

"So what's your story?" the woman inquired, leaning on her elbows.

"What do you mean?" Isaac asked looking over at her through glazed eyes. He was definitely tipsy now.

"You said you were having a bad day. You're obviously trying to drink your sorrows away over something. I'm here if you need to talk."

Isaac looked over at the woman who looked to be no more than 23 years old and snickered. *What does she know about life yet?* he thought. "Thanks, but I doubt you'll have the answer to what I'm going through right now.

"Oh, I don't know about that. I've been through a lot at my

age. Right now, I'm on my way to pick up my grandmother who's being kicked out of her retirement home because she ran out of the money my grandfather left her. It's just me and my dad and we're barely making it ourselves. We live in a one bedroom apartment the size of a shoe box and now we have to try to figure out how to make room for my grandmother and afford her monthly medical expenses. My dad got paid two days ago and gave me half of his check that's supposed to be for our rent next month to drive nine hours to pick her up. It's so easy to want to give up and so many people in my shoes probably would have at this point, but I still believe there's someone up above looking after us. I mean look at me. My car is a total piece of junk, yet I've made it this far without any problems to pick up my grandmother. So if you have a story that can top that then I would love to hear about it," the woman said, sipping on her glass of water.

The woman's story almost sobered Isaac up immediately as he sat his glass back down on the counter. He couldn't imagine experiencing anything like that without having to take a drink, much less having the positive attitude that the woman had in believing things were going to get better. "I'm really sorry to hear that. I pray everything works out for you and your family. Your strength is impeccable. You give me hope and all I'm doing is trying to deal with a broken heart," Isaac said, leaning against the back of his chair.

"Well, I'm happy my mess could be a message to you. I've had a lot of broken hearts too. You can't see it right now, but it'll get better," the woman added.

The bartender returned with her food and a bottle of water for Isaac.

"Thanks," Isaac said, unscrewing the water bottle to take a sip. He needed to sober up before attempting to drive home. He appreciated any bartender who took care of their customers. He has had too many clients come into his office with DUI charges.

The woman started to immediately dig into her burger as if she hadn't eaten in days. Isaac had never seen a woman eat like that before and it was really starting to break his heart.

"Are you driving straight through to pick up your grandmother?" Isaac inquired, hoping not to come across too nosey.

"Yep. Dad didn't have enough money to give me for lodging expenses. I only have enough for gas to pick her up and head back home. I'll just stop over in a safe area and shut my eyes before continuing. It's still light out. I'll be fine," she said.

Isaac couldn't allow a woman to sleep in her car even if he didn't know her from Adam. It just wasn't safe. "Hey, there's a Holiday Inn around the corner. I would be more than happy to go in and pay for you to stay over a night."

The woman looked up from her burger with a suspicious look on her face. "I'm sorry, but I don't get down like that. I may be going through tough times, but I'm not that desperate."

"No, you misunderstood my offer. I was going to pay for you to stay the night, not for me to stay with you," Isaac said, taken aback from her insinuation that he was trying to take her to a hotel.

"Oh, I'm sorry. You just never know what people have in mind these days. Really you don't have to do that. I'll be fine. I have a baseball bat in my car that I'm pretty good with, in case someone decides to mess with me," she said, eating the last of her burger.

Isaac tried. He finished his water and sat the empty bottle down next to the ring he had given Mariah. He picked it up and twirled it around his finger. His relationship with Mariah was over. He was no longer willing to work with her on her marital issues. The trust was gone.

It would be a long time before he would ever be willing to put himself in another position like this again to possibly endure another broken heart. He didn't need the ring anymore. He had the perfect idea of what he should do with it. Some people might think his idea was crazy, but Mariah had thrown the ring in a drawer like it was nothing.

"I don't even know your name, but I really feel for you. Here take this ring. I hope it can help with your family expenses. It'll appraise for $25, 000," he said placing the shiny ring in front of the woman's empty plate.

He rose from his chair and took $20 out of his wallet to leave for the bartender who was now looking at Isaac with a puzzled look on his face. He placed his wallet back in his pocket.

The woman's mouth dropped. "Sir, are you crazy. You're drunk and you're not thinking very clearly," she said, handing the ring back to him.

"I'm in my right mind and well aware of what I'm doing. I'm also an attorney. The bartender is your witness that I gave you the ring willfully if you're concerned that I'm going to report it stolen. If you still don't trust me, wait thirty days if you can and then sell it. There will be no claim made against it because I'm giving you this and free legal advice as a gift. Please keep your head up. I don't think it is a mistake that you walked into this tavern today, so you're right. God is looking over you. I don't need the ring anymore," Isaac said, closing the woman's palm with the ring enclosed.

The woman's eyes immediately started to overflow with tears. The bartender looked shocked, as he folded his arms and leaned against the countertop.

"Take care," he said, about to walk off as the woman jumped up from her seat and ran to give him a hug.

"I-I-I don't know what to say. What's your name? My name is Angelica. Are you some sort of angel? Oh my gosh – thank you so much. I mean it from the bottom of my heart," she said, through tears.

Isaac hugged the woman, said goodbye to the bartender and walked out of the bar. He felt okay to drive home. His heart still ached from the pain of leaving Mariah and he didn't know when it would go away, but he was happy he could have at least helped someone else today.

Chapter Fourteen

Mariah called into work sick the next day and spent the entire day in bed. She didn't even get up to brush her teeth until late in the afternoon, when she finally decided to eat something. As much as she tried to make herself believe that she was better off without Isaac, she couldn't help the fact that she was missing him like crazy. She had tried calling him all last night, but he didn't answer his phone. Mariah walked into her kitchen with her hair all over her head from wallowing in bed. She wore an oversized t-shirt that was clinging to her thin body. She walked over to her refrigerator and pulled out a container of leftover Chinese food. She threw the container into the microwave and started to heat up the contents. Leaning against her island, she started to cry.

The phone started to ring. Mariah looked up through watery eyes at the cordless phone on the kitchen wall. She ran over to answer it, hoping it was Isaac finally returning one of her many messages.

"Hello?"

"May I please speak to Mariah Langston?"

"This is she," Mariah answered, her sudden happy spirits quickly diminishing now that the call was not from Isaac.

"Hello, Mariah. This is Cheri from Macey's Bridal Boutique. I wanted to let you know that your bridal dress is in! Please feel free to stop by the boutique from eight a.m. to nine p.m., Monday through Saturday for a dress fitting," Cheri, the bridal consultant, said with enthusiasm in her voice, as if she had just told Mariah that she had won a million dollars.

"OK – thank you," Mariah said, trying to muster up a happy tone before disconnecting the call.

Her wedding dress was in, but there wasn't going to be a wedding. *So now, what?* she thought. She just couldn't imagine picking up the dress to add it to her other two dresses in her attic. Mariah had to get Isaac back. She missed every ounce of him right now. She refused to face the fact that their relationship was really over. The whole situation just seemed too surreal to her. She thought of driving over to his house and letting herself into his condo, but was scared of being rejected and thrown out. Isaac was already not answering her calls.

Mariah looked up as the microwave started beeping to signal her food was done. Her eyes caught a glimpse of a picture of her and Isaac at a ski lodge in Denver on her hallway table. She had forgotten about the many photographs scattered around the house, images of them in South Africa, Mexico, and Italy together. Unfortunately, she was now going to have to throw them all away. Mariah walked over to the microwave and took her food out. The sudden sight and smell of food made her sick. She tossed the food in the trash can and walked out of her kitchen.

The doorbell rang.

ISAAC. Mariah darted to the front door expecting to see her man. She stopped to fix her hair and tried to straighten up her appearance in the hallway mirror. Mariah opened up her front door with a smile. Her smile was immediately short--lived, because it wasn't Isaac at the front door, but her sister.

"You," Mariah mumbled, her mood beginning to change again.

"Hi, Mariah. May I come in? I wanted to talk to you about yesterday," Tina asked, pitifully.

Mariah stepped back to allow her sister room to enter her house. She didn't really have anything to say to her right now, and wasn't really in the mood to have a second round from yesterday.

Tina led the way to Mariah's family room and sat down on the couch. Mariah walked in and sat at the other end of the couch. She wanted her sister to be very clear that she wasn't going to just shake off what she had said yesterday. Tina, of all people, knows how insecure she feels about her past, and throwing it up in her face like that was not acceptable!

"Mariah, I wanted to come over and apologize to you."

"Did Mom send you over here to do this?" Mariah asked, not falling so easily for her sister's apology.

"No, actually Mom doesn't know that I'm here today. She thinks I'm out meeting a potential business opportunity, which is what I told her when I got up this morning," Tina said, looking away.

"What do you mean when you woke up this morning? You stayed at Mom and Dad's last night? Why?" Mariah inquired.

Tina turned to face her sister with a sad look on her face. "Paul and I have decided to take a break. We're officially separated, and I'm not certain if we will get back together again," she said.

Mariah immediately scooted next to her sister. "What happened? Is this what you and Mom were really talking about yesterday when I walked into the kitchen? I knew it was more to what you were telling me. Is it because money is tight, or is there something else going on?" she asked, sincerely.

"Mariah, Paul and I have been breaking up for years now. We've just become a big balloon that has expanded as far as it can go. We're not getting along, and we both decided it would be best to separate for a while. However, I knew when I agreed to it, that our marriage would be over with. He's staying at the house, and the kids and I are going to stay at Mom and Dad's for a while. This was totally my decision. Paul offered to move out, but I couldn't imagine staying in a house that he was paying for and feeling indebted to him. Plus, I know he can't really afford to make a mortgage payment and pay rent somewhere else. I guess that's why I went off on you yesterday. I really feel like Isaac is such a great guy. You don't have to worry about any of the problems that I have to go through with Paul, and I became angry that you were willing to walk away from it. I'm so sorry, Mariah, that I said what I said to you yesterday. I never meant to hurt you," Tina said as she started to cry.

Mariah pulled her sister into her arms. She couldn't remember ever seeing her sister this distraught, even when they were growing up as kids. Tina even showed pure strength during the one time that Mariah felt she should have fallen apart when they were teenagers. Two weeks before the senior prom, Tina found out her high school Sweetheart was trying to two-time her with another girl at a different school.

Mariah was so impressed to see how her sister handled the situation. She simply dumped the guy without any hesitation, or a tear, and went to the prom with her friends and had a good time. Mariah never heard her speak about the guy again or even complain about anything that happened, so she didn't really know what to say, or how to react to seeing her sister upset like this. Tina was always the strong sister that Mariah went to for strength or advice when something was going wrong in her life.

"Tina, I know you didn't mean it. It's okay, trust me. I'm more concerned about you right now. I had no idea that any of this was even going on. I mean you and Paul didn't seem too chummy at my engagement party, but I just chalked it up as if you guys had a disagreement like any other time. Are you sure it's over and there's no other chance to work things out?"

"I doubt it. Like I said, things haven't been right for years now. And it's not entirely Paul's fault either because I didn't do anything to try to stop it from getting to this point. I should have done more to try to work things out when we first started to grow apart. I allowed things to manifest just like he did. And now I'm not sure if there is any love left on either of our parts to make our marriage work," Tina said, raising her head from her sister's shoulder to wipe her face. "I'm mostly crying for the kids because I don't want to tear their world apart, but I can't expose them to a marriage that's not making their parents happy either."

"I'm sorry to hear this, Tina. I really like Paul and I hope things can work out for all of your sake, but you're right. You both deserve to be happy, which will be better for the kids. How are they handling everything so far? I just can't imagine what they're thinking right now," Mariah inquired, leaning her elbows on her knees in complete awe at the thought of her nieces and nephew suffering.

"The kids are doing great. It happened so fast that Paul and I haven't even had the conversation yet with them. The kids think they're just spending some time with their grandparents now that school is out, but I know pretty soon they'll want to go back home to their own stuff and room. Paul and I plan to speak to them soon though."

"Gosh, this is happening so fast. I can't believe all of the drama that is breaking out between us. Ugh! I would have never guessed at the beginning of the week that all of this would have happened before the week was out," Mariah said, running her hands over her face in pure frustration.

Tina ran her hands over her sister's back. "Hey, cheer up. You and Isaac will be back together again. I'm certain of it. There's no way that the love you two share could have dwindled away overnight."

"You don't know what happened! He came over to my office for a surprise lunch date and I wasn't wearing my ring. I know it was stupid of me to take my ring off, but I was trying to buy myself some time before I told everyone at work," Mariah said, rising from the couch and pacing the room.

She waited for Tina to tear into her for being so stupid, but things seemed different on this day. Tina simply gave her a sympathetic response that Mariah was not accustomed to hearing from her big sister.

"It's okay. We all do things that may not make sense at the time, but it's not like he caught you cheating or anything. All you have to do is give it a few days to blow over and go talk to him."

"He took the ring back, Tina! Come on give it to me. You were right. You told me that I would lose him if I kept playing these stupid games of not being ready and look, I've lost him," Mariah said hysterically, pounding her fist on the corner of her fireplace.

Tina rose from the couch and walked over to her sister. "Mariah, I'm not going to beat you up about this. To be honest, I think I've done that a little too often when we were growing up. Always trying to tell you what to do or how you should feel. I'm sorry. Now that I'm heading toward a divorce myself, I can see how you would feel about accepting a third proposal. You have every right to feel the way you feel. I'm sure if you give it a few days and then go explain yourself to Isaac, he'll see where you're coming from," Tina said, walking to the kitchen for more Kleenex.

"Thank you, Tina. I'm sorry too about what I said yesterday. If Mom and Dad start to get on your nerves, you're more than welcome to come and stay with me. I would love to have you and the kids here while you're figuring stuff out. I could really use the company of my nieces and nephew running around here to take my mind off of Isaac. I just received the call this morning that my wedding dress is in and you have no idea how much that tore me up," Mariah said, sighing.

"Oh gosh, I can't imagine how hard that was for you. I would like to go ahead and take you up on that offer. My old room is a little cramped with me and three kids and you know Mom has too much sewing stuff in your old room to move around to make room. I'll just finish out the week so that Mom doesn't get a complex. She's enjoying her time with the kids. And then when I get here next week you and I are going to work on a plan to get Isaac back. In the meantime, go try on your wedding dress and get it altered because there will be a wedding. And take some time out for yourself as well. Okay?" Tina asked.

Mariah nodded at her sister. She was so happy that she had stopped by. Mariah felt blessed at that moment to have a big sister like her.

Chapter Fifteen

Saturday morning Mariah woke with a heavy weight on her heart. She felt good after her sister had given her encouraging words, but it seemed to only be a Band-Aid to cover the empty hole she had in her heart. She woke up missing Isaac all over again. He hadn't called last night, hadn't called this morning and she still hadn't spoken to him since he left her office three days ago. As much as she hated to admit it, she was starting to believe that he might have really meant what he said that they were officially over with.

Mariah rolled over and looked at her alarm clock. It was 10:00 a.m. She never slept this late on a Saturday. By now she would have either been on her way to her sister's house for their normal workout routine or she would have been meeting her somewhere on her side of town to go work out. Today, she didn't feel up to doing anything. She reached for her telephone to dial Isaac even though she was starting to feel like an idiot. First she dialed his home number and then the cellular phone number. Both calls ringing until the calls went to voice mail.

"Stop it!" she yelled to herself, slamming the phone back onto its cradle.

It was obvious that he didn't have anything to say to her and was deliberately ignoring her calls. It was starting to piss Mariah off. Who did he think he was anyway? She made one stupid mistake and he was going to penalize her for it. *Forget him*, she decided as she climbed out of bed and went to her bathroom to brush her teeth. Mariah looked back at what her reflection had become over the last couple of days. Her normal roller set curls were flat to her head. Her eyes were swollen from crying and she was starting to smell musty from not taking a bath.

Mariah couldn't remember looking this bad since her breakups in her adolescent years. She didn't even look this bad after her divorce to Arthur. She was 36 years old and was acting like a teenager. She rinsed her mouth with mouthwash and grabbed a hair tie from a basket on her shelf to tie her hair back into a neat ponytail. She was done with this crying and depression over Isaac. Yes, she loved him, but she refused to allow herself to fall apart over this separation for another day.

She washed her face and turned on her shower to take a hot steamy bath. She pulled off her t-shirt and looked at her body. She still had a beautiful size four figure that she needed to maintain. She was going to the gym. It was high time that she got back into the groove of things. And like Tina said, when Isaac decides to call, which she was sure he would sooner or later, then she would still look like the woman he last saw the day he stormed out of her office.

Mariah took a long, hot shower and got dressed in some workout shorts and a tank top. She slipped on her Nikes, grabbed her workout bag and filled it with her water bottle and a towel before heading to her car in the garage.

She made it to the gym in twenty minutes. She felt good walking into the gym. The hot shower definitely helped to lift her spirits. Mariah walked up to the front desk and signed the sign-in sheet. As she was about to put the pen down, she noticed five names up, Isaac Stevens had signed in about thirty minutes ago. She swallowed and tried to decide if she wanted to go in the gym knowing he may still be there, or head back home.

"Is everything okay, ma'am?" the woman working the front desk asked.

"Yes, everything is fine. I was just trying to remember if you had a Spinning class today," Mariah lied, moving to the side to allow the person behind her to sign in.

"No, the Spinning class is on Monday, Wednesday, and Friday nights at 7 p.m. We have a calendar up by the main entrance of all of our classes," the woman responded.

Mariah nodded, smiled and turned to go inside the gym. She knew about the location of the calendar and that there was no Spinning class today. She took a deep breath and entered the sweaty smelling gym. She had made a decision before she left the house that she was not going to let her break-up with Isaac interfere with her life anymore. Since she had driven the miles to the gym, she might as well work out. Mariah headed over to the long rows of treadmill and elliptical machines. She grabbed a treadmill in the back and wrapped her bag on the attached handle. She turned to CNN on the attached mini TV to catch up with what was going on in the world, set her machine for a two mile jog and got moving.

Mariah kept her attention on the TV screen the whole time, determined not to scan the room for Isaac. If he was still in the gym, then he was going to see her first and have to make the awkward move of walking out without speaking.

Ten minutes into her jog, Mariah heard a woman laugh at the end of the opposite row. At first she didn't pay it any attention with all the noise that was going on in the gym, but then the woman laughed again as if she was just told the best joke in the world. Mariah couldn't help but look in her direction. What she saw knocked the joy out of her spirit. A beautiful, tall woman with shoulder-length hair was standing on the treadmill, and Isaac was helping her with the machine. Mariah couldn't believe what she was seeing. Isaac was obviously here with another woman. She pulled the emergency plug on her treadmill as it immediately came to a stop. She quickly wiped the sweat from her machine with a Lysol wipe, grabbed her bag and marched over to where the woman and Isaac were standing, still talking and laughing.

Mariah wanted to cry as a big knot started to form in her throat. She couldn't believe he had already started talking to someone else while she had been home crying her eyes out still believing that they had a chance.

"I see it didn't take you long to move on. How long have you two known each other?" Mariah asked as soon as she approached them.

Isaac looked at her with a startled look on his face.

"Mariah, just walk away. It's not what you think," Isaac suggested.

"What do you mean walk away? So, it's like that now. We've been together for three years, engaged, and now you want me to just walk away, just like that? So, how long have you been messing around with my fiancé?" Mariah asked, turning to the woman who was already stepping down from the treadmill.

"Isaac, I'll let you take care of whatever business you have going on here. Thanks for helping me figure out the machines. It was nice seeing you again," the woman said smiling at Isaac and turning to give Mariah a head nod as to pronounce her exit before walking off.

"Well, isn't she cute? You sure know how to pick em'. She couldn't even stand and defend the fact that she has been cheating with my man," Mariah said pissed off as she folded her arms.

"That's because we're not together. She's an old college friend I knew back in law school, who has moved to the area with her husband. I haven't seen her in over 10 years. It's not like I have to tell you this, but she just had a baby and is trying to get back in the groove of things, so she needed help with the machines in the gym. Now if you will excuse me, I was just about to head out. You have just embarrassed the both of us for no apparent reason," Isaac said, walking off.

Mariah ran after him and followed him out to the parking lot talking the whole way.

"What gives Isaac? I made a stupid mistake. I'm sorry once again for letting my emotions get the best of me. I saw you with a cute girl and I panicked thinking you had moved on or had cheated on me. You would have done the same thing if you had seen me out with another man," Mariah said.

Isaac opened up the trunk of his car, flung his workout bag into the back and came back to the curb to face Mariah. She missed him so much that she couldn't contain it any longer. She threw her arms around his sweaty neck. It felt so good to be in his arms for the moment.

"Mariah, we just broke up a few days ago. I'm not in any position to date or even want to see another woman right now. I still have feelings for you that I'm trying to deal with," Isaac said.

Mariah slowly pulled away to look back at him. Isaac looked sad. He didn't look like his normal happy self.

"Isaac, I still love you too. Why haven't you called me back? I know you have seen my calls," she inquired.

"I've been sorting some things out in my head and I just needed my space. I'm sorry," Isaac said, turning to head back to his car.

"Why? I don't get it!" Mariah asked.

Isaac turned around to face her. "Mariah, you lied to me. All I wanted was to spend the rest of my life with you and I thought you wanted the same thing. You will never know what it felt like for me to see you hiding my ring in a drawer. What you don't understand is, when I was out there living my life as a bachelor, I never lied to any of the women I met. They wanted a relationship and I told them from the beginning that it was not going to happen, no matter how much they tried to show me they were the one. My mother raised me to always be honest, and I always tried to keep that with me. I always said when I was ready to settle down that it would be with a woman that I could trust and I thought it was you, but I now know it's not," Isaac said.

"Isaac, I understand your feelings, but I am the woman you're supposed to be with. I promise you," Mariah said.

Isaac took her by the hand. "Mariah, I've been thinking these last three days if we had a chance and I just don't think it's going to work. I'm sorry. You have issues with getting married again and I have to respect that. I would go back to dating you if I felt that would be enough for me, but it's not. I've been thinking about having kids lately and a wife at this point in my life. I know it's going to be hard thinking about these things without you, but I don't have any other choice. I know that now," Isaac said.

"Isaac, I want to be with you. If I have to have children, then I want it with you and nobody else. Please don't give up on us," Mariah said tearing up in the parking lot.

"If you have to have it…see Mariah, we want two different things. You don't have to change for me. I know you love me and I know you didn't mean to hurt me and I forgive you. But we can't hide the fact that you don't want to get married again. I should never have put you in that position. I'm sorry. Please take care," Isaac said, getting into his car.

Mariah ran up to his driver side window. "Isaac, my dress is in. I've already paid a $500 dollar deposit on it. What am I supposed to do about that now?" she asked, speaking as tears were streaming down her face.

Isaac reached into his glove compartment and pulled out his check book. He started to write Mariah a check for the $500 dollars, but she stopped him.

"You know what? Never mind. Keep your money. I feel like an idiot. I'm sitting out here crying for you and you're still going to walk away from me. I'll see if I can return the dress or if not, pay it off and sell it. Take care, Isaac. You don't have to worry about me calling you anymore," Mariah said, turning on her heels to head back towards the gym.

"Mariah!" Isaac called after her, but she didn't turn around.

It was officially over with and Mariah knew it now for sure. It was time for her to move on and begin the healing process. Isaac had made it perfectly clear that there was nothing left for them to build a future toward. Mariah went back inside to sign out of the gym and headed to her car.

She was going to make a quick stop by the bridal boutique before heading home. She knew she would lose her deposit from the contract she signed, but she hoped to at least be able to return the darn thing. If not, it would just be an expensive investment that she would see if she could turn into a party dress. She planned to hit the streets and have some fun because she was now a bachelorette again.

Chapter Sixteen

Sunday afternoon, Isaac pulled up to the Hudson Recreation Center near his house to play basketball with his closest friends – Christopher, Kurt, and Tim. All of them had demanding careers, so they tried to get together whenever they could to play basketball. Unfortunately, Isaac was running late. He grabbed his gym bag from his back seat, and ran over to the basketball court where he could see his friends had already begun playing.

"Hey man, we didn't think you were going to show. Maybe we can play a real game now. Isaac, let's show them something," Christopher called out as Isaac approached the court.

"Sorry about that you guys. I got caught at my parents' moving some furniture around. Let's do it, Chris," Isaac said, dropping his bag and getting into defense mode against Kurt.

"I see…trying to delay the inevitable pain of getting your ass kicked on the court," Tim joked, as he passed the ball to Kurt to start the game.

"Whatever," Isaac said jokingly. He ran after Kurt with some serious defense to keep him from making a shot.

Isaac was able to block his three-point shot. He ran after the loose ball and passed it to Christopher before falling to the ground.

Christopher caught the ball and did a quick lay-up.

"Late but brought your A-game! That's how you do it!" Christopher yelled at Isaac.

Tim attempted to pass Kurt the ball from the sideline. Isaac caught the ball and dribbled it across the court, doing a fake around the back move on Kurt, before heading straight to the hoop for a lay-up.

"Hold up, we need a time out. I think I need to talk to my teammate," Tim said shooting Kurt an irritated look.

"Nah, you two got it covered, remember? My man just ran you down the court and you couldn't stop him," Christopher said patting Kurt on the back jokingly, as he nudged him off.

"We're good, Tim. I'm ready for him," Kurt said bending down on his knees to catch his breath.

Isaac was feeling great. He was hanging out with his friends and having a great game so far. He hadn't even thought about Mariah once.

Tim tried to pass Kurt the ball with the heavy defense Isaac was putting on him. He ended up missing the pass because Isaac caught it again, and he passed the ball over to Christopher, who made a three-point shot.

They played for what seemed like an hour with Christopher and Isaac winning by 10 points. Isaac wobbled over to the bench from exhaustion as a group of kids came onto the court. They finished in perfect timing to prevent having to share.

"That was a good game. Sorry, we had to kick your butts," Isaac said giving Christopher a high-five before falling down onto the bench. He relaxed back against the bench and allowed the sun to beat against his face.

"Whatever," Tim hissed at them. He was the most competitive of them and hated to lose at anything.

"So are you guys bringing dates to my housewarming party next weekend?" Kurt asked, guzzling down a bottle of water.

"Why bring sand to the beach if you're going to have other women there. Hey, you should invite that Amanda girl from your office. She's cute. Besides you owe me," Tim said, referring to the loss he had just incurred from the game.

"Hey, speak for yourself. You know this one here will be bringing his fiancée," Christopher said, defending his best friend, Isaac.

Isaac quickly sat up and possibly too fast because he felt dizzy all of a sudden. He hadn't told his friends about calling off the engagement yet, and he wasn't really up to sharing the news at this moment. He just had a great game and didn't feel up to rehashing the whole break up with Mariah.

"Oh, that's a given. Eight months away before you take the big plunge. I never thought I would see the day," Tim said smiling at his friend.

"Me too, but out of all of the women you have dated, I must say you picked the right one to settle down with. Mariah's pretty cool," Kurt said reaching over to give Isaac a high-five. Kurt was the only one who was married and for three years now.

Isaac high-fived Kurt, but was starting to feel guilty about lying to his friends. The news was going to come out sooner or later when they inquired about going for their tuxedo measurements, so he figured now was as good of a time as any to break the news.

"Thanks, Kurt, but there isn't going to be a wedding anymore. Mariah and I are no longer together."

"Whoa...when did this happen?" both Christopher and Kurt said in unison.

"Don't worry about it, my man. Kurt will invite someone for you as well to the party," Tim responded.

"Hey, chill," Christopher said giving Tim an eye to be more considerate. "Are you alright?" he asked Isaac.

"Yeah, thanks. It's just not going to work out with the whole marriage thing, after all. Mariah has hang-ups about getting married for the third time. And no matter how much I tried to reassure her that I was in it for the long haul, I think the thought of marriage was just too much for her to handle," Isaac said.

"Three times Isaac? Wow, I didn't know about all of that. Well, maybe she was trying to keep you from experiencing what the other two husbands had to deal with. It sounds like she has major issues, and it may not have been the guys' fault," Tim said as everyone tossed their sweaty towels at him.

"Hey, I liked her for you too. She was fun to be around, but there are always two sides to a story, and you haven't heard what the other ex-husbands have to say," Tim said, defending his comment.

"Tim, thanks for your concern, but the situations in her past were nothing like that. We only started to have problems after I put the ring on her finger. She's still a good woman. She's just insecure about marriage and didn't want to be judged by anyone," Isaac said, shooting Tim an eye in regard to his statement. "But it doesn't matter anymore, because no matter how much I tried to make her feel comfortable about it, it just didn't work."

"Hey…sorry man. I didn't mean to sound like an ass. Maybe you two can just date then," Tim said, trying to improve his position on the topic.

"Nah, it's better this way. I want kids and the whole family thing now, and I don't think we want the same things anymore," Isaac said.

"Yeah, I feel ya," Kurt said.

"It'll all work out for you, man," Christopher said.

"Thanks, you guys. I'll be at the housewarming though. It starts at 7 p.m., right?" Isaac asked.

"You know it. There'll be plenty of food, so come hungry," Kurt said, gathering his things as they started to walk towards their cars.

The cat was officially out of the bag. Now Isaac had to tell his parents. He didn't feel as bad as he thought he would feel after coming clean to his friends. It was time for him to start preparing to move on anyway. He knew the hardest part was yet to come when Mariah had to come over to his place to pick up her things.

Chapter Seventeen

Mariah walked into her office on Monday morning with her head held high after crying the last of her tears over Isaac on Saturday. She spent Sunday afternoon taking down the pictures they had posed for together, and boxing up his belongings. Tina and the kids were moving in that evening and she wanted to make sure she was ready for their stay.

Mariah unlocked her office door and dropped her briefcase on the desk. She walked over to her window to open up the blinds. It was a beautiful sunny day outside. As soon as Mariah turned around to walk back to her desk, she noticed a picture of her and Isaac sitting next to her computer. She immediately took the picture out of the sterling silver picture frame the company had given her as an anniversary gift and ripped the picture into tiny pieces. She tossed the shredded pieces into the trash can before taking her seat behind her desk. She would put a picture of her nieces and nephew in the frame later.

Mariah's office phone rang from her receptionist's desk.

"Good morning, Cheryl."

"Good morning, Mariah. I have a call for you on line one," Cheryl said.

"Thank you," Mariah responded before connecting to the call.

"Good morning, Mariah," Isaac said.

Mariah froze. She wasn't expecting to hear his voice come through the line.

"I would've called you directly, but I didn't think you would answer," he said.

Mariah crossed her legs and turned around in her chair to face her window. "Ok, so how may I help you? I'm pretty busy," she asked, nonchalantly.

"I'm sorry. I didn't mean to disturb you. I just wanted to let you know that I have a few of your things at my place, and I wanted to know when you would like to pick them up," Isaac inquired calmly.

"Just trash them. I have a few of your things as well, including your house key. I was going to call Fed-Ex today to deliver the box with your key inside to your condo."

"Mariah, I don't want to throw your stuff away. You have two nice blouses here and a pantsuit."

"Isaac, when I move on from something, I erase it from my memory for good. You made your decision, and now I'm fine with it. I have no need for the pantsuit or the blouses, or anything else you may find. In fact, why don't you donate them on my behalf," she added, pissed for leaving her pinstripe Donna Karan suit over there. It was one of her favorite suits, but she refused to go anywhere near Isaac's property…even for Donna Karan.

"Mariah, I'm off today, so I'll just box your items up and leave it on your back stoop. Will that work?"

"Whatever. Well, I have to go, Isaac. Toot-a-loo," Mariah said, hanging up the phone without waiting for a response.

For a split second, she felt sad, but she reminded herself of how Isaac had treated her in the gym parking lot. She was able to get over the sad feeling fairly quickly, and picked up her office phone to dial Sandra's extension.

"Hi. I'm happy to see you're back in the office. I hope you're feeling better," Sandra answered in her usual upbeat tone.

"Yes, I'm feeling much better. Thank you. Sorry I had to call into work sick last week. I'm free until 10 a.m. if you want to catch up on the Aerilis project," she said.

"Okay – sounds great! I'll be over in ten. Let me grab a cup of coffee first," Sandra responded.

Mariah hung up the phone. She knew she was going to have to explain her engagement, or lack thereof, when Sandra arrived at her office. She was happy Sandra didn't really entertain office gossip, so she didn't have to worry about explaining to more than one person. Things didn't work out between her and Isaac, and it was as simple as that, so she was ready to throw herself into what she was good at…work.

℃ℬ

Mariah pulled into her garage at 5:00 p.m. She couldn't help but see a box sitting on her back stoop. She got out of her car and went to retrieve it. Isaac had kept his word on delivering her things to her house. She brought the box inside of her garage and went back to her car to retrieve the Fed-Ex label she had printed off at work. She walked over to the box she had left beside her kitchen door and applied the label to the front of it.

She couldn't resist opening up the box one last time to glance at the items inside. Sitting on top of a pair of basketball shorts that Isaac would slip on to relax was a gold key. Isaac's condo key. She quickly closed the box, resealed it and walked back out to her stoop to leave the box there. She had the Fed-Ex scheduled to be picked up at 5:30 p.m., so the box was soon going to be gone.

She reentered her garage and pressed the wall switch. Mariah watched as the garage door started to go down. It was as if it was separating her from her old life with Isaac. His things were on the opposite side of the door, and would soon be gone forever. Mariah entered her house and closed the door. She went upstairs to take a quick shower before her sister and the kids arrived.

Thirty minutes later, Mariah heard a couple of mini knocks at the front door, and then the doorbell repeatedly ringing until she answered it. Her nieces and nephew were standing there giggling with their hands over their mouth.

"Sorry, they couldn't help themselves," Tina said, entering the house with three large luggage bags.

"Please, I'm so happy that my nieces and nephew are here! Guess what?! We're having p-i-z-z-a for dinner!" Mariah said, chasing the kids into the nearby family room.

"Yay!!! Pizza! Pizza!" The kids started to chant from the top of their lungs.

"Hi Sis, drop your bags. Make yourself at home. I'm going to set the kids up in here, and I have you set up in the sunroom," Mariah said, flopping down on the pull-out couch in the family room, which was about to become the kids bed.

"Oh, that'll work. I really appreciate you letting us stay here," Tina said sitting down beside her.

"So, how are you feeling?" Mariah asked in a low voice. The kids had turned on the television and were watching an episode of Sponge Bob Square Pants.

"I'm okay. I just never thought I would be here at my age moving from my parents' house to my sister's house," Tina said.

"I know, but it will get better. Have you spoken to Paul?"

"Yes, and he thinks we should sell the house so he can help me pay for a place."

"Well, how do you feel about that?"

"I don't know yet. I really like the house, and I like the kids having a backyard to run around in. But it's not something I can afford right now on my own, so I really need to give Paul's idea some consideration," Tina said looking at her kids. They had no idea of what was going on between their parents.

"Well, if you could afford the house note on your own, would you stay in it, or still sell it because it's something you and Paul bought together?" Mariah inquired.

"I would definitely stay in that house, if I could afford the $2,700 a month mortgage payment. I handpicked every design in that house, and it doesn't matter that it was once a house Paul and I shared together. We're no longer in a bad place. We've just made an adult decision that we no longer want to be married to each other, and our relationship has been much better ever since we came to that conclusion," Tina said.

"Well, I have an idea. My division at work is doing their annual summer picnic, and I'm in charge of picking the caterer this year. I have a $12,000 budget, and I would like to hire you. I'll ask my boss if he's fine with this arrangement, since you are my sister, but I'm sure it will be fine. You have a reputable business," Mariah said, beaming at her idea.

"Really, Mariah?! I wouldn't want to mess anything up when it's at your job," Tina asked, jumping to her feet with excitement, but then turning to look at her sister with doubt on her face.

"I trust you. I know your capabilities and this will be a walk in the park for you," Mariah said, squeezing her sister's hand.

"Mariah this could be the big break I have been looking for, and possibly a way to allow me to keep my house. The fact that you would do this for me…I can't thank you enough," Tina said, bending down to hug her sister.

"No problem. You would do the same for me. We're sisters and we have to stick together. Your dream is going to come true this year, Tina. I just know it. Your catering business is going to take off. There'll be some influential people at the picnic who love to throw parties, and you can pass along your business card. The picnic is in three weeks though."

"Not a problem! If your boss signs off on this, I'll definitely be ready."

The doorbell rang.

"The pizza is here! Yay!" PJ said jumping to his feet and running to the front door.

"I'll pay for it. You have done enough," Tina said reaching for her purse.

"No way…I've got this," Mariah said heading to meet PJ at the front door.

"Okay – Thanks! Come on Lexie and Leshia. Let's go have some pizza!" Tina said taking each of her daughter's hands and walking them to the kitchen table.

"I got cheese for the kids and meat lovers for us," Mariah said placing the hot pizza boxes on the kitchen table.

"I want meat lovers," PJ said jumping up and down.

"You can have a piece of meat lovers then," Mariah said,

pretending to tickle him.

"I'll get the plates," Tina said.

Mariah took a seat and waited for her sister to bring the plates to the table.

"I know you don't like the kids to have soda, but I need to go grocery shopping," Mariah said unscrewing the top off the two-liter Sprite that had arrived with the pizza.

"No problem. Mom broke every rule I ever tried to maintain while staying there last week. I say no to candy, and she gives them a piece. I say no to eating ice cream before dinner, and these two were able to get some," Tina said pointing to the twins.

"Well, I can't promise you that I won't spoil them with kisses, but I will definitely obey your non-soda rule after tonight," Mariah said biting into a slice of pizza.

"I just realized there are no pictures of Isaac around here. Where are they?" Tina asked.

Mariah looked up from her pizza and gave her sister a wink to let her know she was fine. "I have to fill you in on the update tonight after we get the kids to bed. I took them down this weekend though."

Tina mouthed the word, "OK," and changed the subject. They were always good about not bad-mouthing anyone around the kids. Although Isaac was not going to be in Mariah's life anymore, he was always good to the kids, and she didn't want to change that image in their heads.

Mariah enjoyed a nice dinner with her family, listening to the kids talk about what they did over the weekend with her parents at the park. She was so glad they decided to stay with her. It was as if life had been brought back into her house, and she was no longer thinking about Isaac.

Later on that night, Mariah got the kids nestled into bed after saying their prayers.

"Night, Auntie Mariah," Lexie and Leshia said together.

"Night, Auntie!" PJ yelled out.

Mariah giggled as she gave each one a kiss on the cheek. PJ tried to separate himself from the twins a lot more these days, to keep his own identity separate. If the girls said Good Morning, he would say Morning.

"Good night. I love you all," Mariah said turning off the light. She headed to the nearby sunroom to visit Tina before going upstairs to her room.

Mariah stopped at the doorway because she could see Tina talking on the phone. She seemed to be having a decent conversation with Paul, with no arguing. Mariah pointed upstairs to let her sister know she would be in her room if she needed her, and Tina nodded. Mariah walked away and headed upstairs. She couldn't help but remember Tina's remark about how she and Paul were getting along now that they had decided to end their marriage.

This was another example of what she had been saying all along. Marriage definitely changes things. She was happy that she hadn't gone through with marrying Isaac, after all. She couldn't imagine being in her sister's place right now, preparing for a divorce with kids involved. The only way to avoid ever having to experience a divorce was to not get married in the first place.

Chapter Eighteen

Isaac knocked on Kurt's front door for his housewarming party. He and his wife Bianca had just bought their first home together, a ranch-style near Solana Beach. Isaac knocked on the door again, hoping they could hear him over the loud music playing inside.

"Hi, Isaac. Come on in," Bianca said, answering the door with a martini glass in her hand.

"Hi, Bianca. Nice neighborhood. It's not too far from the beach," Isaac said, handing her a housewarming gift.

"Thanks! We got a good deal on it. It's quiet out here too, so we're happy about it. There's plenty of food to eat, so please make yourself at home. I'll let Kurt know you're here. He's responsible for the tours. I'm in charge of the drinks, so can I get you anything? We have beer, wine, wine coolers, mixed drinks…," Bianca asked.

"I'm fine for right now, but I'll let you know," Isaac responded as he made his way over to the buffet table.

Isaac filled his plate with hot wings, vegetables and dip, shrimp pasta salad and mini quiche rolls. He made his way through the crowd of people that were already there laughing and drinking, to look for his friends. Kurt and Bianca were the most social friends he had due to their professions. Kurt worked as a Realtor for a well-known real estate company in the area, and Bianca worked in her family furniture business. As he turned the corner toward the living room, he noticed Kurt heading in his direction.

"Hey man, thanks for coming and for the gift. Bianca told me you were here. Let me show you around," Kurt said leading him around the house.

The house was spacious inside with a lot of rooms. Kurt and Bianca had a few pictures on the wall and a small amount of furniture was scattered sporadically throughout the house. They had moved from a one bedroom apartment, so they had quite a bit of space to fill up.

"This is a nice house. So are you two ready for kids now?" Isaac asked after they did a walk through.

"Yeah, we're ready for kids. You'll be the first to know when it happens," Kurt said as they approached Christopher and Tim.

"I'll hold you to it. What's up fellas?" Isaac asked, stuffing another wing in his mouth.

"Nothing much. Kurt, these are some good wings. Did Bianca make these?" Tim inquired.

"No, she bought them from some wing place up the street...pretty good, huh? I told her we're going to have to go back to get some for one of our game nights. They have some good food places around here," Kurt said, bobbing his head to Party Rock Anthem by LMFAO, as it came through the stereo.

"Kurt, where are the single ladies in here? Everyone here

seems to be with someone," Tim inquired, scanning the crowd.

"Don't worry I invited Amanda and Bianca invited a few of her single friends as well. It's still early. Just relax," Kurt said.

Isaac excused himself and headed over to the kitchen to get a beer. Bianca was making margaritas and chatting with a few people who were waiting for their drinks to be finished. Isaac was happy for his friends. Kurt had found the love of his life, and they were now in their first home together, ready for their next step. If anyone could find love in this crazy world, they should be so lucky. For a second, Mariah came back into his mind. He thought he had found all of that with her and was ready to embark on the same journey. The house and the kids, but he guessed he was wrong.

"Isaac, would you like a margarita?" Bianca asked interrupting his thoughts as she filled glasses.

"No, thank you. I got a beer," he said, raising his bottle to her before walking back over to the food table for a second helping of the nice spread they had laid out.

Isaac pushed the whole Mariah thought out of his head and went back over to have a good time with his friends, who were teasing Kurt about something funny he did when they were in college.

An hour later, Isaac started to feel sick. He went and sat down on the couch right next to the speakers, which he later realized was a bad idea, as the music pounded against his head. He had consumed more beers than he would have normally, although he knew what it was all about. He was starting to miss being with Mariah and wanted to erase her from his memory.

Isaac got up and moved over to the sitting area near the bar and relaxed back against the couch. Luckily, he still looked like he had his composure. He never liked to look pure drunk and unable to control himself like some people. He was too old for that.

Just as Isaac was starting to relax, he saw Tim walking up with a blond haired, blue eyed woman and her friend who looked like she was mixed with Hawaiian and Black. He had his arm around the blond haired woman. He led her over to the couch next to him to sit down, while the Hawaiian woman sat next to her friend.

"Hey, Isaac this is Amanda and her friend Kirsten. Hey Kirsten, why don't you go sit next to my friend Isaac? You two can get to know each other," Tim suggested, giving Isaac a wink.

Isaac knew that wink too well. Tim wanted Isaac to run interference for him with the tagalong friend. Isaac shot him a quick, disgusted, look back as Kirsten got up and sat down next to him. Isaac wasn't in the mood to talk to this woman, but Tim didn't seem to care as he turned around and started to chat with Amanda.

"Hi, nice to meet you, Isaac," Kirsten said, extending her hand to his.

Isaac shook her hand. She was a beautiful woman, but her beauty wasn't enough to take his mind off the one person he wanted to be with right now.

"Same here," he responded.

"I love this house. I like how it looks small and quaint from the outside, but it opens up and is really spacious once you get inside. Sort of like an illusion," Kirsten said.

Isaac looked back at her and smiled.

"So, what do you do?" she asked.

"Excuse me?" Isaac asked again over the music, not really interested in the conversation.

"I asked what you do for a living," Kirsten repeated herself, seeming to be very interested in Isaac.

Isaac didn't want to appear rude, so he turned slightly towards her and responded. "I'm a lawyer."

Kirsten's eyes lit up like she was just informed that she had won a million dollars. "Really – well that's an intriguing career. What area of law do you practice?"

At this point, Isaac knew what time it was with Kirsten. She thought he had money and thought she had met someone who was good marriage material. This is what most women their age were looking for, or at least the ones he had come across before settling down with Mariah.

When he first started dating Mariah, she wasn't Vice President of Marketing yet. In fact, she hadn't gotten promoted until the end of their first year together, and not once did she react like this when she found out what he did for a living. Actually, she felt like an equal and never looked at Isaac to do anything for her, which he really liked about her personality.

"Um...I'm in criminal law," he responded, looking across the room to distract himself from the conversation.

"Ohhhh – that's good. We need more attorneys to get the bad guys off the street. Do you want to know what I do for a living?" Kirsten asked, nudging Isaac's leg with hers.

Not really, Isaac thought. "Do tell," he said anyway, wondering why he had to ask if she really wanted to tell him in the first place.

"I'm a business consultant. You know, with Federal Government contracting," Kirsten added.

Isaac looked over to Tim, who was lip-locked in a kiss with Amanda. He felt like he had had enough at this moment. The party was still going on. People were up mingling and dancing, but Isaac felt like the one space he had found, in a secluded corner to ride out his buzz, had been violated with Tim and his latest catch. He really didn't appreciate Tim asking him to run interference with the girlfriend like they were still in college. This was definitely enough to sober him up really fast.

"Kirsten, it was great talking to you, but I'm going to head out now. I'm getting tired," he said rising from the couch.

"No problem. It was nice to meet you. Do you want my

number so we can continue this conversation another time?" she asked eagerly.

"I'm just getting out of a relationship so I'm not really ready to start dating just yet, but it was nice talking to you. I'm sure we'll see each other again at the next event," Isaac said hoping to conclude the conversation there, but Kirsten was already reaching into her little handbag for a business card.

Isaac couldn't believe this girl. He tried with every ounce of energy to keep from laughing. She was definitely one who goes after what she wants and doesn't know how to take No for an answer, even if she looks silly in the process. Anyone could see that he wasn't interested.

"Well, call me when you're ready to talk," Kirsten said smiling as she handed him the card.

Isaac took the card so he didn't look rude. He quickly hit Tim on the leg to let him know he was leaving and headed over to where Kurt and everyone else were chatting to say his goodbyes.

As soon as Isaac stepped out onto the front porch, he smelled the nearby ocean. Bianca and Kurt had placed a bag of trash by the front door to take out after the party was over. Isaac bent down and tucked Kirsten's card inside of it. He walked over to his car and got inside for his lonely drive back home.

Chapter Nineteen

On the first Friday in June, the Armstrong & Associates Division 40th Annual Picnic was scheduled to kick off at Crescent Grove Park. Mariah had dressed in a company t-shirt, khaki skirt, and matching khaki slip-on shoes. She had her hair scooped up in a neat ponytail in hopes of staying cool on that hot day. It was supposed to be cloudy, with on and off showers at a muggy 89 degrees, although the sun was currently blazing. Mariah hoped the rain would hold off for the picnic. She wanted everything to be perfect for her sister today.

She turned her car into the entrance of the community park where they had reserved space. She couldn't wait to see how Tina was doing. Her sister had been preparing all week for this occasion purchasing food, reserving equipment and recruiting help from two former employees she worked with at the seafood restaurant.

Mariah was super nervous even though she knew her sister was going to do a fantastic job. This was her biggest contract and Tina had confided in her last night that she was nervous. As Mariah pulled her car into an empty parking space, she saw her sister's van and the tent she had set up to prepare the food. There were about a dozen cars already there from other Armstrong & Associates employees. Most of them were senior managers from her division. Mariah got out of her car and walked over to speak to her colleagues before checking in with her sister. She was certain that

Tina had everything under control and didn't need her to hover over her while she was trying to work.

"Hello, all," she said walking up to Keith, her boss, Mora, the Vice President of Finance, and Carlton, the Project Manager over the new Aerilis account.

"Hi," they all said in unison.

"I heard your sister is catering this event. I can't wait to try the food. Where is the location of her business?" Mora asked, sipping on a bottle of water.

Mariah simply smiled. She had prepared herself to answer this question. No, Tina didn't own her own facility or have a laundry list of clientele. But, she was confident in her sister's skills and she knew that pretty soon everyone else would be too – as soon as they tasted her food.

"She's a private chef. She used to be the executive chef at the Atlantic Seafood Restaurant on Ocean Beach for fifteen years, before venturing out on her own last year," Mariah said hoping to divert any other questions, especially pertaining to her sister's current clientele or any other company events she has done.

"I love that spot. They have the best seafood. My wife and I celebrated our 20th wedding anniversary there last year. I had no idea your sister used to be head chef there. Very impressive," Keith said as the others nodded in unison. They would have agreed to anything Keith said.

A couple other managers walked up at that moment and the conversation quickly shifted to work related business such as proposals, bids on new work, and upcoming plans for the Aerilis contract. At this point, Mariah figured it would be a good idea to go check on her sister. The crowd was really starting to pour in at this point and she wanted to know when the food would be ready.

As Mariah approached the food tent, she saw her sister dressed in her white chef's coat providing food orders to one of her cooks.

"Hey Tina, how's everything coming along?" Mariah asked as Tina wrapped up her conversation. The cook ran off to finish beating something on the stove.

"Well, it's coming. I hope everyone likes it," Tina said nervously, using her arm to wipe the sweat beads from off her forehead.

"Yeah, it's a hot one today. So are you okay? Do you need help with anything?" Mariah asked, attempting to speak over the loud air conditioning fan her sister had set up to keep the tent cool.

"The barbecue chicken and ribs are ready to go!" one of the cooks called out.

"No, we got a good start prepping this morning. I'll be ready to put the food out in another ten minutes. I put out water bottles and little finger snacks, so that should hold them until we get the food out," Tina said.

"Okay, well, I will let you get back to work. Tina, you're going to do great. This is just the beginning," Mariah said, giving her a hug. She could tell her sister was still a little nervous.

"Thank you. I can't thank you enough and your boss for giving me this opportunity. This could definitely make or break my career with all these people here. Word of mouth is big in this field. I have to go get the baked beans and corn on the cob ready to take out. I love you," Tina said, giving her a wink.

"I love you too, Sis. And you're going to rock today," Mariah said putting up two thumbs before heading out of the tent. She was so proud of her sister. She knew everyone was going to love her food just as much as she does.

About thirty minutes later, the food was put out and Mariah couldn't remember ever seeing so many people go back for seconds and thirds. Tina did an excellent job in overestimating the numbers because there was plenty of food available for her company. Mariah was even impressed with the fruit display that her sister had designed. The watermelon was cut in the shape of a whale, surrounded by a bed of fruit, giving off the illusion that the whale was rising out of the ocean. As she sat and ate her food, she saw people taking a picture of it with their cameras and smartphones.

"Everything is wonderful, Mariah. It's two for two for you this year. First sealing the deal on the Aerilis contract and now putting together a magnificent company picnic. I tip my hat to you," Keith said as they were sitting at the picnic table eating.

"Thank you, Keith. But I cannot take all of the credit for today. Timeless Catering definitely owned up to their name," she said, making sure to stir the attention toward her sister's business.

"And I hear the owner is your sister. Way to take a risk if things didn't go right today. Lucky for you, you have family who's able to follow through. I've seen this sort of thing not run so smoothly in the past when working with family," Stephanie, one of the senior managers, said as a few others at the table shook their heads in agreement.

Mariah tried not to shoot her an eyeful. Stephanie had only been with the company for two years, yet she walked in the door always saying exactly what she felt without any sort of filter for her mouth. There were times when Mariah would be in a meeting with her and would gasp at some of the comments she would make. Today was definitely no different for Stephanie to speak her mind about her hiring her sister for this big event.

Secretly, Mariah was just now able to breathe a sigh of relief. She knew her sister was talented, but if anything went wrong today, she knew she would hear about it and possibly be ridiculed for it at work. It was evident from Stephanie's comments.

"Well, I know my sister is talented, and she has done other events of this magnitude, so I wasn't worried," Mariah said as she forked some baked beans in her mouth. She was embellishing just a tad, but so what, her sister had already shown through her work today that she could handle an event like this.

Tina walked over to their table. "Hello Everyone. I hope you are enjoying the food. The dessert table is available when you're ready," she said.

"The food is great. Do you do children's birthday parties? My son is turning five in September, and we're looking for a caterer for the party. My husband and I are trying to bring Disneyland to our backyard with all the characters, amenities and things like that," Madeline Harper asked at the end of the table.

Mariah looked up at her sister who had the biggest smile on her face. "Sure, we do all events. I'll get you my business card so we can make an appointment and discuss the details," Tina said.

Mariah was so happy for her sister. She knew she would be well on her way now. Tina just needed a little push and for someone to believe in her. Mariah secretly hoped this would uplift her spirits too. Being separated was just as bad as being divorced in her opinion; it put you in a standstill to endure the reality that you are in a failed marriage. *At least after the divorce is finalized, you can move on and try to look for a brighter future as you piece your life back together*, Mariah thought. She ate the last of her corn on the cob and watched as other people at the table complimented the chef.

☙

Later on that night, Tina and Mariah dropped the kids off at their parents' and decided to go celebrate at a nearby lounge where a jazz band played on Friday nights. Mariah felt weird getting dressed to go out, without meeting Isaac. She settled on a shimmery turquoise tank top, black capris and a pair of black stylish pumps with a large turquoise feather on the back, to help jazz up her outfit. She definitely wasn't trying to overdo it, but her sister did not share in her thoughts.

Tina decided to wear a white, purple, and black printed fitted tube dress and black 3-inch skinny heel sandals. The outfit took Mariah by surprise. She had never seen her sister dressed in something fitted like that since before she had had the twins, much less in high heels.

"You look great," Mariah said as they got back in the car to head to the lounge. "You make me want to go back home and change my outfit."

"Thank you. I feel really good. Today was a successful day and I have two possible job opportunities lined up. I'm feeling better now about my whole situation," Tina said as she pulled down the visor to look at her makeup in the mirror.

"Yes, today was a big day for you. You seemed to be even more excited about going out tonight. Have you spoken to Paul?" Mariah asked as she turned onto the entrance ramp to the interstate. She couldn't help but catch a glimpse of her sister's left hand to see that she wasn't wearing her wedding ring tonight.

"Nope. We have pretty much ironed out the details of what we need to discuss at this point. With the money I have made from this job, I can afford to make a few house payments. I spoke to my old boss from Atlantic Seafood this week. I'm going back part-time just until I can really pick up more catering jobs and establish myself. The kids and I will start moving back home next week, and Paul is going to get an apartment," Tina said matter-of-factly with a shrug.

"Wow, it sounds like you two have everything figured out. Are you sure there is no way you guys can work it out? I saw your mood sort of change last week. I wasn't sure if it had to do with the separation."

"Gosh no. The separation is the best thing Paul and I could have done. I think it was more of me feeling sad about how we're going to tell the kids, but I know it will work out somehow. I mean I love Paul, but I know there is not enough there between us anymore to continue with this marriage. Now, enough about that, let's go and celebrate," Tina said, turning up the volume on the radio and dancing to Single Ladies by Beyoncé.

Mariah looked over at her sister through shocked eyes. *Who is this person sitting in her front seat?* she thought. Her sister was definitely in high spirits tonight. Five minutes later, they pulled up to the Red Goose Lounge in Gaslamp Quarter. A crowd of people already stood in line waiting to pay to get into the lounge. Red Goose is a big establishment with downstairs and upstairs seating areas and a balcony that overlooks the dance floor and stage. Mariah really liked this spot because most lounges she had experienced were small. The spacious atmosphere at the Red Goose allowed for more movement around the venue without bumping into anyone.

Mariah and Tina headed upstairs after paying the $5 cover charge to get in and got a perfect seat by the balcony. They reserved their seats and headed straight to the bar to get something to drink.

"I would like to make a toast to my big sister for doing an amazing job today!" Mariah squealed as she tapped her glass to her sister's.

"And I would like to toast my baby sister for giving me such an amazing opportunity and for standing behind me and my dream. You trusted in me today and I wanted to make sure I did my very best to not let you down. Here's to you, Mariah. I love you girl," Tina said lifting her glass up in the air.

Mariah mouthed the words I love you too, clicking her glass as the band started to play a fast rendition to On & On by Erykah Badu.

"This is so much fun! I haven't been out in years," Tina said sipping on her blue motorcycle.

"Are you serious? You and Paul don't go out?" Mariah asked, looking at her in amazement for what seemed like the one-hundredth time already that night.

"No. We haven't done much of anything in the past three years except pay bills, take care of the kids, work, and oh…have sex every other month it seems like," she said moving slowly in her seat to the jazz band playing. The band was a local well-known band with a lead singer who sounded like Jill Scott.

"I'm not trying to get in your business, but I think I can see now where you two were heading for problems. You two needed more intimacy with one another and time together away from the kids. Why didn't you ever drop the kids over at my house so you two could have a date night?" Mariah inquired.

"Well, it's over with now, so I'll take that advice for the next one," Tina said as a gentleman approached their table in a nice sky blue dress top and slacks.

"Hello Ladies. Would you like to dance?" he asked, extending his hand to Tina.

"Sure," Tina said, eyeing the tall man with a close shave and bald head.

Mariah leaned against her chair and sipped on her glass of wine as her sister sashayed off with her new friend. She couldn't help but think of Isaac and what he was probably doing on a Friday night. She imagined him possibly out with his friends not thinking about her, so she decided to push him out of her thoughts and listen to the band.

"Hi. You're too beautiful to be sitting here alone. Are you here with someone?"

Mariah looked up and almost did a double take at the gorgeous man who had approached her table. She couldn't imagine

185

thinking about looking at another man right now after the way things ended with Isaac, but this man was just too handsome to not pique her interest.

"Hello and thank you. I'm here with my sister who's on the dance floor right now."

"Oh, well hopefully your sister won't mind me sitting in her seat until she gets back. I just wanted to make sure you weren't here with another guy," he said with a chuckle as he sat down.

"I like your accent. Where are you from?" Mariah asked.

"I'm from Cuba. I lived there until I came to the states for college. So what's your name, beautiful?"

"My name is Mariah Langston and yours?"

"Alberto Hernandez. So do you come here a lot?"

Mariah sat up in her chair and crossed her legs. "I've been here quite a few times with…um, yeah quite a few times. I like the atmosphere. It's a nice mellow place to relax," Mariah said trying to cover up how she almost mentioned coming here with her ex-boyfriend Isaac.

"Well, I'm happy you came tonight so I would have an opportunity to meet you. I must say you're the most beautiful woman here tonight," Alberto said.

"Wow, you have a way of making a woman feel special," Mariah said. She didn't feel like she had put her best foot forward tonight in her attire, but she was definitely enjoying the compliments from a handsome gentleman who had the ability to take her mind off things.

"Hey, I speak the truth. So, are you currently in a relationship with anyone?"

Mariah was back at this stage of the game again. She decided to give the same line she used to give when she was out and a man would approach her.

"I'm here with you now, so that's all that matters right?" she asked with a wink.

"I like that and you're right about that. Well, I know you're here with your sister and I do not want to impose on your girl's night out with her. Would you mind if I take down your phone number so I can give you a call sometime?" Alberto asked.

Mariah didn't know if she was really ready to start dating or even talking to another man just yet. She was just now getting used to the single life and going to bed without talking to Isaac first. However, if there was going to be a man who she held a conversation with, it definitely needed to be the Cuban hunk that had approached her table tonight.

Mariah took her wallet out of her purse and took out a business card. She marked through her office number and wrote her cell phone number on it. "It was nice to meet you, Alberto," she said, handing him her business card.

Alberto smiled at her showing off his straight pearly white

teeth. "I will definitely give you a call. Enjoy the rest of your night with your sister, Beautiful," he said giving her a wink as Tina started to approach the table.

She sat down breathing hard as if she had just run a marathon. The last couple of songs were pretty upbeat and everyone was either jamming on the dance floor, between the aisles or was just moving in their seats.

"Who was that eye candy that just walked away from this table?" Tina asked looking back in Alberto's direction as he disappeared into the crowd.

"That was Alberto Hernandez. He has the most erotic accent I have ever heard. He asked for my number and I gave it to him," Mariah said with a shrug as she sipped from her glass of wine.

"Hmm so you're ready to start dating again?" Tina asked, fanning herself with a napkin.

"Not really, but I have to move on. I'm sure Isaac has already," she said.

Tina reached over and rubbed her hand. "You don't know that."

"It's not like I'm trying to settle down again right now. If Mr. Alberto calls and we have dinner, at least my eyes will be in good company because he's gorgeous. Enough about me, Missy. You were really getting your boogie on out on the dance floor. I saw you out there moving around with that man," Mariah said jokingly.

"Hey, your big sister still has it," Tina said, laughing as she started to move around in a dance motion in her seat.

"Did you think about Paul when you were out on the dance floor? Maybe wish that the guy you were dancing with was him?" Mariah inquired.

"No, not really, but I can tell you're still thinking about Isaac. This time shall pass, Sis. You'll be okay. I'm here to support you in whatever you decide to do, whether it's to date again, take time out for yourself, which is what I highly recommend right now, or see about reconciling with Isaac," Tina said.

Mariah decided not to answer her sister as she looked over the balcony at the other couples slow dancing on the floor to the sound of the saxophonist doing a solo. There was not going to be another Mariah and Isaac episode and she had already accepted that fact a long time ago.

The ladies listened to the band for about another hour and a half before calling it quits and heading back to Mariah's. They were both exhausted and decided to leave the kids at their parents' until the morning.

Chapter Twenty

On Sunday around 11 a.m., Mariah woke up to an empty house. Her sister had left her a note saying she went to their parents' house to pick up the kids and to take them to their house to see their dad. Mariah got up, freshened up and decided to tackle her least favorite chore – laundry. She was loading the washer with her whites when her cell phone started to ring. She dropped a few more shirts into the machine and went to the kitchen to get it.

"Hello," Mariah answered, even though she was not familiar with the number flashing on the screen.

"Hello. May I speak to Mariah?"

Mariah started to smile as she recognized the familiar voice from last night. "This is she," she said, leaning against the island.

"Hello, Mariah. This is Alberto. How are you doing this morning? I hope I didn't catch you at a bad time."

"Actually, I woke up late this morning and missed church so I'm just doing a load of laundry. How about you?" she inquired.

"That sounds like two things I need to do. I'm a real estate agent and work seven days a week. I had an appointment this morning that just canceled, so I'm home right now. I saw on your business card that your office is on Seventeenth Street. I work two blocks from you.

"Wow, what a small world. So how's the housing market coming along? Is it still a good business to get into with the current economy?" Mariah asked.

"Yeah, the market is getting better slowly, but I do pretty well, so I can't complain. I also sell properties for companies. It always seems like someone is trying to relocate and buy bigger spaces, so it keeps me busy. Enough about me though. Tell me about you," Alberto said.

Mariah poured herself a cup of coffee and sat down at her kitchen table. "What do you want to know?" she asked.

"Well for starters, tell me how a beautiful woman like yourself hasn't been taken off the market yet. I had no idea agreeing to go out with a few friends would put me in a position to meet you last night."

"You're full of compliments. A girl could get used to this. I was recently engaged and we called it quits not too long ago, so that's why I'm single. We just wanted two different things out of life. As far as work goes, I'm Vice President of a marketing department, which I'm sure you saw on my business card. And I don't have any children, so it's just me. Why are you single?"

"Gosh, engaged. Well, I can't say I'm sorry for the fella, or else I wouldn't have had the opportunity to meet you last night. Personally, I'm single because I haven't found the right woman for me yet. As I stated, my career is pretty demanding so I don't get a lot of time to go out and meet anyone. So, Ms. VP of Marketing, do you think I could meet you for lunch this week?"

"Sure, you're in luck. My schedule is not as busy this week with meetings. How about Tuesday at 1 p.m.? We can beat the lunch rush hour if we leave at that time," Mariah said, sipping her cup of coffee.

"Tuesday sounds great. I can't wait to see that beautiful face again. How about Luigi's Café on Wilson Blvd? They have a variety of food selections unless you would like to go somewhere different."

"I know exactly where that is. I've heard great reviews about their café, but haven't had a chance to try it for myself," Mariah said.

"I'm glad you'll be trying it for the first time with me," Alberto responded.

They chatted for a few more minutes before getting off the phone. Mariah couldn't believe she was actually enjoying his conversation and didn't think once about Isaac, which was getting harder to do lately, regardless of how hard she tried. She wasn't sure if it was Alberto's adoring voice or his alluring sex appeal, but nevertheless, she planned to move on with her life and have fun in the process.

Mariah placed her cell phone back onto the charger and sat

back down at the kitchen table to read her newspaper. Generally on Sundays she met Isaac for brunch after church was over. Today she looked around at her normally tidy house to see toys scattered around and a load of laundry she needed to tend to before the week started. She smiled as she thought of her nieces and nephew. She had really enjoyed having them here for the past few weeks. Although she never wanted to have any children of her own, she enjoyed being an auntie. She shopped for them just like they were her own. She had even set up a savings account for them to have access to the funds when they turned eighteen years old. Mariah hoped they would use the money to help with any college expenses.

The buzzer went off on the washing machine, so Mariah got up to take the clothes out and put them in the dryer. She was hanging up her blouses to dry on the dryer racks when she heard the front door open and close. Then within seconds she heard sniffling. Mariah quickly sat the remaining blouses down on top of the dryer to go see what was going on. Tina walked into the kitchen, flung her keys down on the island and plopped down at the kitchen table crying.

"Tina, what's wrong?" Mariah immediately asked. She didn't recognize this person from last night who was so full of life dancing on the dance floor.

"It's all a mess now and it's all my fault. I took the kids over to the house and Paul and I finally told them that we're separated and are not getting back together. The kids started to cry and asked if it was because of them. And of course we said no. You know Leshia who is a pure daddy's girl turned to me as she was holding her father's hand and said, "It's your fault, Mommy. You don't treat Daddy right," Tina said mimicking her daughter's voice before bursting into tears again.

"Tina, you know it's not your fault. Stop blaming yourself. It takes two to mess up a marriage and Paul is not innocent in all of this. The children are going to probably pick sides in the beginning, and I'm not surprised that Leshia took Paul's side. You know how close she is with her dad. But she will come around. Don't let them guilt you into allowing them to disrespect you. You and Paul will be great parents, even if you are not in the same household," Mariah said pulling a chair closer to her sister to sit down.

"Look at you. I was the one always providing the big sister advice and now you're helping me out. I can't tell you how much I have appreciated everything you have done for me. From opening up your home to us, to being there for the kids the way you have. Thank you, Mariah," Tina said, wiping the tears from her eyes.

"You're welcome. And you don't have to thank me. That's what family is for," Mariah said.

Tina blew her nose into a tissue. "I honestly thought I had it all figured out. I now see how hard this must have been for you."

"No, you definitely have it way harder than I ever did. I didn't have kids to think about. When I needed to cry, I could without worrying about being strong for the little ones. I know you're moving back home next week, but if you ever need to drop the kids off here to unwind, please let me know."

"The way I'm feeling right now, I'm sure I'll take you up on that offer. Paul wanted to keep the kids until this evening since he has to go to work tomorrow, so I'm going to go lie down. My head feels like it's about to split," Tina said rising from the table.

"Sure, go lie down. Take all the time that you need. I'm sure after a good nap you'll feel a lot better. Would you like me to make you a sandwich or some tea?"

"I'm not really hungry right now, but I could go for some of your raspberry mint tea," Tina said.

"One cup of raspberry mint tea coming up," Mariah said, smiling as her sister headed to the sunroom to lie down.

Mariah walked over to the sink to fill up a kettle with water. She placed it on the stove and prepared to make her sister a cup of tea. Though she felt bad for her sister, she couldn't help feeling happy to be out of her own funk for a change. She was really looking forward to her little lunch date with Alberto. Could this be the guy who could actually pique her interest enough to help take her mind completely off Isaac? She didn't know for sure as of yet but was definitely interested in finding out.

Chapter Twenty-one

Mariah walked into the office on Tuesday morning and was immediately slammed with questions from her proposal team for an upcoming contract the company was bidding on. It seemed even when she thought she was going to have a slow day, something still managed to come up.

Mariah didn't get to come up for air until 11:30 a.m. She had planned on leaving for her lunch date at 12:30 p.m. to get a good parking spot. Since her office was in a heavily populated business area, parking can be hard to find near the restaurants.

Mariah picked up her mirror from her desk to check her appearance. She had worn one of her favorite business suits today. A cream-colored suit with a cream and chocolate scarf and matching patent leather Nine West pumps. She had pin curled her hair last night to ensure she had bouncy curls for today. She was running her fingers through her curls when a knock sounded at her office door. It was John Peters, her boss' executive assistant.

"Hello, John. Come on in," she said waving him into the room as she put her mirror away in her top drawer.

"Hello, Mariah. Keith is in a meeting that's running over, and he would like you to take his place on a status ECO conference call he has scheduled at 12 p.m. It should only be about 10 minutes," John said.

"Oh – okay," Mariah uttered, thinking about her lunch date.

"Thanks, Mariah. I will let Keith know that you'll be calling in for him. I'll forward you the email meeting-invite so you can have the call-in number and agenda. As I said, it should only be 10 minutes," he said before disappearing from her office.

Mariah blew air out of her mouth. She knew firsthand how Keith's status meetings could go with the other senior managers handling the ECO contract. She has witnessed it go from 10 minutes to an hour on multiple occasions. She sometimes felt the senior managers liked to hear themselves talk, by going off on a tangent into a discussion that had nothing to do with the topic of the meeting. She was definitely going to have to control the conversation so she could get off the call in time.

Mariah got up to get a cup of coffee before the conference call. She was happy that Alberto worked near the restaurant in case she had to give him the heads up that she would be running late. She couldn't help but notice how quiet the office was today as she made her way back from the break room. Everyone obviously had the same idea in mind to take their summer vacation at the same time. She and Isaac used to take a vacation the week of July 4, which was a week away, whether it was a cruise or fly to an island somewhere. She shook her head as she sat back down at her desk. She couldn't believe she was still thinking about Isaac and her experiences with him.

Enough already Mariah, she thought to herself as she opened

197

up the email John sent her to get the number for the conference call. The call started on time with everyone on the line, but ended up going an extra 15 minutes due to pertinent action items that needed to be discussed. Mariah didn't care because it was 12:25 p.m. and was enough time for her to leave the office. She grabbed her purse, reapplied some gloss to her lips, and headed toward the elevators before anyone else could stop her for something else.

The drive over to the café wasn't bad since it was only a couple blocks from her building. However, she had to circle the block a few times to wait for a free parking spot. One of her biggest pet peeves was to always be on time, and she expected the same from anyone she agreed to date. That was another trait that made her and Isaac such a perfect match. Punctuality was important to him as well. He always said he never liked to keep his lady waiting. She sure hoped that Alberto shared in this belief or else this could very well be their last date.

Mariah spotted a car pulling out in front of the building, so she sped up to grab the spot before anyone else got it. Before exiting the car, she took one more look at her appearance in the mirror. A lump began to rise in her throat as a sudden wave of sadness washed over her. She was about to go out on a date with another man. And this man was not Isaac. What was she doing? Was she ready for this?

Maybe I should call Alberto and tell him I had a late meeting, she thought as she looked at the front door of the café. Come on

Mariah. You know that wouldn't be the right thing to do, she said to herself. She opened the car door.

For all she knew, Alberto was probably already inside waiting for her. She wouldn't want to stand him up at the last minute unless she absolutely had to. Mariah blew air out of her mouth, grabbed her purse from the passenger seat and walked over to the front door of Luigi's. The smell of Italian food hit her in the face as soon as she walked through the door. The café was semi busy at this point with the lunch rush hour ending, so Mariah was able to get a good seat near the back. Alberto hadn't shown up yet, so it allowed her some time to get herself together.

"Will it just be you dining with us today?" the hostess asked as she handed her a menu.

"No, I'm meeting someone here. I'll take a Diet Coke while I wait," Mariah said. The hostess placed another menu on the table and walked off to get her drink.

Mariah crossed her hands on the table while she looked out the window to the busy streets of downtown San Diego. The sidewalks were busy with people bustling back to work from lunch and pedestrians walking their dogs.

The front door opened, and Mariah could see Alberto walk through it. He looked even more gorgeous than the night at the lounge. Mariah waved from her table, and he gave her a warm smile, which melted her like butter as he walked over to meet her. Alberto was dressed in a cream colored business polo shirt with black business slacks. The color of his shirt went brilliantly with his skin tone. Mariah also couldn't help but fall in love with the scent of his cologne. Seeing Alberto again was enough to make her say, Isaac who?

"Hello, Beautiful. You beat me here. I wanted to be the one to greet you when you walked through the door," he said. Mariah stood to give him a hug.

"It's cool. I couldn't wait to leave the office today. I thought it was going to be a quiet day, but it seems like I've been pulled into every possible meeting. Anyway, enough about me - you look really nice today," Mariah said.

"Thank you. I knew you would look beautiful like the first time I met you, so I didn't want to disappoint you. But just so you know it could never be enough about you. I want to get to know all about Mariah Langston, including your crazy days at the office," Alberto said with a chuckle.

The hostess showed up at the table with Mariah's coke. "Hello, I'm Mary and I'll be your waitress today. What can I get you to drink, sir?" she asked Alberto.

Mariah sipped on her Coke to make sure it wasn't flat as Alberto quickly looked at his drink menu and ordered an ice tea.

"So, how is work coming along for you today?" Mariah asked after the waitress left their table.

"Not too bad this morning. I set up a few appointments for

this afternoon. I have to take a potential client to Broderick today. Do you know where that is?" he asked.

"No, I've never heard of it," Mariah said with a shrug.

"I didn't think you would. I had no idea about this place until my client suggested it to me this morning. It's in the middle of nowhere in a town called Culpepper with a population of about 500 people, believe it or not. It'll take me a couple hours to get there from here. But for some reason, this client wants to purchase a building there to open up a nightclub, to draw people from around the neighboring areas," he said with a confused look on his face.

"But that doesn't make any sense. Why would he or she want to open up a nightclub in an area that's not really populated? There's a big chance that they'll lose out on their investment," Mariah asked, confused as well.

"Your guess is as good as mine. He says he wants to draw in customers from the neighboring areas. There is a casino that's about 40 minutes away that attracts a large crowd on the weekends, so maybe he thinks he can benefit from that. Who knows? The guy is a rich kid with a lot of money to burn. Hey, I told him my take on it, but if he wants it, then I'll write up a contract for it."

"Well, I'm glad you're telling me about this so that someone knows where you'll be going. I'm not trying to call your client crazy, but there are a lot of people who like to lure people off to weird places so they can have them for dinner, if you get my drift," she said, shivering at the thought.

"That's very nice of you. You care about me already," Alberto said with a smile.

"Not really. I just don't want it on my head if I could have warned you and I didn't. I can at least go down for saying I told you to be careful," she said with a funny smirk.

"Yeah, you're right. And with 500 people listed in the town, I'm sure that would make it to the top of their newspaper headlines by morning," he said.

"Yeah, the headlines would read, 'Someone actually tried to sell a property here and got eaten in the process'," Mariah said as they both started to laugh at the idea.

"Thanks for shedding some humor to my crazy appointment. I'll be sure to think about this conversation when I'm taking the long drive to Culpepper," Alberto said.

"Anytime," Mariah said, taking a sip of her soda. As she placed the glass down on the table, her hand accidently brushed against Alberto's wrist. The heat that generated from that one touch caused her to quickly withdraw contact from him.

Alberto smiled. He reached across the table to touch her hand. "It's OK. I don't bite," he said in his sexy voice that sent chills down Mariah's back.

"I know. It's our first date, and we're just getting to know each other that's all," she said, trying to avoid eye contact.

"I know it's just our first date, but I have to be honest. I'm really feeling you. I want to get to know everything about you, Mariah. What you like and what you don't like," Alberto said, as their waitress approached them to take their order.

Neither Mariah nor Alberto had a chance to even look at the menu. They had started talking as soon as he arrived. Mariah quickly ordered a turkey and provolone sandwich on wheat bread and Alberto ordered the chicken alfredo.

"Well, I see you're going to be a cheap date," he said.

"Ha – there'll be other times," Mariah said with a smile. And at that moment she realized she had given Alberto the inkling that she was interested in seeing him again. He didn't seem to mind at all, because he immediately started talking to her about where he wanted to take her next. On a real date that was not between office hours.

Mariah relaxed in her seat and enjoyed her conversation with Alberto. Wondering when it would be a good idea to bring up her two failed marriages and that she never wanted to get married again.

After lunch, Alberto walked Mariah out to her car since she was parked in front of the café. He was lucky to have found a parking spot across the street.

"I enjoyed lunch with you. I can't wait for us to do it again. I'll give you a call tonight to see how your day finished out, okay," he said as he took her hand and kissed the back of her palm.

"That sounds like a plan. Have fun driving out to Culpepper. I'll talk to you later. Thanks again for lunch. I had fun," Mariah said smiling as she got into her car.

"I'm glad. Okay, Beautiful."

She watched through her rear view mirror as Alberto crossed the street and got into his SUV. Still smiling from cheek to cheek, Mariah turned on her car and reached for her seat belt. She was marveling over the first good date she had had after ending things with Isaac as a familiar van drove past her. It was her sister. Mariah wondered what she was doing downtown because Tina hated coming downtown due to the traffic. She reached for her cell phone and tried to call her. After numerous rings the call went to voice mail. Mariah sighed, wondering why her sister did not answer her phone. She pulled out of the parking space and decided she would give her a call again later.

Chapter Twenty-two

July 4th was always a big time for the Langston family. This was the one holiday that Mariah's father actually enjoyed taking part in and didn't mind leaving his favorite chair in the family room. By the time Mariah arrived at her parents' house for the cookout, her father was already in the backyard with his brother, Uncle Sammy, and his wife, Margery, grilling steaks, hamburgers and hotdogs, and listening to old school music.

Mariah walked into the kitchen and placed a grocery bag on the kitchen table full of her contributions to the cookout – baked potato chips, a vegetable tray, and a homemade fruit bowl.

"Hello, Mariah. How's everything going, Honey?" Mrs. Langston asked, walking through the sliding door from the backyard carrying a roll of Reynolds Wrap.

Mariah walked over and gave her mom a hug. "Hello, Mom. Everything is fine. I'm just ready to have one of Dad's juicy steaks."

The front door opened and closed. Mariah turned to see her sister walking into the house carrying a homemade strawberry cake. PJ, Lexie, and Leshia followed, each carrying a liter of Sprite and Coke, and a container of homemade sweet tea.

Mariah couldn't help but notice as she and her mother bombarded the kids with hugs and kisses that Leshia had a serious attitude. After she bent down to give her a hug, which was returned without any affection, Mariah quickly looked over to her sister who simply shrugged and waved her hand in the air as to not even ask her what's wrong.

"Are you kids hungry? Papa has burgers and hotdogs that are about to come off the grill," Mrs. Langston said, leading the way back to the backyard.

"Hey, Leshia, wait a second. I would like to talk to you about something," Mariah said, touching her shoulder.

Leshia turned around and they walked over to the kitchen table to sit down.

"How are you doing? Is everything okay?"

"I'm okay. I just didn't want to come to this cookout today, but Mom said I had to come. I would have rather stayed at Dad's house and played with my friends," she said nonchalantly.

Mariah was surprised to hear that Leshia had made friends so fast. Her Dad had only been living in the apartment for a short period now, and the kids were only going over there on the weekends. She tried to shrug it off, thinking kids enter into friendships fast these days. Although deep down she hoped Leshia wasn't trying to tell them something. Maybe she was preparing to go live with her father permanently.

"You would rather hang out with your friends then to come see your family? I haven't seen you since you guys moved back home," Mariah said, with a playful pout.

Leshia looked across the kitchen as if she was bored with the conversation. "Can I just go in the living room and watch TV now?"

Wow, Mariah thought, *this kid has a major attitude problem.* She almost didn't even recognize her niece.

"I tell you what, if you go outside and mingle with the family for a little bit and have a bite to eat, I will talk to your mom about letting you come inside to watch TV," Mariah said.

"Deal," Leshia said, her little face lighting up.

"Hold on a second – You have to do one more thing for me. You have to promise me if you ever need to talk or feel down about something, that you will reach out to me. I know you and the other kids are going through a tough time right now, but your parents still love you."

Leshia rolled her eyes. "Auntie, you just don't understand. If they really love us then they wouldn't be breaking up our family. I mostly blame Mom for this. I think Lexie and PJ and I should live in the house with Dad and let Mom go live in an apartment. Dad was the one who really paid for the house anyway," she said.

Bingo! So Leshia no longer wanted to live with her mother.

Mariah tried to cover her disappointment in her niece's tone. She couldn't believe Leshia had spoken about her sister in this way. She knew that Leshia was a big time daddy's girl, but she had no idea to this extent, that she would sell her own mother down a river to support her father. She wanted to chastise her for saying such a thing but decided against it. Mariah wanted to get to the bottom of what was going on, and if she yelled at Leshia for talking like that, then she would never come around to share her inner feelings with her again.

"Leshia, I'm going to tell you what my grandmother, your great-grandmother Annie, used to tell me when I would get upset with my mom because she wouldn't let me do what I wanted to do. You only get one mom in this world, and it's never good to think bad thoughts about her. She also told me God's word tells us to honor your father and your mother. Sweetie, at the end of the day your mother loves you very much, and what's going on now with your parents will not affect how they feel about you and your siblings. For whatever reason, BOTH of your parents have decided that they would make better parents living apart than together. This has nothing to do with you and your siblings. You should never think that you all are to blame for them deciding to get a divorce," Mariah said, hoping that she made sense to Leshia's seven-year-old ears.

Leshia shifted in her seat, fumbled with her hands in her lap and nodded. The silent treatment Mariah received after making her comment let her know the conversation was over with. She didn't know if she had gotten through to her niece, but she did know that this was something that Tina and Paul needed to discuss with the kids. She didn't want to overstep her boundaries as the aunt. The music kicked up outside and they heard laughter coming from the backyard. It seemed like everyone was having a good time, and they were inside missing out on all of the fun.

"Come on. Let's go outside and see what all the commotion is about. I promise I'll speak to your mom about letting you come inside. However, you never know you may end up having some fun," Mariah said.

Leshia simply nodded again and led the way to the backyard. Mrs. Langston, Tina, Aunt Margery, and Lexie were at the picnic table. PJ was playing catch with Uncle Sammy and Mr. Langston was pulling the last of the meat off the grill. Mariah walked over to the table and took a seat next to Tina, who was enjoying a bowl of fruit that Mariah had made.

Mariah watched as Leshia went over to the hammock and rocked back and forth.

"Tina, I'm worried. I spoke to Leshia and she doesn't seem to be taking the separation very well. I don't want to be the one to tell you this, but she told me she blames you for it. I really wish she wouldn't talk like that," Mariah whispered in Tina's ear.

Tina didn't seem to be phased. She popped a grape in her mouth and looked back at Mariah with tired eyes. "You will never know how much it hurt me to hear her blame me for everything. I just can't deal with it right now. I have two other kids to tend to as well. I will not allow Leshia to disrespect me, but I cannot harp on the fact that she wants to take her father's side right now. It will literally drive me crazy if I do that."

Mariah smiled a sympathetic smile at her sister and rubbed her back. Her sister was really going through more than she thought or had ever experienced in her last two divorces. This was just confirmation that she made the right decision to never get married again. It just wasn't worth dealing with this sort of pain. Life can be hard enough as it is without adding these sorts of issues to the mix.

"Enough about me. How are you and Alberto doing? It's been almost a month now, right?" Tina asked, changing the subject abruptly.

Mrs. Langston and Aunt Margery had been giggling at something they were discussing, but immediately zoomed into their conversation.

"Who's Alberto?" Mrs. Langston asked.

Mariah looked up at her mother and aunt who were sitting waiting anxiously to hear about the new man in her life.

"He's just a friend. Nothing serious," Mariah said, figuring less is best at this point. She couldn't reveal to everyone that she talked to Alberto every night on the phone before going to bed. They were also spending more and more time together as their schedules permitted.

"Honey, I didn't know you were seeing someone new," Mrs. Langston said.

"What happened to that nice fellow you used to date? I really liked him," Aunt Margery asked, drinking a cup of ice tea.

OK...here we go, Mariah thought. She knew the question of Isaac was bound to come up. Needless to say, she had a quick response for that one too. "Aunt Margery, Isaac and I have decided that we should go our separate ways. It was for the best," Mariah said with a shrug.

Mrs. Langston looked over at the kids playing because she knew the truth and Aunt Margery looked like she was disappointed to hear this news.

"I'm sorry to hear that. I always thought he was such a respectful gentleman. I actually thought you two may decide to tie the knot one day. But I understand how relationships sometimes go. You should have invited your new friend to the cookout so I could have met him today," Aunt Margery said.

Mariah was taken aback by her aunt's response and was so glad that she could avoid coming up with another excuse because her dad yelled out that dinner was ready. As much as she was enjoying Alberto's company and listening to his sexy voice, she wasn't ready to do the whole meeting the parents' thing yet. They had only been dating for a few weeks now, and she really didn't think her mom was over the fact that she and Isaac had split up.

"Well, I'm going to help myself to one of Dad's juicy steaks. Do you want me to help fix the kids' plates?" Mariah asked her sister as she jumped up from the picnic table.

"I'm well ahead of you, Sis. If you make PJ's plate, I'll make the twins'," Tina said.

Mariah grabbed two paper plates and started to load her plate with steak, potato salad, her dad's famous baked beans, and grilled corn on the cob. She made PJ a hot dog and baked beans and headed back to the picnic table. She looked around for Leshia, who was nowhere in sight. She must have snuck off and went back into the house to watch television. She figured she would let her sister handle it.

By the end of the dinner and a great conversation at the picnic table, the family started to prepare to watch the fireworks that they were able to see perfectly from the backyard. It has been this way ever since Mariah and Tina were kids. The fireworks are held at the nearby park. However, they could always bypass the big crowd growing up by just sitting on blankets in their backyard and watching it from there.

"I'm going to head out now," Mariah whispered to her sister who was helping her mom wrap up the food to take back into the house.

"Where are you going? We always watch the fireworks together."

"I know, but I have a date. Alberto wants to take me to the baseball field near his house to watch the fireworks together," Mariah said, trying to hide the excitement in her voice.

"Well, excuse me. In that case, I don't blame you. Go have yourself some fun. You deserve it. I just don't know what you're going to tell Mom," she whispered, but, of course, their mother picked up on the tail end of their conversation.

"Tell Mom what?" Mrs. Langston asked.

"Just that I'm about to head out. I'm meeting Alberto to watch the fireworks near his place," Mariah said quickly.

"OK. I'll miss you. Be careful. We'll have to talk about this Alberto fellow another time," Mrs. Langston said as Mariah placed a kiss on her cheek.

"Will do. Love you lots," Mariah said, heading over to say her goodbyes to everyone before going through the back gate to her car.

"Mariah, you left your bowl!" Mrs. Langston called out after her.

"I'll get it later, Mom!" she yelled back to her as she unlocked her car door. She had to drive over to the baseball field to meet Alberto and she didn't want to be late. Last year she remembered sitting under the stars watching the fireworks with Isaac at Liberty Station Park. For a split second, she wondered how his 4th of July was going, but then she refocused her attention back on Alberto. This year she would be sitting under the stars watching the fireworks with him, and honestly, at this point, she wouldn't have had it any other way. He was definitely the new interest in her life.

Chapter Twenty-three

Mariah shifted through her bedroom closet looking for a black cover up for her dress. She was packing for her job's banquet in Las Vegas where she was going to be honored. She needed her cover-up to go with the brand new strapless dress she had bought.

"What did I do with that thing," she said to herself, looking to see if it had fallen on the floor between the racks of clothing.

The doorbell rang.

Blowing air out of her mouth in frustration, Mariah went downstairs. She opened the front door to see her sister smiling from cheek to cheek with a huge duffle bag on wheels.

"Hello! I'm so excited to be going to Las Vegas with you. Thank you again for inviting me," Tina said all in one breath as she rolled her luggage into the house.

"No problem. If I could find the cover up for my dress I would be able to share in your excitement," Mariah said. She headed back up the steps to her bedroom to continue to look for it in her closet.

"You haven't finished packing yet?" Tina asked, scanning the messy bedroom. Clothes were thrown all over the bed and shoes were scattered on the floor. "OOOO-h these are so cute. I may have to borrow these for the trip," Tina said, eyeing a pair of

Mariah's shiny purple platform 3-inch pumps.

Mariah turned around and smiled at her sister trying on shoes before directing her attention back to her closet. She was so happy that she had invited her along for the two-night stay. Her job provided her two tickets to Las Vegas leaving Friday morning and returning Sunday evening. As the winner of the Spotlight Senior Executive of the Year award, she also received hotel accommodations at Caesar's Palace and a limo ride to the banquet at Mandalay Bay hotel. With all the stress that her sister had been under with the separation, she really needed a trip, even if it was a weekend getaway.

"Found it!" Mariah yelled. The cover up had been wrapped around a dress that she had worn some months back.

"I've never been to Las Vegas before. In fact, I can't remember the last time I have been on a plane. The last trip we took was four years ago when we drove to Disney Land with the kids. PJ was small at the time and it was the longest trip ever. I believe I was still nursing him then, which made for an even longer trip! Anyway, the kids are hanging with their father this weekend, and I will be hanging out at the slot machines. I cannot wait!" Tina squealed.

"Same here. This will be my second time visiting Las Vegas. I had to go for a conference a while back. But it is definitely a city that everyone should visit in my opinion. There is so much to do. I'm happy we're going together and that you decided to stay over

215

so we can make our 5:45 a.m. flight," Mariah said, putting the last shirt in her luggage before zipping up the bag.

"Oh, you know I would've been on time either way. There is no way I would miss an all-expense-paid trip to Vegas, Baby," Tina responded.

Tina walked over to the love seat in the corner and sat down wearing one purple pump and one red one. She crossed her legs and looked at her nails. "Sis, I'm so proud of you. This is an amazing award that you're accepting this weekend."

Mariah hopped on her bed with gratitude in her heart. It felt good to hear her big sister tell her how proud she was of her, no matter how old she was. "Thanks, Tina. It really means a lot to hear you say that. I've been going over my speech all week practicing what I'm going to say when they call me up to the podium. I'm so nervous. I may come across as confident, but public speaking is not really my thing. Would you like to hear it?" Mariah asked.

"Sure, I would love to hear your speech. I'm sure it's fine," Tina added.

Mariah got up to get her speech from her desk as her doorbell rang. It was six o'clock in the evening on Thursday. She didn't know who that could be.

"I'll be right back," Mariah said, running down the steps to answer her front door. It was a flower delivery man.

"I have a delivery for Mariah Langston," the man said,

holding a bouquet of two dozen red long stem roses.

"Thank you. Have a good night," Mariah said accepting the beautiful flower arrangement. She closed her front door and ran back upstairs with the flowers in her hand. She couldn't wait to read the attached card to see who the sender was.

"Wow! Who sent you those?" Tina inquired, immediately admiring the arrangement.

Mariah looked at the card. "Mariah, congratulations on your award. I wish I could be there to see you accept it, but I want you to know you will be in my thoughts. I can't wait to see you when you get back. Have a safe trip~ Alberto.

"Very nice, Alberto. I'm starting to like him more and more," Tina said with a wink.

Mariah couldn't help smiling as she took the flowers to her nightstand and sat down on her bed to admire them. She was starting to like Alberto more and more too. "Yes, Alberto has definitely grown on me. He wanted to fly out to Vegas and attend the banquet, but he has to work on Saturday and couldn't get out of it."

Tina hopped on the bed and sat next to her sister. "I'm happy you have found someone to share your time with. I know the break-up with Isaac wasn't easy, but I knew everything would work out for you in the end."

"Yeah, it wasn't easy, but I know it was for the best. Alberto's work schedule can sometimes be a little challenging, but we're both just taking it one step at a time getting to know each other. I just didn't know when I would feel like this again after Isaac and I ended the way we did."

"We have a lot to celebrate. Let's go grab a bite to eat. New beginnings for the both of us! You're moving on from Isaac to an obviously nice man, and I'm moving on from Paul. And this marriage that I've been holding onto for far too long," Tina said with determination in her voice.

"Sounds like a plan. Just one thing first," Mariah said.

"What's that?" Tina asked.

"Could you please change your shoes first? I'm not going anywhere with you looking like that," Mariah said as they both looked down at Tina's feet and burst into laughter.

Tina nodded and proceeded to take off the one purple pump and red pump to put back on her silver flip-flops.

"You're right. I doubt very seriously that it would be a good look to go out dressed like this," Tina said between giggles.

"Indeed," Mariah said, wiping the tears from her eyes that had formed from laughing. She got up to go get her purse so they could grab a bite to eat. She was so happy that she and her sister were going away together. Her personal life was looking upward and she and her sister were closer than ever since their last argument.

"I'll meet you downstairs!" Tina said as she left the room.

"I'll be right there," Mariah responded. She walked over to her flower arrangement and took out a single rose to smell it. The arrangement was definitely a nice gift to receive before leaving for the banquet. She would have to give Alberto a call when she got back home to thank him.

Mariah placed the rose back in the vase. She slipped on a pair of sandals and headed downstairs before Sergeant Tina gave her warning siren that it was time to go eat.

Two Years Later...

Chapter Twenty-four

Standing in the middle of the kitchen looking around at moving boxes scattered on the linoleum floor, Mariah tried to figure out her next move. She needed to clean out the refrigerator, pantry, and cabinets before packing up the appliances. Mariah grabbed an empty box and walked over to the silverware drawer. As soon as she opened it, she cringed at the sight of the messy appearance. Forks, spoons, and knives were mixed together. Spatulas and large cooking utensils were thrown overtop the silverware holder.

She gave a loud sigh and grabbed three zip lock bags to start putting each piece of silverware with its type before placing them into a moving box. She was starting to regret ever volunteering her services to help Alberto move out of his condo, especially since it seemed like she had been doing seventy-five percent of the work since Friday afternoon.

The front door opened and closed. The sound of the door closing echoed throughout the condo, since everything had been packed up in the living room. Alberto walked into the kitchen with a greasy fast food bag. He sat down at the kitchen table and started to empty the contents of the bag.

"Hey, Baby. I brought you some lunch," he said as he unwrapped a cheeseburger that had chili dripping from the sides of it.

"Honey, you know I don't like eating fast food," Mariah said scrunching up her nose at Alberto's burger.

"I know…I know…I brought you a Greek salad. This burger is so good, though. You have no idea of what you're missing," Alberto said, closing his eye as he salvaged every bite of his high-calorie cheeseburger.

Mariah shook her head as she sat at the table to eat her salad. "I'm not saying that you don't look good, but I remember you being 20 pounds lighter when I first met you two years ago…so what's up with that?" she joked.

"Now that we are down to two agents in the office, I don't have time to hit the gym anymore. I'm pulling in mad hours just to keep my head afloat. Fast food has become my lifeline, which isn't good, but if I spend time cooking my meals than I would have to deduct it from the few times a week I get to spend with you. I know you wouldn't want that now would you?" Alberto asked, reaching for his super-size orange soda.

"No, I wouldn't want you to do that, but I don't want you to fall over from a heart attack either. How about I cook at my house on the days that we spend together instead of you feeling like you have to take me out to eat on those days? We've been seeing each other for a while now. We can spend time together at each other's house without going out to spend money all the time."

"Mariah, I just feel bad because I don't get to see you as much as I'd like. I hate the fact that you have to take your sister to places that you would like to take me. I missed your banquet two years ago in Las Vegas because work got in the way. I couldn't escort you to your cousin's wedding last summer, and this year you wanted me to escort you to a corporate event that I had to miss," Alberto pointed out as he starting to work on his large size French fries.

"Okay, the banquet in Las Vegas doesn't count because we had only been seeing each other for two months, and the wedding was also understandable. You missed it for a big commission job that has allowed you to purchase the beautiful house you're moving into next week. And I've decided to let the banquet last month slide. My sister and I had a good time. I just want to be with you, whether it's at my house or a nice restaurant. You have already impressed me," Mariah said.

"Yes, but I have to keep it going. That's what a man does. And anything that is important to you is important to me," Alberto said.

Mariah's heart started to soften. She was no longer regretting the fact that she was doing most of the moving tasks for Alberto. He was a great guy who obviously cared about her so much that he was willing to stretch himself thin to spend time with her.

"Okay – Break time is over for me. I'll start boxing up the kitchen gadgets," Alberto said, getting up from the kitchen table to throw away his trash.

223

Mariah forked over her feta cheese and lettuce before placing the lid back over her salad. She might as well get back to work too. She was going to meet her sister for girl's night at her house this evening, and they still had a fair amount to be done to meet the move-out date set between him and the new owner.

Chapter Twenty-five

Tina added the last of the fresh spinach to her spinach dip before pouring it into a serving bowl. She placed the dip on a silver platter along with the homemade hot wings she had prepared and took the platter to the family room.

"Okay, kids. Your dad will be here shortly to pick you up for the night so get up from the TV and go get your bags ready," Tina said to her children who were sitting on the floor watching a movie.

"Okay, Mommy," Lexie and PJ said, climbing off the floor to go to their room and get their overnight bags ready. Leshia on the other hand continued to sit and watch television as if she hadn't heard a word Tina had said.

Tina placed her hands on her hips. "Um…excuse me Leshia. I told you to go to your room and get ready because your father will be here soon to pick you up," she said before heading back to the kitchen. Tina got to the doorway and turned around to see Leshia still sitting and laughing at something on television. Tina walked over to the television and turned it off.

"Maybe you can hear me now that the TV is off. Go to your room and get your overnight bag together."

"I hate you," Leshia said jumping to her feet with an attitude before marching off to her room.

Tina stood with a perplexed look on her face trying to figure out if she had heard what she thought she had heard from her daughter's mouth. Tina walked down the hallway to the girls' room.

"Lexie, could you go check on PJ and make sure he packs his toothbrush, please?" she asked her daughter who was busy stuffing her favorite blanket into a bag.

"Sure, Mommy."

Tina waited until Lexie left the room before closing the door. Leshia huffed at her mother's presence and went to her drawer to take out her pajamas.

"I'm only going to tell you once that I will not tolerate you disrespecting me in my house. When I ask you to do something, I expect you to do it without any lip. I don't know what has gotten into you, but you better get it together!" Tina said, firmly.

Leshia turned around to face her with her arms folded. "I don't want to live with you. I'd rather go live with my father. It's your fault that he left us anyway. Why don't you leave and never come back?"

Tina immediately marched over to her daughter and smacked her in the face. "You are so disrespectful! You have no right to speak to me this way, especially when you have no idea what you're talking about. I'm your mother, and you will respect me! Do you understand?!"

The doorbell rang. Leshia started to cry, cupping her red cheek.

"You hate me?! You wish I would go away and never come back! How dare you speak to me in that manner? I break my back for you and your siblings. You think your father is so innocent? Well, we've only been divorced for one year, and he is already dating someone else!" Tina screamed to the top of her lungs as the bedroom door opened.

After the words had come out of her mouth, she cupped her hand over her face. She should never have said that to Leshia about her dad dating someone else. None of the kids knew about his new girlfriend, which was still a sensitive topic for Tina. She still didn't know if this was someone he had met while they were still married.

"What's going on in here?" Paul asked, standing in the doorway.

"Why don't you ask your ungrateful daughter," Tina said in a voice closest to a whisper as she left the room. She was sure Leshia would pour it on strong and make her look like an incompetent mother, so why should she bother explaining anything to Paul.

Tina rushed past PJ and Lexie, who were standing in the hallway looking nervous from all of the screaming. Tina went to her bedroom and slammed the door. She fell face forward onto her bed and started to cry.

How could Leshia treat her this way? She didn't mean to slap her, but she didn't know what else to do at this point. Since the divorce was finalized, and the kids knew there was no chance that their parents were going to get back together, Leshia's attitude had gotten worse toward her mother. Talking back to her, not doing her chores until she felt like it, and being just downright rude every chance she could get. It was starting to feel like she was trying to punish her because she felt Tina was the real cause for the divorce.

Paul knocked on her bedroom door. Tina rolled over and quickly sat up on her bed. She reached for a Kleenex and dried her face before telling him to come in. The look on his face wasn't pleasing at all.

"Tina, what the hell is going on here? Did you smack my daughter? What could she have done to deserve that sort of treatment? She's a kid for Pete's sake," he asked, closing the door so the kids wouldn't hear them.

"Listen, I have been telling you how your daughter has been getting out of hand, and you have set back and done nothing, so don't come at me with this attitude. She told me she hates me and wishes I would leave and never come back. Apparently, I am to blame for our divorce."

"Tina, the kids are going through a lot. They may say things that you know they don't mean, but we have to be the adults here. You could have grounded her or something. I think it would be best for everyone if I take the kids to live with me for a while until you can get a grip on things. I can't have them in an abusive environment," Paul said firmly.

"Are you freaking kidding me, Paul? You cannot take my kids away from me. Don't you see this is what Leshia wants? She's playing us to punish me? You can take Leshia, but PJ and Lexie will reside with me. She's welcome back in my house when she's ready to show me some respect."

"You need to pull yourself together. I also didn't like the fact of you telling the kids that I have a girlfriend. You were totally out of line to do that," Paul added.

"Me out of line – HA! I admit that came out of my mouth out of anger. That was wrong for me to tell her in that way, but you're the one out of line with a girlfriend, one month after our divorce was finalized. I'm sure you were probably cheating with her while we were still married," Tina said, angrily.

"Tina you can say what you want, but I have never cheated on you and that's all I intend to say about that matter. As far as what I do now with my personal life, it's none of your business. I will keep Leshia past this weekend, but if I hear or see you ever put your hands on my kids in that manner again, I will take them from you permanently," Paul said.

Tina hopped off the bed and got in Paul's face. "Don't you dare threaten me, Paul! Do yourself a favor and get out of my, emphasis on my, house. I'm a good mother to our kids, and if you were any type of father, you would go in there and tell that girl that she needs to respect me."

"Tina, I'm aware that this is your house. I helped you build this house, remember? And you got it through the divorce without any fight from me. I'm not trying to be the bad guy here; I'm just

229

trying to look out for everyone's best interest. I know you're a good mother, but this whole fiasco between you and Leshia has got to stop. She's the child and needs to act as such. I will talk to her about her attitude, and you can expect to hear an apology from her," Paul said.

Tina backed up from her ex-husband and sat back on the bed. "Were you looking out for our best interest when you decided to get yourself a girlfriend one month after our divorce was finalized? Oh, look at the calendar. It's almost been a year for you guys. Congratulations," Tina said, smirking.

Paul shook his head and left the room. Typical – He never liked to engage in any confrontation. Tina exhaled and stood up to say goodbye to her kids. Leshia was already at the front door holding her father's hand. She tried not to make any eye contact with Tina. Lexie and PJ on the other hand ran over to give their mother a hug.

"Bye, Mommy. Love you. See you tomorrow night," came out of Lexie and PJ's mouth.

"Bye, Kids. Mommy loves you too. Bye, Leshia," Tina said while bending down to give Lexie and PJ a hug.

Leshia didn't say anything until her father shook her hand to make her say something. "Bye."

"Okay – Have fun. Paul, as always it's a pleasure to see you," Tina said with a sarcastic smirk.

"Have a good night, Tina," Paul said dryly. He led the kids out the front door.

Tina exhaled again and shook her head. She just couldn't get a break no matter how hard she tried. After all this drama, she wasn't in the mood to have a girls' night, but she knew it was too late to cancel. Mariah had probably already started on the 45-minute drive over to her house.

Tina walked into the kitchen and opened the cabinet above the refrigerator – one place that the kids could not reach. She pulled out a pack of Newport cigarettes and a cigarette lighter and walked out to her back deck. She lit a match and sat down on the iron chair to savor every ounce of the toxicity she was allowing to enter her body.

Tina started to smoke right after her divorce was finalized, when she found out Paul had a girlfriend. Paige was her name. She had long flowing blond hair, was a former San Diego Charger Girls' cheerleader, with the figure still intact and was now working as a physical therapist. Tina bet Paul was getting a lot of physical therapy these days. The thought made her cringe. Tina took another draw of the cigarette and held the smoke in her lungs as long as she could hold it before blowing it out. She started to cough. Nobody knew about her new smoking habit or how her divorce was taking a toll on her emotionally.

Tina's catering business picked up tremendously the first year during her separation. However, after the divorce was final, and the reality set in that she was now alone, her world started to spiral out of control.

Tina would receive catering calls that she would turn down because she was too depressed and didn't have the desire to do what she loved to do most – cook. Pretty soon the catering calls stopped coming in as much, the bank account started to decrease, and Tina recently had to go back to work full time at the restaurant to make her mortgage payments.

Paul was promoted right before the divorce was finalized, but Tina didn't want any spousal support. She didn't want anything from him except for him to carry the kids on his health insurance and continue to pay for the girls' private school tuition, which he agreed to do without any hesitation.

It seems like everything in Paul's life seemed to be going uphill, while Tina's was taking a nose dive into the water. She took the last drag of her cigarette and walked over to the flower pot she had in the corner of her deck. She pulled the ashtray out that she secretly kept hidden behind the huge plant leaves and squashed her cigarette butt. She pushed the ashtray, which was getting full, back behind the plant. She would dump it later when she took the trash out. Tina went back inside to brush her teeth and wash her face before her sister arrived. The clock on the wall said 7:30 p.m. so she knew she would be there shortly.

CB

Ten minutes later, Mariah stood outside her sister's house waiting patiently with a bowl of her famous bean dip and a shoulder bag filled with additional goodies for the girls' night. It was the second weekend in September, and the weather was a bit cooler than usual. Mariah had to put on a light jacket.

Tina finally opened the front door with a huge grin on her face. "Hi, Mariah," she said.

"Hi. I brought the wine that you love," Mariah said as she followed her sister to the family room. She placed the bowl of dip on the coffee table and took her bag off her shoulder. It contained the wine and a bag of baked nachos for the dip.

"Great! I could use that right about now. I'll go get the glasses," Tina said, rushing off to the kitchen to grab the wine glasses. She decided that she was not going to tell her sister about what had transpired earlier. She wanted to forget about anything negative right now and just relax and have some fun for a change.

Tina walked back into the family room as Mariah was fixing her plate.

"Work was horrendously busy this week. I was sooooo looking forward to tonight. How was your day?" Mariah asked, dipping her bread into the spinach dip.

"I spent the day with the kids. I went grocery shopping, and that's pretty much it," Tina said, trying to avoid her sister's eye contact.

"Oh, that's good. I was hoping to get over here to see them

before Paul picked them up. How's everything going with Leshia nowadays? Is she still mouthing off?" Mariah inquired.

"Leshia is still Leshia. It hasn't gotten any worse if that's what you're asking," Tina lied before trying to divert the conversation to something about her sister. She didn't feel like bringing up the events from earlier. "How's everything going on at Alberto's condo? Has he finished packing yet?"

Mariah exhaled. "I got a lot done for him today. I left him packing up his bedroom before I came over here, so hopefully he will finish everything tonight. I told him I would stop by after church tomorrow to help with the last bit of cleaning. To be honest, I feel like I'm the one who is moving."

Tina raised an eyebrow at all the work her sister was putting into helping Alberto move out of his place. She didn't have a problem with Alberto personally; however, she didn't necessarily like him dating her sister anymore. She felt Mariah always had to make too many accommodations for him, but she never wanted to bring it up in fear that Mariah would think she was judging her relationships again. Since their last falling out concerning her break-up with Isaac, Tina decided she would tread lightly with her opinions regarding her sister's personal life. She never wanted to experience another fight like that, if she could help it.

"Well…what do you want to watch tonight? I took the liberty of renting a few DVDs earlier today," Tina said, pointing to the stack of movies on the end table.

Mariah started going through the DVDs before getting up to put *Safe House* starring Denzel Washington into the DVD player. "Before the movie starts, I would like to talk to you about something," Mariah said.

Tina looked up nervously from her plate of wings. She hoped she didn't smell like cigarette smoke. "About what?"

Mariah sat down on the couch. "I've been strongly thinking lately about talking to Alberto about making things a little more official between us. No, I don't want to get married, but I do want to know that we're in a committed relationship. What do you think?"

Tina swallowed the last bite of her wings before responding. "To be honest, I was under the impression that you two were a couple already. You have been dating for the past two years now. You pretty much do everything together. I think this is something that should have happened a long time ago, especially on his end. Do you think he will object to the idea of you two becoming exclusive?"

"I don't know, Tina. It does seem a little weird that he has never brought it up or called me his girlfriend. He brings up everything else that's on his mind. I'm not dating anyone else, and he isn't either. We're pretty much exclusive in my mind. "

"What does he call you when he introduces you to other people? Have you met anyone in his family yet?" Tina inquired.

"His parents moved back to Cuba ten years ago. He mentioned they're due for a visit once he moves into his house, so maybe I'll get the chance to meet them soon. He has a sister who lives in Florida who I have never met, but he does have an uncle who is local. I met him once while riding with Alberto over to his house to take him a drill. I sat in the car and his uncle came to the car door. Alberto introduced me as Mariah, and that was it. I have met all of his friends though. We've gone out together on numerous occasions. I met them early on when it was cool for me to be introduced as Mariah. There hasn't been anyone new recently to test a change in the introduction," Mariah said matter-of-factly.

Tina sighed. "I don't know…it just doesn't sit right with me. I think you should address the sincerity of your relationship at this point. Marriage or not, you still need to know if you're formally his girlfriend or not. Some men just need the women to bring up the conversation. He didn't seem to mind meeting mom and dad when we had Sunday dinner over at their house, so I'm sure the conversation will go in your favor. For all we know, he may very well have you two in an exclusive relationship already and think you're on board," Tina said, trying to give Alberto the benefit of the doubt. He better not be two-timing my sister while dating someone else on the side, she thought reflecting on Paul and his new girlfriend Paige.

Mariah started to smile and feel better about her relationship with Alberto. "Thanks. I'm sure you're right. Besides he's always with me so it's not like he would have time to date anyone else," she said with a shrug, as the opening credits finished and the main menu popped up on the television screen.

"Now that we got all of that out in the open, let's officially start our Girls' Night!" Tina said, pushing the play button on the remote.

"Sounds good to me," Mariah said, moving to the sound of her favorite song from Safe House as the movie started.

Chapter Twenty-six

Wednesday evening came, and it was Mariah and Alberto's usual night to get together before the weekend. Alberto worked late Monday and Tuesday nights, so Mariah looked forward to seeing him on Wednesday evenings.

She decided to cook for him instead of going out to dinner that night. Mariah chopped up green onions to add to the spaghetti squash she was preparing. The aroma coming from the marinara sauce and its thyme, rosemary and pungent garlic simmering on the stove made her hungry. She added the green onions to the pot and replaced the lid.

Mariah wiped her hands on her apron and looked at the clock. *Alberto should have been here by now*, she thought, leaning against the island. Maybe it was a good idea that he was running late. This would give her some more time to decide how she was going to approach the whole relationship conversation. She still didn't know whether she should bring it up over dinner or afterwards when they were watching their favorite Wednesday night television shows.

"I'll wait until after dinner," Mariah said aloud as the doorbell rang. She took her apron off and went to open the door for Alberto.

"Hey, Honey. Sorry I'm late. Traffic was a beast getting from my last appointment. Mmmm, it smells good in here," Alberto said, entering the house with some flowers.

"Thank you for the flowers. How thoughtful of you," Mariah said, carrying the blossoms to the kitchen to put them in a vase. This was another reason she loved Alberto so much. He still did things that some men stopped doing after the first few months of dating.

Alberto went to the bathroom to wash his hands as Mariah took the spaghetti squash from the stove and the garlic bread from the oven. She set both on heating mats on the kitchen table. She had already taken the liberty earlier, while everything was cooking, to set the table with her fine dishes and wine glasses.

"Everything looks nice, Honey. Is there a special occasion that I should know about?" Alberto inquired as he joined her at the table.

"Nope, you take me to fancy restaurants all the time, so I just wanted to show you that we can still have five-star presentation at home," she said, giving him a wink.

"Well, everything looks nice. Thanks for cooking for me," he said as they started to dig into the food.

Alberto immediately started to tell her about the craziness of his work day, while Mariah zoned out thinking about his reaction to her wanting to take things to the next level. She was confident that he would be on board. It was obvious that she was the only woman he was seeing and cared for her, but the fact that he hadn't approached the topic himself still made her feel uneasy. Nevertheless, despite the fact that he hadn't brought it up yet, she was going to do so tonight and finally get everything out in the open about the way she was feeling.

Mariah nodded to something Alberto said and tried to play catch up and understand the nature of the conversation. After dinner, Alberto helped Mariah load the dishwasher and then they went into the family room to watch television.

"Dinner was delicious. I've never had spaghetti without noodles before," Alberto said, putting his arm around her to move her closer to him on the couch.

Mariah gave him a kiss on the cheek. "It's a much healthier way to eat it if you're trying to avoid carbs. I told you I was going to help you get back on track with eating healthy instead of all that fast food stuff," she said, poking a finger in his midsection.

"I appreciate you taking good care of me," he said.

Mariah liked the sound of that and figured now was as good time as any to say something to Alberto. Besides, she wouldn't take care of someone who wasn't her man, so it was time to make things official.

Mariah turned around to face Alberto on the couch and took a deep breath. Here goes nothing...

"Alberto, we've been together for two years now, and I want to know where we're going with this?"

Alberto gave Mariah a puzzled look. "I thought you said you never wanted to get married again?"

Mariah did a double take. She hoped that he didn't think she meant for the two of them to get married. "No, I'm not saying let's get married. And you're correct – I have no interest in getting married again. However, I would like to know that I'm in a committed relationship with just one person, and I want that person to be you."

Mariah watched as Alberto looked downward uncomfortably. "Mariah, I think we're in a good place, and there's no reason to put a title on anything. I'm enjoying only your company, and you're obviously enjoying my company, right? So why can't we just leave things as they are for now?"

This was not the response Mariah was looking for. In fact, her heart sunk farther and farther into her stomach with every word he said. The words of a man who spent all of his time with her was starting to make her feel like she was back in high school trying to get someone to be her boyfriend who wasn't interested in her.

"I'm confused. We spend all of our time together. I'm not seeing anyone else, and you're not seeing anyone else. We're technically together exclusively, so what's the big deal about making it official?" Mariah asked, starting to get angry.

"Mariah, calm down. I love you. You're my best friend. However, putting a title on what we have right now makes things too serious for me. I'm already feeling bad because I can't spend as much time with you as I'd like to. If I ask you to be my girlfriend, I'll feel pressured to give you more than I can give right now. Things were different when we first started to date. Now, I'm working hard to move up in the chain at work, and it'll be another five years before my boss retires and I can take over the District Manager position. But until then, I have to prove myself against the competition. You're VP of your department, so I know you understand goals and priorities," Alberto said.

The sexy voice Mariah loved to hear was making her sick with every word he spoke. This was her first time hearing that he was trying to get a District Manager position that could take five years to acquire! What if his boss decides not to retire and stays on for another five years? She had seen it time and time again with the senior execs in her company. The retirement date gets closer, and people change their minds when they realize all they have to look forward to is waking up in the morning with time on their hands and nothing to do. She had seen men in her company push their retirement date back numerous times. What was she supposed to do, sit back and wait for Alberto's career to take off? She also didn't like that she had been demoted in his list of priorities. This definitely didn't look good for what she thought they had developed over the past two years.

"Alberto, I didn't put my life on hold while I waited to get promoted, and I don't think you should either. I had no idea that I didn't have to worry about competing with another woman, but the culprit was your job. I don't know how I feel about this right now. It seems the priority is your job, and I'm on second base waiting until your job moves up, so I can run toward the home plate. I'm much more than that. I must be stupid because I never thought you felt this way about us. What is it really? Is it easier for you to leave me alone without breaking up with me if we're not exclusive? Is it easier when another woman asks you if you're in a relationship to tell her no without feeling guilty? Or are you a player because I know you know how fine you are?" Mariah asked.

"Now wait a minute, Mariah. You're overstretching right now, and I think you need to stop. I told you what the deal is, and if you can't accept it, then I don't know what else to tell you. I'm just not ready for that level of commitment in my life right now," Alberto responded.

Mariah got up from the couch and sat across from him in her loveseat. She wanted to see every part of his face when he responded to her next question. "So when will you really be ready? Because if you think I'm going to sit back and wait until five years pass by to put a title on us, then you have another thing coming."

Alberto got up. "I think it's time for me to leave. I'm not trying to argue with you. I came over to have a good night with you, not to feel interrogated. You've hauled out some pretty attacking things at me tonight when all I've tried to do is treat you with respect. Have a good night Mariah and thanks again for dinner," he said, turning to head out of the room.

"Answer my question, Alberto. When are you going to be ready?!" Mariah yelled after him.

But the only answer she got was the sound of her front door closing as Alberto left her house abruptly.

Chapter Twenty-seven

Tina walked into her therapist office on Thursday for her 12:30 p.m. appointment. She couldn't wait to talk to Cynthia about the dramatic episode that had transpired on Saturday. Tina quickly signed in at the receptionist desk and took a seat in the back of the waiting room. She still didn't like the fact that she was seeing a therapist, but after she and Paul had separated, she started to have a hard time coping with the reality of her marriage ending.

Now that her divorce was final, she was really having a hard time adjusting to doing everything on her own without Paul's help. No one told her that life after a divorce could be so tough. She thought since she was no longer in love with Paul that it would be easy to move on without him. But the day she signed the final divorce papers and the moving truck showed up to pick up Paul's items entitled to him by the divorce decree, brought about an empty feeling that she would never forget.

Tina remembered looking around an empty house and feeling so alone. At least when she and Paul were still married and they were in one of their bickering moments, she still knew she had someone there with her who would protect her if someone tried to break into the house, or was there if she needed to talk. However, August 22, 2011, the date their divorce was finalized, marked the end to what was supposed to be her new beginning – starting over fresh without Paul.

Tina tried to put all of her energy into the kids in the proceeding weeks, but that only lasted until it was time for the kids to visit their father on the weekends, and she was left alone questioning whether or not she had made the right decision. That's when the depression started to set in, and she fought to try and get a grip on her life.

Tina still remembered it like it was yesterday, the substantial weight that was dropped on her as she was informed that her now ex-husband was seeing someone else. This news was tragic to her ego. She had felt like she was the only one still holding onto the past when Paul had obviously moved on with someone else. This news almost sent her over the edge and running back to her therapist office.

Tina couldn't talk to anyone about the way she was feeling, not even Mariah, so she desperately leaned on Cynthia for support. She felt too ashamed to let her family know that she didn't have it all together. She was always known for having everything together. As Tina waited patiently for Cynthia to finish up with her appointment, she couldn't help but reflect back on the day she found out about Paul's girlfriend…

Tina wrapped up a call with a former client who wanted her to cater her parents' 50th wedding anniversary. This job was going to provide a good piece of revenue since her customer wanted this to be a very memorable occasion by providing a lot of high-end dishes. Tina jotted down the last of her notes and placed the pad on the coffee table next to a stack of mail. It was Saturday and the kids were away at Paul's for the weekend. He had picked them up yesterday, and she forgot to give him his mail that had come in earlier that week.

Tina grabbed the two envelopes and placed them in her purse. She decided to drop them off on her way to work. She didn't want to be accused of holding onto the last of his mail or be the cause of a bill getting paid late. After their last dispute at their court proceeding prior to their divorce finalization, she was sure that this would be exactly what Paul would think if she didn't give him his mail. Since Tina had to be at the restaurant at 2 p.m. to help prep before the dinner crowd, she got up to take a quick shower and change so she could drive over to Paul's first.

Paul moved to an apartment about 20 minutes from the house to still be close to the kids, so the drive over wasn't bad. Tina parked in the visitor's spot, which was adjacent to Paul's building. She grabbed the mail from her cup holder and got out of the car. As Tina was making her way toward the open entrance, she saw Paul outside talking to someone in a red sports car. As Tina got closer, she noticed it was a blonde haired woman. Paul leaned into the car and gave her a kiss on the cheek. The woman smiled at him and proceeded to pull off. Paul turned around and started to climb the steps to the third floor.

Tina couldn't believe what she had just witnessed. Who the hell was this chick that Paul was kissing while her kids were inside? And had she just been inside with her kids? Tina immediately started to speed walk toward Paul. He heard the heavy pounding of her feet against the pavement and turned around.

"Who the hell was that?" Tina inquired.

Paul looked startled and immediately got defensive. "Tina, what are you doing here?"

Tina started to fan the mail in the air. "I was trying to be a good ex-wife and bring you your mail, but obviously this is not important anymore. What's more important is the woman you were just kissing on two weeks after we signed our divorce papers. Have my kids been around her?"

Paul came back down the steps and pulled Tina away from the stairway. Although his apartment was on the third floor, the stairs leading to all of the apartments were outside, and he didn't want the kids to hear them fussing.

"Tina, please keep your voice down. Unlike you, I don't have a 3,500 square foot house anymore. The kids are right there in the living room. Listen, I didn't want you to find out this way, but the woman you saw is my girlfriend, Paige."

"Whoa, wait a minute. Your girlfriend?! Huh — I mean when did this happen? We just got divorced, like, yesterday. When did you start dating her?" Tina inquired sarcastically, feeling hurt and devastated all at once.

"Tina, does it really matter? We're no longer married, remember?"

"Was she the reason you started to disconnect from me in the first place? I know why I got divorced, but obviously there was someone else in your corner. I know I never broke my vows to you. I remained faithful the *entire time we were married. Can you say the same?" Tina asked.*

"Listen Tina, I can assure you that I have never cheated on you. I met Paige right after the court had us do our one-year separation. We remained close friends throughout our separation and divorce. I refused to act upon any feelings until after our divorce was final. I just asked her to be in a relationship with me a week ago," Paul said.

"Man, I'm glad we're divorced because you are as bright as a burnt-out light bulb. Do you really think it's wise to get into something serious so soon after a divorce? And here I was using our separation time to reflect on our marriage like we were supposed to be doing, to see if there was any possibility of reconciliation. And you had already moved on with someone else…a blonde at that. Get out of my face you make me sick. Take your mail and make sure your address change orders go through with the last of your mail because I will not bring you anything else in the future," Tina said, shoving the mail into his chest and storming off.

She remembered something else and turned around abruptly before Paul could make it up the steps. "And another thing, I do not want her around my kids!"

"The kids do not know, Tina, and I want it to stay like that for right now. I was only out here giving Paige something that she had left here this week. She hasn't been around the kids. I would talk to you before bringing anyone around the kids," Paul said.

"Well, I would NEVER approve of Ms. Paige being around my kids, so you and your girlfriend can stay in hiding," Tina said, turning around and storming to her car. As soon as she got inside, she locked her

door and started to cry. She didn't know why she was crying right away. She and Paul were over, and she knew that this would happen for either of them as their lives moved on. However, seeing that Paul had possibly had an affair while married to her was too disheartening to take in at the moment, especially if Paige was the reason he fell out of love with her in the first place...

"Tina," Cynthia said, standing in the doorway of her office.

Tina came back to reality and looked up to see Cynthia waiting for her. She placed a phony smile on her face and got up to walk into her therapist's office.

"Hello, Tina. You seem to have been deep in thought today. How's everything going?" Cynthia inquired, immediately getting down to business.

Tina sat on the couch facing Cynthia and placed her purse on the wooden coffee table. "Hello, Cynthia. I was just thinking back to my past that's all. I don't know why it still bothers me that Paul has a girlfriend. It's not like I want him back or anything."

Cynthia scribbled something down in her folder and looked up, pushing her red, thin-rimmed glasses above her nose. "As I have said in our other sessions, it's normal to have these sorts of feelings in the beginning. You're fresh out of a divorce, and it's going to take some time getting used to seeing your ex-husband with someone else. It's no different than when you're dating someone in college, and you break up and then see them out with another woman at a coffee shop. The wounds are still open and as time goes on it will heal. Has anything else happened since our last session that you would like to touch on today?" Cynthia asked.

Tina's thoughts reflected back to her confrontation with her daughter. Frustration and anger started to build back up inside her chest as she shifted on the couch to try to get comfortable.

"Well, my daughter, Leshia, pushed me to the edge this weekend. I asked her to get ready to go because Paul was coming over to pick them up, and she ignored me. When I finally got her to go to her room to pack her clothes, she told me she hated me and blamed me for the divorce. Can you believe it? I was so livid and fed up with her disrespectful ways that I hauled off and smacked her in the face."

Cynthia raised her eyebrows as Tina continued telling her story.

"Paul walked in afterwards and blamed me for losing it and not being the adult in the situation. He decided that Leshia should stay with him for a while and threatened to take the other kids for good if I ever hit PJ and Lexie in the face. He has some nerve, right?" Tina asked.

Cynthia leaned back in her chair with a serious look on her face. "Did Paul say all of this in front of the kids?"

"No. I walked off, and we had the conversation in my bedroom."

"Good. I don't want the children thinking they can play you

two against one another. I have to say that Paul is right to suggest taking the kids to live with him if the situation could not be resolved under your roof. I have explained in prior sessions the importance of not letting someone else's behavior determine your response to a situation. Leshia was born with two parents living under the same roof, and now she has to adjust to a life that she's not familiar with. She's with her mom during the week and with her father on the weekends, so she's taking out her frustrations on you. It's not fair, and I'm not condoning her disrespectful behavior, but there is a better way to handle it then resorting to smacking her. As your therapist, I have to inform you that by allowing yourself to feed into Leshia's outburst instead of redirecting your anger could have cost you your other two children. You're lucky that a neighbor didn't hear the commotion and call the police. And I can assure you, once child protective services gets involved there's a good chance you could lose all of your children for good," Cynthia said, matter-of-factly.

Tina sat in shock. She was just so upset and fed up with Leshia's behavior that she stooped down to her level. "You're right. I didn't even think about that. I would never want to do anything to jeopardize my kids. I love them. They're mine. After Leshia said that I was the one to blame, I told her about her father's girlfriend as Paul walked into the room. It's all a mess now. Every time I think I'm doing something right it ends up being wrong. I don't know what to do, Cynthia," Tina said, running her hands over her face in frustration.

"Tina, first I want you to stop beating yourself up. You've made the right step to come to therapy, so you're not doing everything wrong. It may not have been the way that you and Paul wanted to tell the children about his girlfriend, but now you two can take the children out to the park and sit down and have a conversation with them about daddy's new friend. Let them know that you are still their parents, that they will always come first, and that you're there for them no matter what happens. Encourage them to share their thoughts about their father having a girlfriend too. This was a conversation that you all were going to have anyway, so stop beating yourself up about it."

"That's a good idea. I'll suggest that to Paul. The kids love going to the park, so a familiar place that they enjoy may soften the sting of their father now being with someone other than their mother," Tina said.

"Remember the kids are going to act out. Try not to feed into their behaviors because it's more about them adjusting and less about you. It's no different than going into a grocery store and having a rude checkout person. You haven't done anything to this person. You don't even know this person and may never see them again in your life. However, they're having a bad day because of something going on in their life, and you're feeling the impact of it. It's better for you to wrap up your sale and walk away then to engage with the person because their behavior has nothing to do with you. You just happened to have walked to their line to check out."

"You're right. It's just so hard to remember that when Leshia is pushing my buttons. I work hard to provide a roof over her head, and Paul gets all the credit."

"Trust me. She sees the work you're putting in. She's just angry right now. I would recommend a different disciplinary action such as taking away her favorite toy, television or having her write a letter explaining what she has done and how she to intends to not let it happen again. I could also refer you to a colleague of mine who specializes in pediatric therapy. Discuss it with your ex-husband and let me know if you're interested, and I can give you her number."

"I'll talk it over with Paul and see what he says. I think Leshia may need to sit down and talk to someone."

"Okay – well, this was a good session. Try to incorporate the suggestions I have made today, and I'll see you next week."

"Cynthia, before I go I wanted to ask you something about Paul."

Cynthia looked down at her watch. "I have a few minutes before my next appointment. What about Paul?"

"Why am I thinking about him and his girlfriend more and more lately?"

"Like I said before, it's normal as you adjust to the fact that you're now divorced. You and your husband did share a good amount of years together. However, I don't want you to get stuck on it. I would like to see you get out more and do something with your sister or friends or pick up a hobby that you wanted to try, but didn't have time to do before. Try investing more time in your catering business now that Paul has the kids on the weekend. If you gear your attention somewhere else, Paul and his girlfriend will become a second thought to you. Try doing that and let me know how it goes next week, Okay?" Cynthia rose from her seat to walk Tina out.

Tina shook her head, reached to grab her purse and headed for the front door. She wished her therapy sessions were longer. She really didn't feel like she had scratched the surface concerning her new-found feelings for Paul. At least she had another week to try and figure out why she was feeling jealous for someone she originally couldn't wait to walk away from.

☙

Later on that evening, Tina prepared spaghetti for dinner. She fixed the kids' plates and sat it on the kitchen table.

"PJ! Lexie! It's time to eat!" she called out to the children in the nearby room. Tina took her apron off and sat down at the table. PJ and Lexie walked into the kitchen and joined her at the table.

"Mmmm, spaghetti is my favorite," PJ said as he picked up his fork to dig in.

"Wait, PJ. We have to say grace first. Lexie, would you say grace, please?" Tina asked, bowing her head over her plate.

"Thank you God for this meal we're about to receive. I pray it provides nourishment for our bodies. Amen," Lexie said in a subtle voice.

Tina looked at her daughter. "Lexie is everything okay?"

Lexie shook her head slowly as PJ started filling his mouth with food.

"How was your day, Lexie?" Tina inquired because her motherly instincts told her that something was wrong.

"She's just mad because Leshia isn't here," PJ said as Lexie turned around and shoved him.

"Shut your mouth, PJ!"

"Lexie, do not shove your brother. Apologize to him," Tina instructed her daughter.

Lexie reluctantly apologized to PJ, who in return gave her a ha-ha, you got in trouble smirk.

"Lexie, I understand that you may be upset that your sister is not here. It's just temporary, Honey. Leshia will be back soon," Tina said, trying to be as gentle as possible to Lexie's feelings. But deep down Tina didn't want Leshia back under her roof until she learned some respect.

"Nah-uh. Leshia told me last weekend that she is never coming back here. How can I be a twin if my twin doesn't live with me?" Lexie asked as she started to cry.

Tina tried to control her anger and think about what her therapist had said earlier about how to handle Leshia. However, she was getting sick of Ms. Leshia and her mouth causing trouble. Tina took a deep breath before responding.

"Honey, Leshia is upset and is just telling you what she thinks she knows, but the truth is that Paul and I are the parents, and we decide where she will live. Leshia is staying with your father temporarily until she can get her act together to come live back under this roof."

"Well, she told me that she has a new mommy now. Somebody named Paige. She said Paige, Daddy, and her are going to live together happily ever after. She said that they have so much fun when PJ and I aren't around. She said that Paige buys her things. She said that Daddy takes her shopping all the time. They go to theme parks and skating. She says that Daddy is so much happier now with Paige…"

And that's all Tina heard. Her cup had runneth over with anger. She could feel her body begin to get hot as her heart started to beat faster. Paul had Paige around her kids without consulting with her first. LESHIA IS CALLING HER MOMMY NOW! She was about to lose it. All Tina saw at this point was red.

"Mommy, Mommy," Lexie said, shaking her.

Tina snapped out of her thoughts. "Huh – I'm sorry Leshia…I

mean Lexie. Do you all know who Paige is?"

PJ and Lexie both shook their head no.

"I've never met her," Lexie said.

"Me either. Who is she?" PJ asked.

Tina ran her fork over her spaghetti. "Good, because you never will, Sweethearts, as long as Mommy has anything to do with it," she said with a deceitful smile, as she placed a forkful of spaghetti into her mouth. She munched down on it, as if she was squashing Paige's existence away with every bite. Tina rose from the table. "Kids I have to go make a quick phone call. Finish your dinner, and then we'll play a board game together."

"Yay! I want to play Chutes and Ladders," PJ said.

"No, Candy Land," Lexie responded.

"No, that's for girls!" PJ yelled back at his sister.

Tina raised both hands in the air to calm her children down. "We can play both. Please just finish your dinner, and I'll be right back," she said, walking to her bedroom.

Tina immediately closed the door and locked it. She stormed over to her nightstand and picked up her phone. She started to dial the number to Paul's place so fast that she almost dialed the wrong number. Paul answered the phone after the third ring. Tina knew from therapy that it wasn't a good idea to call when she was upset, but she was so mad that she wasn't thinking rationally. She could spit fire right about now.

"Hello."

"Hello, Paul. Does your girlfriend live with you now?" Tina blurted out.

"Huh – what are you talking about?"

"Don't play with me. You said you wouldn't bring your girlfriend around my children without talking to me first," Tina said, pouncing back on her bed.

"Tina, I really don't have time for this. I haven't brought Paige around the kids."

"Save it, Paul. Your chicken has been cooked. The kids told me tonight how Leshia has been bragging to them about her new mommy, "Paige," and how you all spend so much time together. How could you let her think that Paige is her mother! I'm her mother!" Tina yelled, lowering her voice at the end in hopes to keep the kids from hearing her.

"She did what? No, that's not what happened. I'm going to have to talk to Leshia. She has gotten out of hand," Paul said, sighing in the phone.

"No, really, Paul? I have been telling you about your daughter for some time now. This behavior didn't just happen overnight. But you didn't believe me now did you? You blamed everything on me until she ran her mouth about something related to YOU," Tina said.

"Tina, I was on the phone the other night and I said Paige's name when Leshia walked into my room. I guess she put two and two together after hearing you say that I have a girlfriend. I will talk to Leshia about the lying to her sister and brother, but I think it is time for us to discuss when it will be a good time for the kids to meet Paige. She's going to be a part of my life, so I don't think it's fair to keep her hidden away when the kids are around."

"Have you lost your freaking mind? We just got divorced, and you're ready to bring another woman around our kids? You've lost it! You've really lost it. Listen here with what sense you have left in your brain. That woman will never come around my kids. Do you understand me?!"

Tina didn't even give Paul a chance to reply before slamming the phone back onto its cradle. She didn't even get a chance to discuss the pediatric therapy for Leshia. She slid on the floor and started to cry. Tina cupped her face in her hands and started balling as she rocked herself back and forth. She didn't know if her tears had something to do with the fact that Paul had moved on with another woman, or if it had something to do with the fact that the woman was no longer her. Whatever the reason was, she knew she owed it to herself to finally figure it out.

Chapter Twenty-eight

On Monday morning, Mariah walked into her office and sat in front of her computer fuming. She hadn't spoken to Alberto since their argument. She was beginning to wonder if whatever they had was over with, since he hadn't called her yet. Mariah blew air out of her mouth in frustration as she tried to start her work day without thinking about Alberto. She turned on her computer and tried to busy herself with a proposal she had started on Friday.

Moments later, it seemed no matter how hard she tried, she just couldn't shake the desire to want to call him. Mariah got up from her desk to get a cup of coffee from the break room. When she returned to her desk, she looked at the clock and realized it was 11:00 a.m. – Lunch time. She desperately needed to get out of the building to clear her mind. Reaching for her telephone, she called her sister to see what she was up to for lunch. Mariah knew Tina worked on Mondays, but maybe if the restaurant wasn't busy she could stop by there to chat.

Tina answered her cell phone after the third ring. "Hello, Sis. How are you doing?"

Mariah didn't hear any pans clinking in the background, so she wondered if she had made it to work yet. "Not so good. I wanted to know if you could do lunch at your restaurant if you had some time to spare?" Mariah inquired while playing with the phone cord.

"That would be nice. I'm just overseeing the prep right now for this evening, so I can get away for thirty minutes. Come on over," she said.

"Sounds good. I'm on my way out now," Mariah said. She grabbed her jacket and purse, logged off her computer, and headed for the door.

The drive over to the restaurant wasn't bad with the early afternoon traffic, or maybe it had something to do with the fact that Mariah was oblivious to anything going on around her right now. She was too focused on Alberto, and why he hadn't picked up the phone to call her since their argument. Mariah turned into her sister's restaurant and quickly put her jacket on to shield herself from the cool October air that was surfacing from the oceanfront. She grabbed her purse and headed into the restaurant, which already had a small lunch crowd inside. Mariah immediately walked over to the hostess podium and asked for her sister.

Tina appeared within minutes giving her a hug. Mariah couldn't help trying to hold back tears. Tina could tell by the look on her face that something wasn't right, so she took her over to a corner of the restaurant where the employees sat for a break away from the customers.

Tina removed her chef's jacket and placed it in the seat next to her before sitting down.

"What's going on, Sis? Are you hungry?"

Mariah shook her head no and immediately started to spill her beans. "Tina, you're not going to believe this," she hurled at her sister.

"What's wrong?" Tina inquired.

"I haven't spoken to Alberto since last Wednesday. We have never gone this long without speaking. He has some nerve. I honestly feel if he truly loves me like he says he does then he wouldn't have any problems committing to me," Mariah said all in one breath.

"This is true. However, I'm a bit confused now. I thought you didn't want to be in a serious relationship," Tina said.

"Huh? What are you talking about Tina? When I asked you your opinion last weekend, you thought it was time for us to have this discussion," Mariah added, confused.

Tina sighed. "You know I'm always going to have your back, and I do think you two needed to have the discussion about where you stand. However, I didn't expect you to be upset like this if he said he didn't want to be in a committed relationship. I recall you wanting to end things with Isaac because he wanted to get too serious, but now you're mad at Alberto because he doesn't want to be serious enough. Do you really know what you want?" Tina asked, as subtle as she could be.

Mariah couldn't believe her sister had just said that, much less brought her old relationship with Isaac into this. "Tina, I came over here to see you hoping you would make me feel better, not worse. And of course I know what I want. I want to have a committed relationship, but not have marriage tagged as the end goal. That was the reason Isaac and I didn't work out," she said wryly.

Tina reached across the table and touched the side of Mariah's arm. "I'm not trying to make you feel worse, and I'm sorry I brought Isaac into this. I'm really just trying to understand where your head is at right now, so I can better help you. Now I'm not saying you should leave Alberto, but I do think if he can't see what an amazing woman you are then you don't need him."

Mariah exhaled loudly as a tear fell from her left eye. She knew her sister was trying to soften her response after what she had initially said concerning Mariah's outlook on relationships, but she couldn't help but admit that Tina might be right. Mariah had the perfect relationship with Isaac, who would have never treated her like this. She could remember the times they would have a disagreement and Isaac would show up at her doorstep with a present or would at least call to try to make amends. Alberto, on the other hand, had the audacity to storm out of her house in a hissy fit and not even call back to see if she was alright.

Tina took a napkin out of the napkin holder on the table and handed it to her sister to wipe her face.

"I'm sorry to come to your job crying over a man. I just can't believe he is using his job as some sort of excuse to hide from committing to me. You always told me that if a man wants to be with you, then he will do whatever he has to do to make that happen. Maybe Alberto just isn't the one I'm supposed to be with," Mariah said, dabbing at her eyes.

Tina gave her sister a sympathetic smile. She knew firsthand that this comment was true. Not only because she used to say it when she and her sister were dating, but because Paul seemed much happier now with Paige in his life then he had been in the last few years of their marriage. Nowadays when Paul came by to pick up the kids for a weekend, he seemed to be back to the old Paul she used to know when they first started dating. He was back to dressing nice, and his attitude was much better.

"I would suggest that you call him if you feel strongly about it, but just know that he has pretty much told you where you two stand. If you're not okay with that, then I think it's time for you to move on," Tina said.

"I don't know if it's the urge to want to call him to have closure, but I know deep down that you're right. He's just in a place right now where his priorities do not include pursuing anything more serious with me, and I have to be fine with it," Mariah said, knowing deep down that she was blowing smoke. She was pissed off and wanted answers. She knew she was going to call Alberto as soon as she got back to her car and then after that she was going to be done with him.

"Okay, Sis. Well, I have to get back to work. Are you sure you don't want me to bring you something out, so you can take it back with you?" Tina asked, rising from the table.

Mariah shook her head yes. "I would love one of your crab cakes," she said, with a smile on her face.

"You got it! One order of crab cakes coming up. I'll add our spicy vegetable dish to it for your side," Tina said. She got up from the table and headed for the kitchen. Mariah waited patiently.

Afterwards, as soon as Mariah got back inside her car, she placed the bag of food on her driver's seat and immediately reached into her purse for her cell phone. She dialed Alberto's number. Normally, he answered her calls after one or two rings; however, today he didn't answer until after the sixth ring – close to going to voicemail. Mariah found herself starring back at the receiver as if to say, "*No, he's not trying to act like he doesn't recognize my number now.*"

"Hello," Alberto answered. His normal enthusiastic tone whenever she called was nowhere to be found. Mariah almost hung up on him because she was getting the impression that he didn't want to be bothered.

"Hello, Alberto. Did I interrupt you or something?" Mariah asked.

"No, I'm not busy," he said, nonchalantly.

That did it for Mariah. She didn't intend to waste any more of her time dealing with this man. He sounded like he didn't want to be bothered with her call. And to top it off, he wasn't busy and still couldn't find the time to call her after leaving her house five days ago.

"I wanted to call to see where we stand after the disagreement at my house, but I think I have my answer. Excuse me for calling," Mariah said, attempting to hang up.

She heard him sigh and then say underneath his breath, "Whatever, Mariah."

"You know what, Alberto? You pursued me for months before I decided to give in to dating you. And now after two years have gone by and I've climbed on board, you're ready to act like I'm delusional or something to want to make our relationship more official. What's the problem here?" she inquired, trying to keep her voice down.

"Mariah, the problem is that you do not respect what I have going on right now. Things have changed in my life. Yes, I did pursue you when we first met because you're an attractive woman with a lot of qualities that interest me. I still feel the same way now, but I'm not going to be pressured into giving you more than I can commit to right now. To be honest, I don't think being friends right now is going to work either. I know how you women are. As soon as you decide you want to tie a man down you'll say you're fine with just being friends to hold on to him, but what you really want is the commitment. Pretty soon we'll be back at this same point, in another argument, six months later or however long you can go before you explode again," he said, matter-of-factly.

"Hold on a second," Mariah said, ready to interject and read him his rights.

"I thought we could work through this period in my life. I honestly thought you would understand this arrangement of being together without all that title jazz. I mean, isn't this what you said you were down for when we first met? You said you weren't the marrying type. I've just been flowing with the tone you set from day one," Alberto added.

Mariah was furious. She didn't even know where to start with her response. "You're not going to put this one on me. I didn't confuse you. You just thought you could continue to get the cow for free without a commitment. Well no more. I'm so glad this happened so now I can see you for who you really are — someone who likes to hide behind his work and use it as an excuse to deter a commitment. Who does that? It doesn't make any sense! And for the record, I never told you that I wasn't the relationship type. I just said that I never wanted to get married again and there is nothing wrong with that. Have a nice life, Alberto. We're done. And just so we're clear…do not call me anymore because I don't want anything else to do with you," she said and pushed End on her cellular phone before he could respond. She immediately deleted his number from her phone list.

Another one bites the dust, she thought as she pulled out of the parking lot to head back to work. Single yet again. And this time she intended to stay this way. She needed a long break from men.

Chapter Twenty-nine

Tina leaned against the headboard of her bed and tossed the cards she had in her hands onto the covers. Another boring Friday night alone without any interaction from anyone else in the house. Paul had picked up the kids at his usual time to take them back to his apartment for the weekend. Tina ordered herself a pizza after they left and ate it alone at the kitchen table before heading to her bedroom to play cards.

The big house she always dreamed of having felt unnecessary now with two kids there only four full days out of the week. This is a house for a married couple with children. She looked around her massive size bedroom with a sitting area, walk-in closet for two, and oversized bathroom with his and her sinks, shower, and Jacuzzi tub and started to hate it. Paul must be really happy that he didn't get stuck with this place. His three-bedroom apartment was just enough room for him, the twins and PJ. Even when Lexie and PJ weren't there, he still had Leshia there to keep him company during the week.

Tina exhaled loudly as she tried to interest herself in another card game. Was this what her life was going to be like going forward? She had no interest to go out and meet someone new, which baffled her how Paul could feel so ready to jump into another relationship so soon. Tina looked over at the clock on her nightstand. It said 8:00 p.m. "Ugh," she moaned out loud, running her hands roughly across her bed, scattering the cards onto the floor.

Divorce was supposed to bring peace and happiness back to her life. She didn't realize the split would bring about peace and loneliness instead. She didn't have her kids anymore to hang out with on the weekends, and her mood had become so disgruntled lately that she didn't have any interest in focusing on her catering business.

All the hard work she had put into starting her empire was now all for nothing. It seemed like all she does is go to work, come home, spend time with her kids after school for three hours at the most, and then kiss them goodbye on Fridays when Paul comes to whisk them away for a fun weekend. She was left to being stuck in this big house with no one to talk to, feeling empty and desperate.

Tina was starting to wonder if it was doing her any good to continue with therapy. All her therapist ever advised her to do is use this time to do things for herself, such as focus on her business or pick up a new hobby. But what she loved doing the most was spending time with her children, which she couldn't do every day now because of the stupid divorce. She was starting to wonder if she had made a big mistake by going through with the divorce in the first place. Even though she wasn't happy all the time with Paul, at least she didn't have to worry about being alone and without her kids every day.

Now that the holidays were here with Thanksgiving next

month and Christmas a month later, Tina wondered what she would do now. Yes, she could go to her parents for Thanksgiving dinner, but Christmas would be split with her children at two different households. Who would she wake up to on Christmas morning to open gifts with or attend Christmas service with at church? This was not the life she had envisioned when she agreed to go through with the divorce.

Tina hopped off her bed and went to her closet. She shuffled through the clothes on the hangers until she came across a black fitted short dress. It was Paul's favorite dress. She took out a pair of black high heel boots from a shoe box and carried the attire back to her bed. She slipped off her sweatshirt and jogging pants and slipped into the dress. As she zipped up the back of the dress, she noticed the dress was a little loose around her waistline. She walked over to her floor-length mirror and modeled in it back and forth to see if the fact that she had lost ten pounds made a difference in the look of the dress. It was supposed to be fitted. She shrugged and decided it looked fine. Tina walked over to her bed and slipped on the three-inch heel boots.

The last touch would be to do something with her hair. She took the clip off that was keeping her thick hair out of her face and watched as her hair fell to her shoulders. Tina took her comb and styled it the best she could around her face. She proceeded to slip on a few pieces of jewelry to add a touch to her outfit and applied a small amount of makeup to her face. She then sprayed herself with a few squirts of her favorite perfume, which used to make Paul drop to his knees.

Tina looked at herself in the mirror and felt good. She felt alive again. She smiled back at herself before blowing a kiss at the mirror. "Sorry Paige, but I'm going to see my husband tonight and there is no way he will be able to turn all of this down," she said aloud, turning off her room light and heading to the front door.

She and Paul took vows that said until death do us part. Neither of them were dead, so just because some paper in a courthouse said they were over, didn't change the commitment that they took before God. Tina grabbed her jacket from the hall closet, grabbed her car keys and headed out to her car.

The entire ride over to Paul's apartment was smooth with no worries. For once in a very long time Tina felt good about herself. She didn't feel alone. She felt in control and that she was doing what she wanted to do without any input from her therapist. By the time she reached Paul's apartment, it was 10:00 p.m. She was sure the kids were in bed by then, which was perfect for the night she planned to have with her husband.

Tina pulled into an empty visitor's parking spot near the entrance to Paul's building and got out of the car. It was 60 degrees outside with a cool breeze, but Tina left her light jacket inside the car. Her body didn't feel the cool night air because she was heated up inside with excitement to spend a night with Paul, away from the four walls of her house.

Tina tried not to make too much noise with the clicking of her boot heels against the wooden steps as she made her way to Paul's door. She knocked softly on the door and waited for Paul to answer. She hoped he was sitting in the living room and would hear the knocks. She didn't want to wake the kids up. No answer. Tina knocked again this time a little louder. A few seconds later, Paul answered the door. Tina's heart started to beat so fast that she was sure that Paul could hear it. She tried not to smile too hard as she looked at Paul looking handsome in a t-shirt fitting closely to his muscles and a pair of drawstring pants. He must be working out these days because she couldn't recall seeing those bulging muscles when they were married. He seemed to have just had a haircut too. Tina did always love how he would keep himself nicely groomed.

"Hey, what are you doing here? Is everything okay?" Paul inquired, looking at her with a confused expression on his face.

"No, everything is not okay. May I come inside?" Tina asked.

"Yeah, come on in. Are you going somewhere?" Paul asked, stepping back so Tina could walk through the door.

"Where are the kids? Are they asleep?" Tina asked. She looked around the living room, which was dark. The lights were off in the apartment except for the light coming from Paul's bedroom.

"Yep, they are asleep," Paul said, waiting patiently with his hands in his pockets for Tina to tell him the nature of this visit at 10:00 p.m.

Tina immediately headed for his bedroom without his approval. She could hear Paul asking where she was going, but it didn't matter. She walked past the kids' rooms where their doors were closed and into Paul's bedroom. This was her first time in his bedroom. All he had was a queen-sized bed, dresser, a nightstand and a lamp and a TV stand with a big screen television. She noticed some clothes on the floor in the corner, but this was his place so he could do as he pleased.

Paul walked into the room with an angry look on his face, but Tina immediately walked over to him and pressed her lips against his before he could say anything. She grabbed his hands and forced him to rub against her thighs pushing the short miniskirt above her waist.

"Tina, what are you doing?" Paul asked, trying to get out of her hold.

"Paul, I miss you. I need you right now. You're my husband, and I don't want to be alone tonight. Please, let's make love, Baby," she begged.

Paul got loose and backed up to the door. He closed it so the kids wouldn't hear them. The angry look he had when he first entered the room had changed to a confused expression. "Tina, you know I can't do that. I have a girlfriend now, and you're not my wife anymore."

Tina couldn't believe this. Tears started to come to her eyes. Paul had never turned her down before, even when he was upset

274

with her after one of their many arguments when they were married. Was this really happening?

"Paul, who the hell cares about Paige? You made a commitment to me, remember? She can't take care of you like I can. Trust me," Tina said. She unzipped the back of her dress to reveal her naked breasts and a shimmery thong. If Paul could walk away from this, then he was a fool.

Paul turned his head and spoke sternly trying to keep his voice down. "Tina, you don't want me. You haven't for years. Why now? Please put your clothes back on and go home."

Tina walked over to Paul and tried to grab his hands to cup her breast, but they wouldn't budge. He was much stronger than she was. She then decided to give him a strip tease to let him see what he had been missing. She walked backward seductively in her boots toward his bed and then turned around leaning against the edge of the bed to stick her butt out in midair moving it back and forth to try to get him aroused.

"Come on Paul, you know you want this," she mumbled.

Paul opened the door and left the room closing the door behind him. Tina immediately turned around and fell onto the bed in pure shock. She felt humiliated. She couldn't do anything to stop the tears from falling from her eyes this time. She wiped and wiped, but they wouldn't stop falling.

"No, I can't give up on us. I won't be alone," she mumbled to herself as she punched the bed.

Tina took her boots off and then slid out of her thong. She climbed into Paul's unmade bed and pulled the covers over her naked body. She wanted the smell of his sheets to be on her body. She missed having him next to her at night. Tina turned off the light on the nightstand and rolled over onto Paul's pillow. She could smell his cologne on the sheets.

Paul reentered the room ten minutes later. "What the...," he started to say as he saw Tina lying in his bed. He closed the door and then walked over to the bed to pull the covers off her naked body.

"Tina, get out of my bed right now. It's time for you to go home. I have called your sister, and she's coming over to get you," Paul said sternly, picking up her thong and dress from the floor and handing it to her.

Tina sat up in the bed. She didn't feel good. She felt sick to her stomach. Her head started to spin as she became overwhelmed with shame of what she had just done. Her children were only a few feet from the bedroom.

"Paul, I wish you hadn't called my sister. Was that really necessary at this time of night?" she asked, snatching her clothing from his hand. "I'm a grown woman. I can take care of myself."

"Apparently not," Paul said, leaning against the bedroom wall with his arms folded as she got dressed.

"Excuse me, so you think your life is so much better than mine. Why, because you have someone to keep your bed warm at night when Lexie and PJ aren't here, and Leshia is in bed? Ugh and to think I was naked in that bed. I need to go home and take a shower immediately. I'm sure you don't clean your sheets as often as you should," Tina hurled insults at him.

"I see the old Tina has returned – the one who loved to insult me to make her own self feel good, and the one who ruined our marriage because she's truly not happy with her own life. You didn't want me tonight. You just didn't want to be alone. Get out of my house, Tina, and go get some help," Paul said, leading her out of his room.

"Paul, I did want you, but I see it was a mistake. You're willing to be faithful to your new girlfriend when you couldn't be faithful to me. I know you cheated on me with her. That's why it was so easy for you to get in a relationship with her after our divorce was finalized. Admit it! Admit it! Admit it!" Tina yelled, running up behind Paul and jumping onto his back. She tried to squeeze her arms around his neck attempting to put him in a headlock as Paul started to spin her around the room in an effort to get her off him.

"Tina, what the heck is wrong with you? Get off me!" Paul yelled as they fell back onto the couch. He immediately jumped up and got far away from her clutching his bruised neck. His eyes were larger than life in disbelief of what had just transpired. Tina had never in all their years of marriage acted in this way toward him.

The door to PJ's bedroom opened, and he came out rubbing his eyes. "Daddy, what's going on out here?" he asked, walking down the hallway toward the living room.

Paul immediately turned around to shield PJ from seeing his mother looking disgruntled on the couch. "Everything is okay, buddy. Let's go back to bed," Paul said, taking him back to his bedroom and closing the door behind them.

Tina couldn't believe what she had just done. How could she have jumped on Paul like that? She got off the couch and tried to fix herself up. Her hair was a mess, and eyeliner marks were smeared all over her face. Tina pulled her dress down and ran her hands through her hair as the door to PJ's bedroom opened and Paul reappeared again, stopping short of the doorway to the living room. He didn't want to come anywhere near Tina at this point, and she couldn't blame him.

"Paul, I-I-I-I'm sorry. I don't know what has come over me," she stuttered.

"Tina, I think it would be best if you leave now," he said close to a whisper.

Tina tried to approach him, but Paul backed away. "Okay — I'll go. I'm really sorry. I guess I cared more than I let on about this whole mess. I'm sorry," Tina said nervously, tears streaming down her face.

"Tina, I told you the truth. I never cheated on you. I didn't meet Paige until after we were separated, and we didn't get involved until after our divorce. I think you need to move on and get some help. I have never seen you act like this before. Please wait for your sister in your car. I don't think you should drive alone tonight," Paul said sympathetically.

Tina nodded. She guessed she had to act like a fool for it to finally click in her brain that he was telling the truth the whole time. After what she had just done, anyone who had done any wrongdoing would have come clean just to get back at her. But Paul said what he has said this whole time, and she believed him.

There was a knock at the front door. She knew it was her sister. Tina didn't want to let Mariah see her like this, but she knew she didn't have a choice. The only way she could get out of the apartment was through the front door unless she leaped over the balcony. And she was sure if she tried to do that, that Paul would have her committed and in a straitjacket by morning.

Tina walked over to the front door and opened it. As soon as Mariah saw how frazzled her sister looked, she immediately took her into her arms questioning what was wrong. Tina wept harder than a child who had lost her favorite toy.

"I'm sorry. Let's just go, okay?" Tina said, raising her head from the crevice of her sister's neck and leaving the apartment before Mariah had a chance to question her again.

Tina ran to the safety of her car not caring about the loud

clicking noise the heels of her boots made as she ran down the wooden steps. She cried and cried and waited for Mariah to come back down. She was sure she was in the apartment speaking to Paul about what had just happened. This all seemed like such a nightmare, one that Tina desperately wanted to wake up from. She felt so helpless! How did she get to a place full of jealousy, anger, and despair all bottled up inside of her body? Tina had never felt like this before and had no idea of how she could get away from it. She felt like it consumed her.

Tina heard a knock on her window. She looked up to see Mariah standing at the passenger door. She unlocked the door and waited for Mariah to drill her about what had happened.

"Oh my gosh. What's going on? Where is your jacket? It's chilly out here tonight," Mariah said, scanning the car for her jacket.

"I don't feel anything right now. I'm numb. I just want to be alone. Oh wait...I have that down packed," Tina said, slobbering over her words as the tears fell from her face.

Mariah found her jacket on the floor of the backseat and wrapped it over sister's bare arms. "Tina, Paul told me you showed up and attacked him tonight. What's going on? And don't tell me it's nothing."

Tina leaned her head against the headrest and tried to wipe her face with the arm of her jacket. "Mariah, I'm lost. I feel so alone. I ruined my marriage. Now I can't even have my children full time anymore. Leshia hates me. Look at me. I'm a mess. Paul doesn't even want me anymore. Do you know I showed up tonight in his favorite dress, which I can't even fit anymore because I've lost so much weight, to try and seduce him? He turned me down. I then tried to make him feel the pain I felt thinking he cheated on me by attacking him. I should have listened to my therapist and just stayed away, but I don't know how. He has everything, and I don't have anything except for that big ole' house," Tina said, as she started to break down again. She accidently slipped out and told Mariah about seeing a therapist. Wow – could her night get any worse?

Mariah took her sister's hand and tried to comfort her. "Tina, you have much more than that. You still have your children and your family. We're all here for you. You're speaking to someone who is a pro in this area. You will bounce back. You're still my strong older sister who will overcome this."

"Thank you. You must think I'm crazy. I have to see a therapist to help me get through this. I have been seeing her for over a year now. Some help she has been. Driving into the city once a week to still end up making a fool out of myself...I feel crazier and crazier every day," Tina said.

"I feel quite the opposite. I think it's commendable that you recognize that you needed help and sought it. It shows how much you are in control of your life. You just had a vulnerable moment, and that's all. I would really like you to come and stay with me tonight," Mariah said.

Mariah thought back to the time she thought she had seen her sister while out for lunch at work. She must have been on her way to a session then. Mariah decided to keep that bit of information to herself. It was obvious that Tina felt uncomfortable about seeing a therapist.

"No, I just want to go home and get in my own bed. Pull the covers over my head and try to forget about this whole night," Tina responded, looking up at her sister through glazed eyes. Her eyes felt swollen from all the crying she had done.

"Okay – then I would like to spend the night at your house. I don't want you to be alone," Mariah said.

Tina slowly nodded her head in agreement. Mariah sat with her a little while longer until she felt OK to drive home. She then followed Tina back to her house. Tina couldn't wait to get home to take off the dress and get into bed. She desperately wanted to put this dreadful night behind her.

Chapter Thirty

Mariah returned home Saturday after staying with her sister for a week following the dramatic episode at Paul's. She arrived home to an empty refrigerator, so she immediately took a shower and got dressed so she could go grocery shopping. She volunteered to pick up Halloween costumes for PJ and the twins, so she figured she would tackle that task as well while she was out running errands.

Mariah hated going grocery shopping on Saturdays because the lines were extremely long. She turned her car into the shopping center. She decided to go to the CVS drugstore next door to the grocery store first to see if they had any nice Halloween costumes left. PJ specifically asked for a pirate costume, and the girls wanted to be princesses with a tiara and wand.

Mariah got out the car and walked into CVS. Halloween decorations and candy were everywhere. She walked down the aisle where she could hear the hackling of a goblin going off and started thumbing through the leftover packs of Halloween costumes. Halloween was next weekend so she hoped she would be able to find what the kids wanted. The goblin went off again as someone came down the aisle. Mariah figured there must be a motion sensor set on it for anyone who walked down the costume aisle.

"Mariah?" a familiar voice asked.

Mariah turned around to see Christopher, Isaac's best friend, standing there.

"Christopher, how nice to see you," Mariah said, surprised.

"Same here. How have you been?" he asked.

"I've been doing well. I can't complain. How are you doing?" Mariah asked.

"I'm doing well. I'm engaged now, believe it or not," he said, smiling.

"Congratulations. Wow time has really gone by. I'm happy for you. Anyone I know?" Mariah asked.

"No, I met her after...um after you and Isaac broke up," Christopher said, obviously trying to find the right words.

Suddenly, the smile that Christopher had on his face faded away as he continued on with the conversation. "Have you spoken to Isaac?" he asked.

Mariah was taken aback by his question about her interaction with Isaac. She was sure he knew how she messed that whole relationship up and that they weren't talking.

"Nope, we don't talk," she said, placing the yellow princess dress back on the hook. She was sure that the twins wouldn't be interested in that color dress.

"I didn't mean to make you feel uncomfortable. I only asked because his dad had a heart attack last week, and he died yesterday," Christopher said.

Mariah felt like someone had taken a sledgehammer and hit her in the stomach.

"Wha-what did you say?" she asked, falling against Christopher.

She hoped she didn't hear him correctly. Mr. Stevens was the sweetest man she had ever met. He always treated her like a daughter. This was another reason the breakup had hurt her so much. She had really gotten close with Isaac's parents.

Christopher helped Mariah back to her feet. "I'm sorry to be the one to tell you. Isaac's not doing well at all. I'm actually out here to pick something up to take back to his mom's house. I think you should call him. He would love to hear from you," he said.

Mariah couldn't believe what was happening in her life right now. First, her sister with her mental breakdown and now to hear that Isaac's dad had passed away. Mr. Stevens was only 67 years old. He was a fit man who loved to play tennis and eat healthy. She just didn't understand how this could have happened. Mariah was certain Isaac was having a hard time coping with his father's death. He and Mr. Stevens were very close.

"Okay. I'll call him," she whispered.

"Are you going to be okay?" Christopher asked.

Mariah nodded and tried to muster up a smile, although she felt like she was breaking down inside. "I need to go see Isaac. Is he at home?"

"Yes, and he would love to see you," Christopher said, giving her a hug goodbye.

Mariah nodded. She was scared to go over to Isaac's house, but she couldn't help but pick up on how Christopher kept saying love to hear from you...love to see you...and she figured if anyone would know it would be his best friend, so she decided to drive over there.

The drive over to Isaac's condo felt surreal for the reason she was going to see him. The familiar turns down the streets leading to his condo brought back so many emotions that she didn't realize was still buried deep inside of her. She pulled into his parking garage and parked her car. She had been going off pure adrenaline from the idea of being able to see him again, but now that she was here she didn't have the courage to get out of the car anymore. What if Christopher was wrong and he didn't want to see her?

The last time they had spoken Isaac was specifically clear that he didn't want to see her again. What could have changed in two years? The pain she was sure he was enduring after losing his dad didn't need to be compounded with the memories of her breaking his heart. *Just leave, Mariah*, she thought as she placed her key back into the ignition. She turned on the car but something kept pulling her to stay.

Mariah turned off the car and got out. The cool air hit her face, and a strong breeze went through her hair as she wrapped her arms around her parka vest and walked toward the elevator. She pressed the number 4 button and got onto the elevator. She shivered as she rode the elevator up. It was really chilly today. Bing! The elevator door chimed as it opened. She walked toward Isaac's door. The hallway was much warmer, so she was able to relax a little bit. She tapped her heels trying to get the courage to ring his doorbell.

She pressed the button and waited for Isaac to answer. If she heard him check the peephole and didn't answer right away, then she would just turn around real fast and get back on the elevator. Mariah could hear him walking toward the door. She took a deep breath as Isaac unlocked his deadbolt and opened the door.

"Hi Isaac, I ran into Christopher today and he told me about your dad. I'm really sorry. I came over as soon as I heard. I hope you don't mind," she said all in one breath, hoping he wouldn't lay into her for coming to his condo.

"I'm glad you came. Come on in," he said, softly attempting to put a smile on his face. Mariah could tell he was hurting. His normal cheerful demeanor was nowhere in sight.

A feeling of relief came over her as she walked into the dark apartment. Isaac locked his door and walked back to his bedroom in silence. Mariah followed him. She almost broke down when she entered the bedroom. Scattered all over his bed were photos of him and his dad from various ages. There were some from when he was a kid in his baseball uniform, to graduation, to recent pictures of them at cookouts, and other various family events.

Mariah immediately ran to him and gave him a hug. She couldn't help but break down. Isaac held onto to her as they sat down on his bed. She had never seen Isaac cry before, but even he couldn't keep from breaking down. He wept in Mariah's arms, shaking with emotions. They held each other for what seemed like an eternity until they both stopped crying.

Isaac wiped his face and relaxed against his pillow looking back at Mariah. She reached for his hand and held onto it tightly.

They sat in silence for a few more minutes just looking at each other and holding hands.

"Isaac, I'm so sorry. Your dad was a great man. I'm glad I had the opportunity to know him," she said.

Isaac nodded his head in agreement. "Thank you."

"I want you to know if you need anything, and I mean anything, that you can always call me, okay?" Mariah said.

Isaac pulled her close to him. Mariah could tell the change in his breathing as he pulled her even closer. It was strong and intense as their lips were inches apart.

"Isaac, what are you doing?" she asked.

"I miss you. Come here," Isaac pleaded as he gave her a lip locking kiss.

Mariah felt a shock go through her body as she became entwined in his passion. The familiarity of how he could make her feel and what she had been missing for the past years made her forget about her reason for coming to his condo. Isaac pulled her parka vest off and started to unbutton her top.

Mariah grabbed his hand to stop him. "Isaac, wait. What are we doing? We can't do this. You're upset, and we're both not thinking clearly."

A grin came over Isaac's face at that moment. He lifted Mariah's hands up to his lips and kissed them one finger at a time. "I know why you came here, and I'm thankful for your concern. But I know what I want right now, and it's you," he said, staring back at her with a sensuous glare.

Isaac bent over to kiss her again, running his hands through her hair. Mariah allowed his lips to cover every surface of hers as they fell back against his bed. Her stomach started to do cartwheels as he ran his strong hands up under her shirt and along her backside and began to kiss every crevice of her neck.

As much as Mariah wanted to push him off her, she fell under his love spell and surrendered her body to his lovemaking. She knew deep down that she was still in love with Isaac and still yearned to be with him. The strong bond that they shared together didn't fizzle away from the years they had been apart. She just hoped that he really missed her and wasn't just using her to feel good for the moment because he was feeling so much pain.

Nevertheless, Mariah decided to let her mind go blank and not worry about what was going to happen afterwards. She was under

Isaac's command, and her body was enjoying every moment of it.

Chapter Thirty-one

The next couple days, Isaac and Mariah spent every hour together, although it was for a sad occasion. It felt like old times being together again and in each other's company. The family decided to have Mr. Stevens' funeral on Thursday at noon. The wake was Wednesday night, and all of the Stevens family and friends met at the funeral home to see Mr. Stevens one last time before the funeral services.

Mariah thought the clothes Isaac and his mother picked out for Mr. Stevens suited him very well. He looked like he was at peace, and she couldn't help reflecting on the last time she had seen him before breaking off the engagement. As she approached Mrs. Stevens after the beautiful wake service, Mariah wondered what her reaction would be like. She hadn't seen her in two years. Mariah waited patiently for a couple to finish giving their condolences and then she walked up to her with open arms.

"Mrs. Stevens, I'm so sorry," she said.

Immediately Mrs. Stevens smiled and gave her a big hug. This response made Mariah melt inside. She realized that his mother didn't hate her, after all.

"Mariah, I'm so happy to see you. Thank you for coming," Mrs. Stevens said.

"How are you doing?" Mariah asked, thinking afterwards that

this was probably insensitive to ask. How do you think she's doing? *She just lost her husband you idiot*, she thought.

"I have my moments. I still can't believe he's gone. It happened so fast that I didn't have a chance to really process what was going on. First, he had the heart attack and was in the hospital recovering, and then he died in his sleep a few days later," she said, dabbing at the corners of her eyes with a handkerchief.

Mariah's heart just ached for Mrs. Stevens. She and her husband were college Sweethearts and always seemed inseparable. An older woman walked up to Mrs. Stevens to speak to her, so Mariah decided to head off and locate Isaac.

"I'm going to go, but I'll see you back at the house," Mariah said, touching her shoulder as she nodded and turned to one of her friends from church.

Mariah scanned the room full of people and saw Isaac by the doorway entrance. She walked up behind him. Isaac looked handsome in his black suit. He turned to her and wrapped his arm around her shoulders.

"I can't tell you how much I appreciate you helping me this week. There have been so many people at the house trying to help my mom that I just needed to get away. Are you ready to go?" Isaac asked.

"Sure. Let's go to your mom's," she said.

"No, I don't want to be around anyone right now. I'll stop by there later. I just want to go home and change and relax for a little bit. The hard part's tomorrow," Isaac said leading the way out of the funeral home.

Mariah followed Isaac out to his car and got in the passenger seat. He was stopped on his way to the car by a few more people who wanted to offer their condolences, so she waited patiently for him to get inside. As she waited, she couldn't help but wonder what all of this meant. Since their romantic night last Saturday, what would happen after the funeral was over, and Isaac came to grips with the fact that his dad was gone. It would be hard to go back to being friends. She realized through all the time they had been spending together that she still loved him.

Isaac opened the car door and got inside. "Sorry about that. Are you hungry? We can stop by my mom's if you want to get a bite to eat, or I can pick you something up," he offered.

"Are you going to eat anything?" Mariah asked. She noticed that Isaac hadn't been eating as much lately.

"Nah, I'm not hungry. But you should eat something," he said, pulling out of the parking lot.

Mariah wanted to push him to eat something but decided against it. She had never lost a parent and didn't know what he was going through personally. She remembered losing her grandmother when she was sixteen, and that was devastating enough, so if he didn't have an appetite then she didn't want to force him to eat. Mariah decided to pick some Thai food up on the way back to his place and would get an extra serving in case he felt like eating later.

∞

The funeral service was beautiful and held on Thursday afternoon. Mrs. Stevens had doves released at the end of the service in Mr. Stevens' honor. Isaac tried his best to make it through the service without crying, but he broke down at the end when it was time for him to serve as a pallbearer and help carry his father out to the limo to be taken to the cemetery. Mariah rode to the cemetery with her mother and sister who attended the funeral services as well. Isaac rode in the limo with his mother.

"The service was beautiful. The pastor was a really good speaker," Mrs. Langston said in the car.

Mariah took her black hat off and tried to fix her hair. "Yes, he's their family pastor. I've attended a few of his church services with Isaac before."

Tina turned around in the front seat to face her sister. "Today was a wake-up call for me. There's so much to life to live for while we're able to. I'm thankful to the both of you for supporting me through my divorce. And I'm sorry for causing you all to worry about me lately."

Mariah reached out and touched her sister's shoulder. "It's okay, Tina. That's what family is for," she said giving her a wink. She knew how hard it was for Tina to admit outwardly to them that she wasn't as strong as she had been letting on and needed help.

"You'll be fine," Mrs. Langston said, trying to keep up with the other cars following the police escort to the cemetery.

"It seemed like old times seeing you and Isaac together again," Tina said as her mother gave a head nod in agreement.

"I'm just being a friend…nothing more," Mariah said, as the images from them being intimate came across her mind. The thought of Isaac running his strong hand up the inner part of her thigh caused a chill to run through her body. She would just keep that tidbit of information to herself.

"You never know, Sis. Maybe this is Karma pulling you two back together again," Tina said.

Mariah gave her sister a strange glare. "His dad died, so Karma decided to bring us back together when he's grieving. No thanks. I don't want us to get back together again based on these conditions."

"I think what your sister is saying is that you two obviously aren't done with each other. It wouldn't hurt to see where this may lead you to, whether it's back together again as a couple or just as friends," Mrs. Langston said, adding her two cents as they turned into the parking lot of the cemetery.

Mariah decided to just let it ride out to put an end to the conversation. She and Isaac broke up for a reason, and that reason had not changed. She couldn't help but admit that some strong feelings she didn't know still existed came out over this past week, but she knew it was best to pull back some after the funeral was over with.

They got out of the car and proceeded over to the burial site. The Stevens had placed roses on everyone's chair to drop into the casket at the end of the pastor's last words. Mrs. Stevens broke down as she said her final goodbyes to her husband and had to be carried away by a family member. Isaac stood off to the side fighting back tears. When it was time for him to say his final goodbyes, he walked over and touched his father's casket and stood there for a while, saying his last words.

After waiting behind the other family members to say her final goodbyes to Mr. Stevens with her sister and mom, Mariah walked over to where Isaac was standing away from the crowd. He was wrapping up a conversation with Christopher and his fiancée who started to walk away just as she approached him. "Ugh…it's over with now. I still can't believe he's gone," he said.

"Same here. It all still seems so surreal. Would you like me to go home with you?" Mariah asked.

"I'm going to ride back to the house with my mom. Spend some time with her. I'll give you a little break. I'm thankful for your support this past week," Isaac said, wrapping his arms around Mariah in a hug.

Mariah hoped this wasn't the sendoff to them going back to the way they had been before. Yes, she knew they weren't back together again, but she didn't expect with all they had shared this week that their interaction with one another would end so rapidly. Wasn't it worth it to see if there was something still there between them?

"Okay…well, let me know if you need anything. It doesn't matter the day or the hour," Mariah said, rubbing his back.

Isaac kissed her on the forehead. "I'll give you a call," he said.

Mariah would have preferred a kiss on the lips, but she guessed a forehead kiss would have to do.

"Well, I'm going to go catch up with my mom and sister. Take care of yourself," she said.

"Please thank them for coming," Isaac said.

Mariah nodded and started to walk toward her mother's car. Her heart began to ache as she walked away from him. She was still in love with Isaac. Had she married him two years ago as they had planned, she wouldn't have to walk away from him right now. She would be leaving with him as his wife. Mariah wanted to break down, but she had to hold it together around her sister and mother. She missed Isaac already, and she had only been away from him for a few seconds now. Some Karma.

Chapter Thirty-two

Weeks went by, and Mariah could count on one hand how many times she had spoken to Isaac. He called her a few days after his dad's funeral, and they talked for about thirty minutes. After receiving that call, she didn't hear from him again until another week. The second call was even shorter. Mariah felt it was okay to check up on him after the second call, even though she really just wanted to hear his voice. However, he was busy with a client and couldn't talk.

A month later, their relationship had become non-existent. And at this point Mariah decided she wasn't going to call him anymore. If Isaac needed someone to talk to, he could reach out to her. She was pretty sure he was sick of people asking how he was doing, and she didn't want to become one of those people.

Returning to the office after the Thanksgiving holiday, Mariah decided to dive headfirst into her work. She was sick of the up and down emotional roller coaster ride with men and just needed a break.

She was typing a memo up to send out to her team when Sandra knocked on her door.

"Howdy," she said, poking her head inside the room.

Mariah glanced up over her reading glasses and waved her coworker inside. "Come on in. I can use a little break," she said.

298

"Great. I haven't seen you since going on vacation. How was Thanksgiving?" Sandra asked, taking a seat in front of her desk.

Mariah took off her reading glasses. "Thanksgiving was nice. We had a big dinner at my parents. I got to hang out with my nieces and nephew, which is always a joy for me. How was Alaska?" Mariah asked referring to the trip Sandra and her husband had taken over the Thanksgiving break.

"Alaska is so beautiful. It was a wonderful trip. You know my parents were disappointed that we weren't home for Thanksgiving, but it was really nice to get away with my husband and just do our own thing this year. I'm so hungry. Do you mind me eating my sandwich here?" Sandra asked, placing a wrapped sandwich on her desk.

"No problem. Please eat. I didn't even realize it was lunch time. I guess I should go grab my lunch from the fridge," Mariah said.

Sandra started to unwrap her tuna fish sandwich and began to eat it. Mariah took a sip of her coffee and immediately felt her stomach began to churn. The smell of Sandra's tuna fish sandwich made her sick, and she could feel her breakfast from this morning trying to come up from her stomach. Mariah grabbed the garbage can from under her desk and vomited into it.

Sandra gasped as Mariah reached for a Kleenex to wipe her mouth.

"Mariah, are you okay?" Sandra asked.

The smell of the tuna fish was still making her feel sick. "I don't know what happened," she said, holding a clean Kleenex over her nose to fight off the strong fishy smell. She loved tuna fish, so she didn't understand what was going on.

"Is it something you ate? Do you need some water?" Sandra inquired.

"No...I'll be fine. Thanks," Mariah said.

"You don't look like you feel well. I'll go get you some water just in case," Sandra said, wrapping up her sandwich and placing it back in her lunch bag before leaving the room.

The smell subsided, and Mariah was able to relax for a little bit. She leaned back in her chair and placed her hand on her queasy stomach. This had never happened to her before.

Sandra returned with a cup of water and Mariah sipped on it. "Thank you so much. I feel better now."

"Geesh, you scared me. I was sitting here and all of a sudden you became sick. I would ask if you were pregnant, but I know you would think I was crazy for asking you that," Sandra said with a giggle.

All of a sudden, Mariah felt like the wind had been knocked out of her. What date was it?

"No, I'm definitely not pregnant. I just think it was a fluke that's all. My breakfast just didn't want to be in my stomach anymore," she said with a nervous giggle as she looked at the calendar on her desk.

"Since you're okay, I'm going to head back to my office to prepare for a meeting. Please call me if you need me," Sandra said, picking up her lunch bag and heading to the door.

"Okay. It was good chatting with you," Mariah called out. She immediately looked at her planner in her purse and looked for the October calendar. As soon as she saw the date, she became nervous. She was a week and a half late. She was never late. Her period always came on time like clockwork and had ever since she was a teenager.

"This can't be," she said to herself out loud. The last time she had intercourse was with Isaac at his condo. They hadn't used any protection. She was so wrapped up with all of the emotions of seeing Isaac again, that she had forgotten to tell him she was no longer on birth control pills.

Mariah turned around in her chair and placed her head between her hands. "Maybe I just had a bad stomach reaction that's all. I'm not pregnant," she said to herself.

But when have you ever not liked the smell of tuna fish? she thought. Mariah finished up her memo, sent it out and grabbed her purse. The only way to be sure was to take a pregnancy test. She decided to go to the local pharmacy to get one.

Mariah was too nervous to take the pregnancy test at work, so she decided to wait until she got home; partly because she didn't want to know if it was true or not. After going to the bathroom and waiting a few minutes, Mariah paced back and forth in front of her bathroom door. She knew on the other side of her bathroom door her life was either going to change forever or remain the same. She hoped she wasn't pregnant, and this was all some big coincidence. Being a mother was never in her plans.

Opening the bathroom door slowly as if she was afraid a monster was going to jump out at her, Mariah walked over to the test stick she had placed on the back of her toilet. The plus sign was bright blue indicating loudly without a doubt that she was indeed pregnant!

Mariah gasped, placing her hands on her flat stomach. She sat down on her bathroom rug in pure shock. This was not happening to her. She was 38 years old and unmarried. She wasn't even in communication with the father anymore. This was just something that happened because emotions were high, and they were sad and wanted to make each other feel better. How could she have been so irresponsible and not used any protection!

Mariah reached for the package in her trash can to inspect the expiration date on the test box. *Maybe the test was old*, she thought, searching for anything that could explain that the test was incorrect, and she wasn't pregnant. But the date had not expired. In fact, the test was good for another year.

She tossed the box on the floor and walked back to her

bedroom. She took off her hot pink yoga pants and climbed into bed. She pulled the covers over her head. As much as she wanted to handle this on her own, she knew she had to go against her promise of not calling Isaac again. He had a right to know that she was carrying his child.

ߢ

A week had gone by, and Mariah still had not called Isaac. She was hoping he would have called her in the meantime and then she could have told him. After seeing the results of the pregnancy test, she decided to confirm it by visiting her OB/GYN. Dr. Pads confirmed after giving her a test and an ultrasound that she was indeed five weeks pregnant. He prescribed prenatal pills for her to begin taking daily. He also wanted to monitor her closely in the first and second trimesters because she was considered high risk due to her age.

Mariah figured at this point she couldn't fight it any longer. She had to call Isaac and tell him the news. She decided to call him on Saturday morning. Isaac wouldn't be at work and would hopefully be home. Mariah dialed his home number and waited for him to answer the phone. She placed her hand on her leg to stop it from shaking; she was so nervous.

Isaac answered the phone after the third ring. "Hello," he said.

Mariah's heart dropped in her stomach at the sound of his voice. "Hi, Isaac," she said.

"Hey, how are you doing, Mariah?" he asked. He sounded enthusiastic as if he was happy to hear from her.

"I'm okay. How are you doing?" Mariah asked, knowing she was stalling for time.

"I'm doing better. Sorry I haven't called. I've just been throwing myself into work since the funeral. What are you getting into today?" Isaac asked, changing the subject.

"I don't have any plans. I called because I need to talk to you about something," she responded, nervously.

There was a brief pause and then Isaac responded. "O-kay– what's going on?"

Mariah tried to find a subtle way to tell him without beating around the bush, but she couldn't find one. She figured just saying it may be easier. "Isaac, I'm pregnant," she blurted out and then held her breath for his response.

"Huh?"

"I said I'm pregnant."

"You're pregnant?" he asked.

"Yes…and it's yours if that's your next question," Mariah said.

"Come on, Mariah. I know you wouldn't be calling me if the baby weren't mine. WOW – I wasn't expecting to hear you say this. I don't mean to sound insensitive, but are you sure? We were together only that one time."

"Yes, I'm sure. I took a home test and then I had my gynecologist confirm it. I don't expect anything from you. I just thought you should know," Mariah added.

There was another long drawn out pause from Isaac. "I can't believe I'm going to be a father. Wow…I'm going to be a dad. This is great news!" Isaac exclaimed.

Mariah could tell he was now smiling through the phone. This softened up the tension in her chest and made her feel more at ease.

"I was so nervous to call you because we're not together anymore," Mariah said, smiling herself for once in the past week.

"Marry me," Isaac said.

Mariah sat back against her pillow, shocked at what he had just asked her to do. "Huh…what did you just say to me?"

"Marry me, Mariah. Don't you see this is a sign that we should be together? I haven't stopped thinking about you since we broke up. I miss you and was so excited to see you come to my door that day. I love you and want you to be my wife when the baby comes," he said.

Those words made Mariah melt inside. She had no idea that Isaac had still been thinking about her for the last couple years. There were so many times that he would pop back in her head, but she made herself suppress those feelings because she thought he had moved on. This is why Christopher said he would love to hear from her. He knew that Isaac still loved her.

"Isaac, how come you never called me? The ball was always in your court! You know I didn't want us to break up," she said.

"I guess I was being stubborn and wanted all or nothing, but you have to see now that we are meant to be, Mariah. You're having my baby so this should make you see that I'm not going anywhere. We're going to be connected for life through our child," Isaac responded.

"Isaac, I love you too. And you're right. This changes everything. I want our baby to have a family…a real one where we're together and not apart. Yes, I will marry you," Mariah said, breaking into tears.

"Mariah, I have been so down over the past month. More than you know. This news has just brightened my day. I can't wait to tell my mom. She could use some great news. I can't wait to marry you. I want to see you now. Are you home?" he asked.

"Yes, please come over here. Just one more thing, Isaac…"

"Sure, anything you want. Are you craving something? I'll go get you whatever you want to eat – chocolate, pickles, you name it."

"No, I don't have any weird cravings yet. I just wanted to say that I don't want a wedding. I just want to marry you. Let's go to the Justice of the Peace and just do it," Mariah said, hoping he would be on board for this.

"Mariah, I'm not really up for a big party these days. That sounds like music to my ears. All I want next to my side is you and my baby, and that's it," he said, smiling.

"I love you, Isaac. Hurry over here. I can't wait to see you," Mariah said as they concluded the call, and she placed it back on the cradle.

She wrapped her arms around her legs and buried her face between her knees. She couldn't believe what had just happened. She and Isaac were back together again and were getting married. Mariah didn't feel any anxiety. In fact, she felt like the luckiest woman in the world.

She relaxed back against her bed and stretched her body out across the comforter. Pulling up her t-shirt she rubbed her flat stomach. She couldn't believe she was going to be a mom.

"Hi, Baby. This is your Mommy. Your Daddy is on his way over," Mariah said to her abdomen. This was the first time she had spoken to her belly. The feeling of becoming a mom was starting to set in. She was now ready to tell her mother and sister. Her life had totally changed in a blink of an eye...

Chapter Thirty-three

Tina looked up at the clock and waited patiently for her turn to go into the pediatric therapist office. The therapist wanted to meet with her and Paul for Leshia's initial appointment. Tina had arrived thirty minutes early to the appointment because she didn't want to walk in when Paul and Leshia were sitting in the room. She preferred for them to come in and address the elephant in the room.

Paul had been avoiding her since the whole fiasco she had made at his apartment. And if it hadn't been for this appointment being made prior to the incident, she was sure he wouldn't want to be around her today. For the last few weeks, he had been blowing the horn for Lexie and PJ to come out to the car versus coming inside to pick them up as usual.

The door to the therapist office opened, and Dr. Madelyn Smith walked out to greet her.

"Hello, you must be Ms. Holmes. Thank you for coming to meet with me. Are Leshia and her father here yet?" she asked, looking around the small waiting room.

Tina shook the woman's hand and looked at the front door nervously. She hoped that Paul and Leshia wouldn't stand her up. She knew that Paul was obviously still pissed off at what she had done, but Leshia needs therapy and it wouldn't be fair for him to hold their daughter back from receiving help just to get back at her.

"I'm sure they're on the way. Let me try calling them," Tina said, reaching for her cell phone.

"Okay – no problem. I do have an appointment right after yours, so I'm afraid I will not be able to go over our allotted time. Just come into the room as soon as they arrive," Dr. Smith said, as she walked back into her office.

As soon as her door closed, Tina immediately dialed Paul's number. She was livid. How dare he miss their daughter's appointment? Oh, that's right…she loves him so of course this wouldn't be a priority of his.

The call went straight to his voicemail. Tina was about to read him his rights until she remembered what her therapist said and just hung up the phone. She couldn't always be in attack mode all the time where Paul was concerned if she wanted things to get better between them for the sake of the kids.

"Ugh," Tina moaned. She tossed her phone back into her purse and got up from her chair. She might as well cancel the appointment and have Dr. Smith contact Paul to pay the cancellation fee because she had arrived on time.

Just as Tina had her hand on the knob of the office door to walk in to cancel the appointment, the main door opened, and Paul and Leshia walked into the waiting room. Leshia took off her jacket and wrapped it around her arm as she stood by her father's side.

Tina exhaled with relief as she walked over to her daughter and gave her a hug.

"Leshia, I'm glad you're here. I thought you two weren't coming," Tina said.

"Sorry, we ran into traffic," Paul said flatly.

"Leshia, go ahead into the office, sweetie. I would like to talk to your father for a quick second," Tina said.

Leshia looked up at her dad and then walked away to go into the therapist's office. After the door had closed, Tina turned to face her ex-husband.

"Paul, I'm glad you decided to keep the appointment. I know we're not on good terms, but I want you to know before we go in there that I'm sorry. I was wrong, and I should have never attacked you. For what it's worth, I do believe that you were telling me the truth the whole time. I was just hurt and felt so alone that I haven't been myself for some time now," she said.

"Tina, I accept your apology. I just want you to be okay for yourself and our kids. I'm hoping we're moving in the right direction today in repairing your and Leshia's relationship," Paul responded.

Tina smiled at Paul and nodded her head. She hoped for the same results herself. She turned around and led them into the therapist's office. Dr. Smith and Leshia had already started talking.

"Hello, Mr. Holmes. It's a pleasure to meet you. Leshia and I were just getting to know one another. She knows that I am a licensed pediatric therapist, and I've been in this profession for over twenty years. She also knows that she can tell me anything, and it will not leave these walls. I've also learned a little bit about Leshia. I learned that she loves to dance and that she takes ballet. She has a twin sister named Lexie, and a younger brother named PJ," Dr. Smith said, looking at Leshia, who confirmed what she said with a head nod.

"Leshia, can you tell me why you think you're here today?" Dr. Smith asked.

"I guess I'm here because my mom wanted me to come," she said with a shrug.

"What's your relationship like with your father? I noticed you arrived here with him today," Dr. Smith asked.

"I love my dad. He loves to come to my ballet classes, spend time with me, helps me with Math, which is hard for me this year, and stuff like that," Leshia said, lighting up like a Christmas tree as she spoke about her father.

Paul smiled as he heard his daughter speak so openly about her feelings.

Dr. Smith jotted something down in her book and then looked back up at Leshia. "This all sounds wonderful. It sounds like you have an amazing relationship with your father. How about your relationship with your Mom?

Leshia's smile faded as she responded, which made Tina's heart drop to her knees. "My Mom doesn't really have a lot of time for me."

"Leshia," Tina was about to interject until Dr. Smith looked over at her and gave a small nod to allow Leshia the chance to explain what she meant.

"Leshia, what makes you feel this way?" Dr. Smith asked.

"Well, it all started back when my mom and dad were married. My mom would get down a lot over her job. I remember she used to take me to dance all the time. One day I had a recital, and I was so excited about it all day through school. I couldn't wait for my parents to see my role as the Swan. Later on that day after school, my dad and I waited for my mom to get off work so we could all ride to the dance studio together. When Mom got home she didn't feel like going and told us just to go without her," Leshia said, looking down at her sneakers.

"Leshia, how did that make you feel?" Dr. Smith inquired.

"It made me mad. We were almost late getting to the dance studio because Dad kept trying to get Mom to come. I could hear her yelling at him from their bedroom. I felt like my mom was being selfish and didn't think about my feelings," Leshia added.

"When did this happen?" Dr. Smith asked.

"I was seven when I was the Swan in the recital," Leshia responded.

"So about two years ago since you're nine years old now, right?" Dr. Smith asked.

"Yes, I'll be ten years old next month; both me and my twin sister," Leshia said, lighting up again like fireworks during the 4th of July.

"Dr. Smith, I remember that day and I wasn't feeling well. Leshia, I didn't know you had been carrying this around with you all this time. I can assure you that it had nothing to do with me not wanting to see you perform. You know I love to see you dance," Tina said, speaking up. She couldn't allow Leshia to make her seem like she was a bad mother and Paul was the greatest father in the world.

"But Mom it wasn't just that. It seemed like you were always unhappy about something after you missed that recital, whether it was your job or something around the house. I heard you and Dad fussing a lot, and it always seemed like you cared about what was going on with you more than us," Leshia said, looking at her mom with hurt eyes.

Tina couldn't believe what she was hearing. She thought she had done a good job in hiding her feelings from the kids. Here she was thinking she was doing a good job faking as if everything was okay and that she had everything under control when everyone around her could obviously see through it. What has she done? Did she ruin her marriage and now her relationship with her daughter too?

"Leshia is this why you turned to your dad?" Dr. Smith asked.

"Yes, because Daddy was always there for me. He started being the one to do things with me and my siblings and asked how our day was at school. Mom just seemed like everything went downhill after she couldn't get her catering business off the ground, and that's why I blame her for the divorce. If she was ignoring me then I know she had to be ignoring my father," Leshia said, exhaling loudly as if she finally got off her chest what has been residing with her for some years now.

Tina had had enough at this point. She dropped down to her knees in front of her daughter and took her little hands. She and Leshia used to be very close and she couldn't understand what had happened until now.

"Leshia, baby, Mommy is so sorry. You're right. I was unhappy with the things going on in my life back then. I tried to shield it from you and your siblings because I love you all so much. I just didn't want you all to see Mommy unhappy. This is why I would have your father step in when I couldn't be around. I thought as long as one of your parents was there at things like your recital, then you would still feel loved," Tina said, a tear rolling down her face.

"Mom, I did feel love from Dad, but not from you," Leshia said, avoiding eye contact with her mother.

"Leshia, you know your mom loves you just like I do. We're both your parents," Paul said.

"Yes, Leshia I do. Please give me another chance. I love you so much, Honey. Mommy is seeing a therapist herself too just like Dr. Smith. And I'm getting the help that I need to understand where I went wrong and how to handle it differently going forward with you and your siblings," Tina said.

Tina realized nobody was putting pressure on her to be tough and in control all the time. This was something she had been doing to herself. This behavior had gone on for too long. And she was fine with admitting that she wasn't perfect.

"Leshia, how do you feel about what your mother just said to you?" Dr. Smith asked, sitting back in her chair with a huge smile. Tina could tell she was happy that they had reached a breakthrough on their first appointment.

"I guess I like it if you really mean it," Leshia said, bending over to give her mother a hug. Tina immediately broke down. She couldn't remember the last time Leshia had given her a hug willingly. She felt like she was on her way to putting the pieces back together in her life.

"It looks like we have scratched the surface in our first session. I would like to see Leshia again to see what progress has been made in two weeks. I would recommend Ms. Holmes and Mr. Holmes that you both attend the appointment again," Dr. Smith recommended as she wrote something down in her book.

Tina unlocked her embrace with her daughter and wiped her eyes. "I think that would be wonderful," she said.

"Okay – Great. It was very nice to meet you Leshia. Thank you for trusting me today. You are a very brave and bright young lady. I'll see you in two weeks, same time," Dr. Smith said, rising from her chair.

Tina and Paul thanked the therapist and exited the room, both holding Leshia by the hand. Outside in the waiting room, Tina turned around to face Leshia. "Leshia, I would really like to spend more time with you this evening. I have to meet your aunt at the store real fast, but your Dad could drop you off at Grannie and Papa's house with your brother and sister. I could pick you all up on my way back from the store. We're going to make homemade pizzas tonight. I would love for you to join us," Tina said.

Leshia looked up at her dad and then back to her mom.

"Leshia, I think that would be a great idea to spend some more time with your mom," Paul said eagerly.

Tina tried to ignore the eagerness in his voice. She hoped he wasn't just saying that so he could spend some more time with Paige ALONE.

Let it go, Tina, she quickly told herself. She needed to focus on what was more important now, and that was rebuilding her relationship with her daughter.

A smile came over Leshia's face. "Okay – That sounds like fun."

"Great – I can't wait. I'll even add in a special mani and pedi night for the girls," Tina said, giving her a wink.

"Now that sounds like even more fun. Just like the old days," Leshia said.

"Okay. I'll go ahead and take her over to your parents," Paul said.

"Thank you, Paul," Tina said giving him a smile as she led the way out of the office.

Chapter Thirty-four

Mariah waited for her sister at the entrance of the Toy Land store. She said she would meet her after her appointment with Leshia's therapist to go Christmas shopping for the kids. She hoped Tina would arrive with good news that the session went well because she had some good news to share of her own. She still couldn't believe that she was expecting a baby, much less with Isaac.

She looked at her watch. Her sister was only about five minutes late so she figured she would be there shortly. Mariah decided to walk around the store. The toy store was already crowded with people shopping for the holidays. Mariah couldn't help but notice that they had their baby toy section right by the entrance. She decided to walk over there to see what they had. At least she would still be able to see her sister as she walked into the store.

Mariah picked up a yellow rubber ducky and squeezed it. It made a squeaky sound as the air came through the hole in the mouth. The toy was meant to help strengthen the baby's motor skills. She placed it back on the shelf and looked at all of the early learning stages books and toys for a baby as early as 0-3 months old. She was in awe of all the gadgets the store had and almost got sentimental right there in the middle of the store. She figured it was the hormones, but Mariah couldn't believe she would soon be

318

buying this sort of stuff for her own baby.

"Hey! What are you doing over here?" Tina asked, coming up behind her.

Startled, Mariah turned around and dropped the book she was looking at called Mommy and Me on the floor.

"Oh gosh, I didn't mean to scare you. Are you looking for something for a baby shower?" Tina asked.

"It's okay. I was just killing time. You're in a good mood. How was Leshia's session?" Mariah asked, picking up the book and placing it back on the table.

"Oh my goodness, I am happy to say I have my daughter back. The session started off a little shaky but ended up being remarkably great! Leshia opened up about everything. She felt like I was neglecting her when I was going through all of that stuff with hating my job, and Paul and I wasn't in a good place. I thought I was shielding the kids from my depression, but I wasn't. It took a toll on my relationship with my daughter. You should have seen it, Mariah. She hugged me without being forced to do so like before. It felt so good. She's even staying over with me tonight," Tina said, beaming from cheek to cheek.

"Oh, Tina this is great news! I'm so happy that things are coming together for you guys after one session."

"Tell me about it. The therapist did a good job of making Leshia feel comfortable to talk about her feelings. Paul and I are happy with the first appointment. So are you invited to a baby shower or something? I remember reading a version of that book to PJ when he was a baby," Tina inquired, referring to the Mommy and Me book Mariah had been holding.

"I need to talk to you about something," Mariah said.

"Shoot. Let's go to the Barbie section while we chat though. Lexie has asked us for some dollhouse that has the pool attached in the backyard."

Mariah walked alongside Tina, who was pushing the shopping cart. She was trying to come up with the best way to tell her sister that she was expecting, but once again she felt the only way was just to say it like she did to Isaac.

"I'm pregnant."

Tina stopped the cart in the middle of the aisle and turned to face her sister with humongous eyes. "You're what?!"

"I'm pregnant. I've already confirmed it with my doctor."

"OH MY GOSH!!! Are you kidding me? I'm going to be an auntie," Tina squealed, hugging her sister.

"Is it Alberto's?" Tina asked, reluctantly as she pulled away from her sister.

"No, Isaac is the father," Mariah said, her eyes beaming with joy.

Tina looked at her sister with inquisitive eyes and lightly pushed her down the aisle away from the other customers looking at all of the Barbie merchandise on the shelf.

"When did this happen? You never told me about this," she whispered.

"It happened the day I went to check on him after finding out his father died. It just happened. Now we're back together, and we're getting married. Not a wedding, just going to the Justice of the Peace before the baby arrives."

Tina started blinking repeatedly as she held her hand over her chest. "Now you're getting married, too. This is unbelievable. I can't take it. I can't believe the type of day I've had. This is the best day ever. You're now marrying the one guy I always wanted you to marry. Wow!" Tina exclaimed.

Mariah rubbed her belly. "Yep, this little guy or girl made sure that me and Isaac were brought back together again and this time for good. Tina, I'm so happy that we are. I never stopped loving him as much as I tried."

"My sister is going to be a mom. I'm going to be an aunt...I...I can't believe it. Have you told Mom and Dad yet?" Tina asked.

"Nope. You're the first aside from Isaac that I have told. I know he has already told his Mom, and she is so excited. She's already talking about helping with the nursery."

Tina gasped. "I have the best way to tell Mom and Dad. They have the cutest little 'My Favorite Grandparents' onesie or bibs all the time in the baby sections that we could get. We could tell Mom we brought her something and put it in a cute little gift bag. When she reaches in to take the gift out, she'll be so surprised. I know Dad is going to be ecstatic as well! They already know my baby factory is over with, so they'll immediately look at you. I'm so excited that we're going to have a little baby in our family again!" Tina squealed, clasping her hands together at the thought of a little baby running around.

"That's a great idea. Let's do it. I can't wait to tell them," Mariah said, following Tina back to the baby section to look to see if the store carried the onesie or bib. She was so excited to have her sister in on the plans to tell her parents. She couldn't wait to share this great news with them.

03

Later on that evening as she arrived back at her house, Mariah couldn't wait to tell Isaac how she and Tina surprised her parents with the news of the pregnancy. Mariah placed her car keys on her key holder by the door. Isaac had just arrived at the house himself. He was pulling the tape off one of the many boxes that were along the wall in the living room. He had started to move his things from his condo to her house this week. They decided to sell his condo and move in together.

"Hey, Baby. How was your shopping?" he asked.

Mariah walked over to him and gave him a big hug and kiss. "Shopping was great. Tina and I picked up the cutest little 'Soon to be Grandparents' keepsake onesie and surprised my parents with it this afternoon. They are so excited! The cat is out of the bag, and everyone knows now who is closest to me," Mariah said, planting miniature kisses on his cheek.

"That's a different way to tell the grandparents. I know they're excited. I have something to tell you that I think will make you even happier," Isaac said. He lifted Mariah up and carried her over to the couch.

"What is it?" she inquired.

"I called the courthouse and I was able to get us a date. We're getting married on Christmas Eve. We just have to apply in person together for our marriage license three days prior to the date, and we can get married," Isaac said.

Mariah gasped and wrapped her arms around him. "Baby, that sounds wonderful! We're getting married on Christmas Eve. I love it!"

"I love you," Isaac said, looking into her eyes.

Mariah smiled back at her fiancé. She couldn't wait to become his wife. Her husband and baby were going to be the greatest gift she received this Christmas! Things were looking up in her favor.

Chapter Thirty-five

On Christmas Eve, Isaac and Mariah were wed before their parents, Tina, and Christopher at the courthouse. The ceremony was simple and just right for Mariah and Isaac. They were able to take a few pictures under an arch after they were married before leaving the courthouse.

Mariah, dressed in a white suit, was now two months pregnant. She waited outside the courthouse for Isaac to get their vehicle while holding the white bouquet Tina had a florist make for her.

"Darling, congratulations! I'm so happy for you and my son. I think he made a great choice in marrying you. Daryl always approved. I know he's watching over us now smiling," Mrs. Stevens' said, referring to her late husband while smiling from cheek to cheek. She gave Mariah a big hug.

Mariah was so happy to hear her say that. She always felt she had Mrs. Stevens in her corner, but those words confirmed it. She thought Mrs. Stevens looked beautiful dressed in a green dress and a black wrap around shawl to celebrate her son getting married.

"Thank you so much, Mom," Mariah said, as they chuckled at her calling her Mom now instead of Mrs. Stevens.

"I wonder how far my son had to park. I don't want you and my grandbaby waiting out here too long," Mrs. Stevens said, looking around for Isaac's black SUV.

"Oh, we're totally fine. Thankfully, my first trimester has been going smooth so far," Mariah said, chuckling.

"My sister's married!" Tina exclaimed walking up with their parents. She took Mariah by the hands and twirled her around.

"Yes, I'm officially Mariah Stevens now," Mariah said, still in shock herself that she had gotten married again.

"I'm so happy that this day finally came. I told you everything would work out for the best," Mrs. Langston whispered in her ear as she gave her a hug.

"Thank you, Mom, and you too, Dad, for coming," Mariah said, reaching out for his hand.

"Baby Girl, I wouldn't have had it any other way," Mr. Langston said, smiling. Mariah knew he meant it because her dad was dressed in a suit and aside from wearing one to church every now and then, she didn't get to see him dressed up like that too often.

Isaac's SUV pulled up to the curb. Christopher, who walked with him to pick it up, got out the passenger's seat as Isaac walked over to hold the door open for Mariah.

"Congratulations, Sis," Christopher said, before joining the remainder of the crew on the curb to wave them off. He had never called her that before. It felt good to hear him say that because he considered Isaac a brother.

"Are you ready, Mrs. Stevens?" Isaac asked.

"Yes, Mr. Stevens," she replied as she hopped into the passenger's seat.

Isaac closed the door and got into the driver's seat. They waved goodbye to everyone as they pulled away from the curb.

"How are you feeling?" Isaac asked, cupping his free hand with her hands on her lap.

"Happier than you will ever know," Mariah said, leaning over to give him a kiss on the cheek.

"I'm glad to hear that because this is the beginning, Sweetheart. I intend to make you happy for the rest of your life."

They drove back to Mariah's house where they decided to live until they found a new house. Isaac had found a realtor who had started the selling process for his condo. Once they finished selling his condo, they were going to look for someone to rent the house. Mariah looked down at her ring finger. She told Isaac not to worry about buying an engagement ring this time. She was happy wearing a simple wedding band, which he insisted had to have diamonds on it. The diamonds on her platinum band flickered every time she wiggled her hand.

Mariah's mind reflected back over the blissful events that took place that day. Not once did she doubt her decision to get married leading up to the ceremony. She knew for certain that Isaac was the one she was destined to be with. The baby made sure of that, she thought as she rubbed her belly.

"How's my little guy doing in there," Isaac asked.

"He or she is doing well. You know this is probably the only trip we'll be able to take before the baby comes. I'm so excited to be able to break away for a little while," Mariah said. They were leaving for their honeymoon the day after Christmas, flying out to Maui, Hawaii for a week and then island hopping to the Big Island for a second week.

"I know…I can't wait to get you in a swim suit before your belly goes out to here," Isaac joked, blowing air in his cheeks and shaping his arms out to form a big stomach when they stopped at a red light.

Mariah started to laugh, hitting him playfully in the arm. "HA-HA-HA…but you better still love me," she said.

Isaac turned to face her with serious eyes. "I will always love you, Mariah. You will never have to doubt that."

Mariah leaned over and gave him a kiss on the lips. "Same here, my love."

The light changed, and Isaac pressed on the gas to continue on their journey home together. This time they had no intentions of ever being apart again.

Epilogue

"**The caterers are** here!"

"Place the flowers over there by the stairway. Hurry! It's almost time for the ceremony to start!"

Mariah got up from her stool to close the double doors to her bedroom from all the noise going on downstairs. She walked back over to her vanity table and sat back down to finish inspecting her face. Her makeup looked spectacular. The makeup artist had done a wonderful job. She took the pin out of her hair and watched as her hair fell to her shoulders. Every roller set curl in place. Her makeup was done, hair done, and all that she had left was to put on her dress.

There was a knock at the door.

"Come in!" Mariah called out.

Tina walked through the door carrying a white garment bag. "Your dress is here. I hope you don't mind, but I had to sneak a peek. It's a gorgeous dress. The seamstress was able to fix the snag in the back without a problem."

Mariah turned around to face her sister. Tina was dressed in a form-fitting black chiffon knee-length dress. She recently had her hair cut in a short bob and dyed it dark-brown with a few caramel highlights. Mariah felt the make-over looked great and truly reflected her sister's restored confidence and happiness from the past years.

"Thank you so much for picking up my dress. Let's get me in it. The ceremony is supposed to start at 4:00 p.m. and its twenty minutes till now," Mariah said eagerly removing her robe. She had already taken the liberty to put on her silk slip, so it was quick and easy to slip into her white dress.

Tina gasped with her hands over her mouth as she saw her sister turn around and pose in her dress. "I thought it was beautiful in the bag, but it looks even better on. Sis, you look amazing!"

Mariah turned to look at herself in the floor-length mirror. She was wearing a white silk dress with rhinestone straps, and a droopy back that had a design made along the sides with rhinestones. The dress was tapered to her size six figure and came right to her knees. It looked perfect as if it was made specifically for her body. Better than it looked in the store.

"I love it. It's perfect," Mariah said.

"Isaac is going to love you in this dress. Look at how sexy the back of the dress looks on you," Tina said admiring the detail.

"Thank you. I can't believe it has been ten years!" Mariah exclaimed, walking over to her closet to get the silk pumps she had purchased to wear with her dress. Since she and Isaac didn't have a wedding when they got married, they decided to renew their wedding vows and have a celebration for their tenth anniversary.

"Yeah. This is your tenth wedding anniversary and what a way to celebrate it. It looks like it's going to be some party downstairs. And to think you didn't want to get married again. I knew you two were destined to be together from when you first started dating," Tina said.

"Ah…here comes the 'I told you so.' You did tell me I was being ridiculous, didn't you," Mariah said, smiling as she slipped on her dangly pearl earrings.

Tina sat on the edge of her sister's bed. "Yeah, a few times, but who's counting. I'm just so glad that I was right about it this time."

Mariah sat down at the foot of her bed, making sure not to wrinkle her dress. "Don't say anything, but when Isaac and I made it to five years, all I could think was how we made it longer than any of my other marriages. But then making it to this point and feeling like I have finally found my soul mate, makes me feel so happy and ridiculous for ever doubting our love in the first place. I just know if it hadn't been for Lil Isaac we wouldn't have ever known what we would have missed out on by staying apart."

Tina smiled and reached over to touch her sister's hand as the doors to her bedroom swung open. Isaac Daryl Stevens Jr. came running into the room dressed in a white dress shirt, black bow tie, and black tuxedo pants. He was ten years old and looked just like his father.

"Mommy, it's time for you to come downstairs," he said running over to give his mother a hug.

"Lil Isaac, doesn't your Mom look beautiful?" Tina asked, rising from the bed.

"Yes, I love your dress Mommy. Dad is going to love it too. It's so soft," he said, touching the fabric.

"Thank you, Baby. It's silk. That's why it's so soft. You look handsome yourself. Go put your jacket on and let your father know I'm on my way down. Love you son," Mariah said, kissing him on the cheek.

"I love you too, Mommy. I'll see you downstairs. Aunt Tina, you look pretty too," Lil Isaac said.

Tina thanked her nephew and gave him a kiss on the cheek before watching him run out of the room.

"Well, are you ready to head down? It's about that time," Tina asked.

"Yep, I'm so ready to marry my husband again. Is Michael here yet?" Mariah inquired, referring to her sister's boyfriend.

"Yes, he's downstairs with Mom, Dad, and PJ. The twins are on their way over from the dorm. I'm going to run and check to make sure my catering crew has everything ready for the appetizers concluding the ceremony. Did you need anything else before I go?"

"Nope, I have everything I need now. Thanks again for allowing me to use your catering company for today. I think I went over budget with the flowers. You know how much I love orchids," Mariah said, chuckling.

Tina gave her a head nod as she wiggled her wrist in the air, showing off the purple dendrobium orchid corsage with baby's breath and a silver ribbon. "No problem. You can use my company anytime. You will always get the sisterly rates with me. You were the first to believe in my business and look at me now. I have two buildings, and we're booked almost every weekend. I can't complain."

"I love you, Tina. And I'd do it all over again!" Mariah said.

"I love you too. Now let's go downstairs so we can get this party started," Tina said, hurrying to the door.

"I'm right behind you." Mariah turned off the light and closed the doors to her bedroom. Standing at the top of the stairs, she looked down and caught a glimpse of Isaac looking handsome in a black, doubled-breasted silk suit. His smooth skin was as clear as the first day they had met, with a fresh haircut and no sign of aging except for the sexy strip of gray in the center of his trimmed goatee.

He wrapped up his conversation with a guest from his office and looked upstairs. He mouthed the word, "Wow," looking at his wife. A smile eased over Mariah's face as she held tightly onto the wrought-iron stair rail gazing into Isaac's brown eyes. A soft classical piano melody started to play downstairs signaling the beginning of their vow renewal. Isaac reached his hand out to her. Mariah's heart started to race as adrenaline rushed through her body with every step she took to meet him downstairs. Excited to reunite with her husband again in front of their family and friends, Mariah knew, as her hand connected with Isaac's that the love they shared together was unbreakable and would last forever.

About The Author

Ayesha L. Shoulders is an ambitious woman who lives life to the fullest. She has a passion for writing jaw-dropping contemporary fiction that is relatable and sprinkled with a life message. After she completed her MBA, she decided to self-publish her first novel, When It's Time to Walk Away, in May 2011. When Love's Knot Enough is her second novel.

In addition to being an author, Ayesha is also an active member of the Northern Virginia Writers Club. Ayesha loves to connect with readers on Facebook (Facebook/AyeshaShoulders) and Twitter (@AyeshaShoulders). She can also be contacted at www.ayeshashoulders.com.